"It ain't fitting for a woman, Kate. A woman's place is with her family, at home."

"I have no family, Cole."

"You could, Kate. One day you could have a fine family. But not if you open that saloon."

Kate blinked at Cole's blunt declaration. He was telling her that no decent, law-abiding man would want a woman who ran a saloon. Especially not Sheriff Cole Bradshaw. It wasn't proper, wasn't what women were expected to do.

"Kate, I'm warning you. Don't reopen the Silver Saddle." Kate didn't miss the threat in his tone.

"Or what?" She planted her hands firmly on her hips, her chin defiantly raised.

He hesitated, peering into her eyes, then bringing his focus lower to her lips. She heard his slight, almost silent sigh. She waited a moment, and when he finally spoke, it was with deep regret. "Or I'll have to arrest you."

THE LAW AND KATE MALONE

CHARLENE SANDS

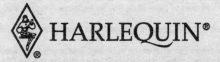

TORONTO • NEW YORK • LONDON
AMSTERDAM • PARIS • SYDNEY • HAMBURG
STOCKHOLM • ATHENS • TOKYO • MILAN • MADRID
PRAGUE • WARSAW • BUDAPEST • AUCKLAND

ISBN 0-373-29246-5

THE LAW AND KATE MALONE

Copyright © 2003 by Charlene Swink

This edition published by arrangement with Harlequin Books S.A.

® and TM are trademarks of the publisher. Trademarks indicated with
® are registered in the United States Patent and Trademark Office, the
Canadian Trade Marks Office and in other countries.

Visit us at www.eHarlequin.com

Printed in U.S.A.

Please address questions and book requests to:
Harlequin Reader Service
U.S.: 3010 Walden Ave., P.O. Box 1325, Buffalo, NY 14269
Canadian: P.O. Box 609, Fort Erie, Ont. L2A 5X3

Dedicated to my sister Carol Pettis,
for all of your love and support, for sharing
a tiny bedroom and an even smaller closet all those years
and for getting me through high school algebra.
But mostly, for being the greatest sister ever.
To your husband, Bill, and my two "other" children,
Angie and Eric. My love to you all.

With love to my sweet mother, Caroline,
and in loving memory to my father, Charles,
who always had a story for me, who always sparked
my imagination and who always made me laugh.
This time the "sheriff" story is mine to tell, Dad.

Prologue

Crystal Creek
Northern California
1868

Mary Kathryn Malone dashed down the school-house steps, her pace never faltering until she reached the creaky wood gate. With haste she unlatched the thick rope holding the posts together and opened the gate.

"And don't you be running all the way home, Mary Kathryn," Miss Ashmore called out from the doorway. "It's not fitting for a young lady to run wild."

"Yes, Miss Ashmore," Mary Kathryn responded, automatically slowing her stride to a sedate walk. She wished her teacher would call her Kate. All of her life, she'd wanted to be just Kate, but Miss Ashmore said "Mary Kathryn" seemed more civilized and if there was anything her teacher thought Kate needed, it was more civilizing. Kate didn't agree, but since she was only twelve, no one listened to what she wanted.

Except for Cole Bradshaw.

Once out of view of her schoolteacher's sharp eyesight, Kate took off running again. She had to catch up to Cole. They'd be heading down to the creek together this very minute if Kate hadn't had to stay late after her lessons to write on the blackboard twenty-five times, "I will not spit in class again. Ladies do not spit." It didn't matter to Miss Ashmore that Toby Benton had done the first spitting, either.

Kate ran behind old Mrs. Whittaker's Millinery, stopping to make sure Mama wasn't across the street, outside the Silver Saddle Saloon, sweeping away debris from last night's brawl. One thing Mama was for sure, was clean. She hated when rowdies paid her saloon a visit and mucked up the place.

Once she was certain all was clear, Kate took off running again, heading toward the creek. She was just past the back end of the livery stable when something long and dark jumped out at her, tripping her up. She went down with a plunk, landing knee-deep in an untied bale of hay. When she glanced up through a web of straw, she saw the leg that had caused her to fall.

"Ha! Fooled ya, Kate." Cole leaped out from his hiding spot behind the wall and stood above her, gloating. "Bet you didn't know I was there!"

"The only way I'd know you was there, Cole Bradshaw, was by the god-awful smell!" Kate lifted herself from the straw and stood, plucking out flaxen sticks from her long braid. She lifted her nose to sniff air. "And I was racing too doggone fast to catch a whiff, but I do now." She waved her hands in front of him and stepped way back. "Whew, you stink."

"Do not." His brows lifted. "Aw, you're just mad 'cause I bested you."

"Feathers will haul off and fly south from one of Mrs. Whittaker's fancy plume hats the day you best me, Cole Bradshaw!"

"I bested you," he said smugly, folding his arms across his middle. "Always do." He stood tall above her and peered down her slight frame. She couldn't wait to grow another four inches to catch up with him. Then she could look Cole right in those piercing blue eyes, valiantly, being his equal in ability and size. But it seemed every time Kate grew half an inch or so, Cole also grew at least one or more. Didn't seem fair to her, not one bit, even though Cole was two years older.

"Do not."

"Do so."

"Do *not*."

"Do *so*. Race me down to the creek."

Kate's hand went to her stomach. She'd just gotten over her monthlies, which tended to make her tired and cranky. But aside from that, she'd been feeling sorta queasy in the gut whenever she was around Cole. Just looking into his face sometimes, or watching how his long hair curled up and teased the tips of his shoulders made her insides churn. Like they were doing now. Kate didn't understand what was happening to her, but she couldn't refuse Cole a race, queasy stomach and all. "I'm getting kinda tired of beating you all the time," she said matter-of-factly.

"I let you win."

"Do not."

He came close and pointed his nose at hers. "Do so."

A small flutter swept through her insides again. Cole didn't smell foul at all. Fact is, with Cole standing so close, Kate liked the way he smelled, like lye soap and earth all rolled up into one. "Cole, I don't feel like racing today."

"Are you scared I'd beat you this time?"

Kate grinned. "You won't beat me. I'm faster than you."

"No, you're not...hey!"

Kate took off running, whipping past the backs of the shops in town, down a lush green slope and around a cluster of pine trees, the wind pushing hair off her face, the air in her lungs near to bursting. Laughter escaped her throat, and she kept on running, feeling alive and tremendously free. "C'mon, slowpoke," she called out, knowing full well Cole was fast on her heels. She heard his breathing, the puffing sound that meant he was catching up.

She could see Crystal Creek in the distance, a hundred yards away. The giant gray stone, their finishing line, lay just ahead. She had to reach it first. She had to win. She couldn't let Cole beat her. She tilted her head and saw him one stride behind. With oxygen exploding in her chest and her legs burning, she pushed herself even harder.

"I win," she shouted, jubilant, when she kicked her boot to their rock. Cole wasn't but a step behind. "I bested you," she huffed out, bending to catch her breath.

Cole did the same. Bracing his hands on his knees, he hung his head and took long slow pulls of breaths. "You did. But I'm catching up. Soon," he said with a solemn nod, "soon, you'll never beat me again."

Kate slid down to the ground, stretching out her legs, and leaned back on her palms, looking toward the creek. Runoff from the Sierras kept the stream flowing, the water deep and blue and inviting. Cole's words sank in and she believed him this time. She was winning the race, each time, by less of a margin. He'd nearly beaten her today and, pretty darn soon, he'd be leaving her in the dust.

The crushing thought saddened her, but she would never let him know her fears. He sank down next to her and picked up an old wrinkled leaf, twisting it to and fro. Both their gazes locked on to that nut-brown leaf, contemplating.

"It don't hurt to lose once in a while, Kate."

"Bet you're used to it."

"I can beat any boy in school."

She grinned. "Just not me."

"It ain't that important anyways," he said.

"What's important is for me to be a fast draw. For when I'm sheriff of this here town."

"I'm going to be sheriff, Cole. Not you."

His face pulled taut as though he'd just eaten the sourest pickle. "Tarnation, Kate. Girls can't be sheriffs."

"Mama says women can be whatever they want to be. It ain't right for a man to say what a woman can or cannot do in life."

"Aw, she's just saying that 'cause she owns the Silver Saddle, Kate. Folks don't take kindly to a woman running the saloon."

"But they still come in, don't they? Mama says you gotta give them what they want. She keeps them happy with better whiskey and the lowest prices in town. Mama knows her business."

Cole nodded. "I ain't got nothing against your mama, Kate. But a woman's got to be at home." His eyes sparked with mischief and he wiggled his brows. "Making babies."

Kate chuckled nervously. She didn't know if they ought to be speaking of such things, but she and Cole pretty much talked about everything. She tilted her head, pondering. "That what you want, Cole?"

"Yep, I suppose. After I'm sheriff, that is. I want a heap of babies."

Cole never really knew his ma and his pa, who died early on. With his older brother raising him on that farm, Kate knew how much Cole missed having a real family. "Mama can't have more babies. She's got no

husband. My pa ran out on us when I was a tot. But
Mama's a good woman, Cole. Goes to church every
Sunday.''

"Still, none of the ladies want to have anything to
do with her.''

"Mama says that's their loss.''

Cole shrugged. "It's why you don't have any gals
as friends, ain't it?''

"I don't need gals as friends, Cole. I got you, and
one day I'm going to sheriff this town.'' She slugged
him in the arm and grinned, determined to change the
subject. She didn't mind not having any gal friends,
not really, but she didn't like Cole bringing it up all
the time, neither. "But you can be my deputy.''

"You got that turned around backward, Kate. I'll
be sheriff and maybe, if'n you're good with a gun
and all, just maybe you can be my deputy.''

Kate made a wide circle with her arms, hitting the
ground with her palms and bringing up autumn leaves
that blanketed the ground. "Ouch!'' Tears stung her
eyes from the jolt of unexpected pain.

Cole was up on his knees, twisting toward her.
"What's wrong?''

Kate lifted her injured hand. Her impetuous swing
had brought up a rusted-out rowel that was hiding
under the thick layer of leaves. Its sharp point was
stuck in her hand.

"Hold on,'' Cole said, quickly examining the
rowel. "This is going to hurt,'' he said, but before

she could respond, he yanked out the sharp piece of spur.

"Darn it, Cole!" she shouted. "That did hurt."

She gazed at her hand, just above the wrist, at the base of her palm. Blood spurted out, coloring her skin red, soaking into her shirtsleeve.

"Sorry, Kate. Had to be done." Without hesitation, he slipped his shirt out of his trousers, ripped off a strip of cloth and dabbed at her hand. "Hold this, press hard. It'll stop the blood."

Kate held back tears. She never cried. But her hand ached with fresh pain. "Okay."

Although she tried, she couldn't put enough pressure on the wound. Blood kept soaking through.

"Here," Cole said, gently taking her hand. He sat next to her, his eyes focused solely on applying pressure to her injury.

Kate felt the trembling inside again. She didn't think it was caused from her wound, but more than likely, from the boy tending to it. "You might have a scar here. Wound's pretty deep."

"It's okay," she said, fighting off the tender feelings stirring up her insides. But she couldn't help noticing Cole's dark lashes, or the deep sky-blue of his eyes, or the kind way he had of caring for her.

He was her only true friend. It didn't matter to him that her mama ran a saloon or that Kate was a girl or that, sometimes, he got teased for playing with the saloon gal's daughter. Cole Bradshaw was her friend.

"Feeling better?" he asked softly.

"Yeah," she said, trying not to look too deeply into Cole's eyes. "I hope we'll always be friends, Cole."

He glanced up at her, his gaze reassuring. "We will."

"But how can you know?"

"I just do, Kate. I know."

"Really, you promise?"

"I promise." A light sparked in Cole's eyes and he lifted up the rusty chunk of metal that had caused her damage. "I'll show you." He opened his palm and with a quick flick, he slashed his hand in the same spot where Kate had been cut. Only, his cut didn't go as deep and just a few drops of blood oozed out.

He took up Kate's hand and pressed his hand, wound to wound against hers. His hand was bigger and rougher, Kate noted as she splayed her fingers to his. The blood mingled and he smiled. "Friends forever," he said seriously. Then he took the strip of his shirt and tenderly wrapped it tight around Kate's hand.

Kate's heart pounded in her ears. Cole had made her queasy again. She felt sick and, at the same time, a pleasant trembling traveled along her entire body.

She reached out to hold his hand in hers, inspecting his line of blood. On impulse, she lifted her skirt, tore off a length of her petticoat and wrapped the white lace over his wound. She applied pressure, just as he had and dared to glance into his eyes.

He swallowed, his Adam's apple riding the length

of his throat and she thought she felt his hand tremble. "Thank you," he said quietly.

"You're welcome," was her soft reply.

He raised up and stretched then bent to offer a hand to help her up. "I got chores to do and my brother Jeb don't like me being late. I'd best get on home."

"Me too," she said, but when she stood, he didn't drop her hand. Instead he pulled her slightly and pressed a kiss to her lips. His eyes met hers only for a moment, before he turned away.

"See you tomorrow, Kate."

Kate stood frozen to the spot, speechless, staring after Cole. He'd kissed her! Her first kiss and it was from Cole. Minutes passed and hundreds of thoughts crowded her mind. She'd been surprised, stunned really, when she'd realized what he'd done. His lips were warm and moist and she'd never felt anything so wonderful in her whole life.

Goose bumps erupted on her arms and she rubbed at them, then she lifted a finger to her lips. They tingled still.

At that moment Mary Kathryn Malone knew what all the queasiness was about. She understood all the stirrings when Cole was near. She realized now, just what it all meant.

She was in love with Cole Bradshaw. And she would never, in her entire life, love any other boy.

Chapter One

Crystal Creek
California
1877

Kate Malone stepped off the train, cautiously glancing around at the town she'd grown up in, the town she'd left at the age of fifteen. It had been six years since she laid eyes on Crystal Creek. Six years since the Silver Saddle had caught fire and she and Mama had to pack up and move on. She'd never been able to squash the feeling that they'd been run out of town. Not by the fire, but by Mr. Wesley's refusal to loan Mama the money to rebuild. Three shops had gone up in smoke that day, but the stone-faced banker had refused only her mama a loan.

"Women make for bad risks," he'd said. It hadn't mattered to the staunch banker that the Silver Saddle had been turning a profit for over thirty years ever since her grandpa John had opened the place during the peak days of the big gold strike.

Louisa Malone had been heartbroken. Kate had always known how much the Silver Saddle meant to her mama. She also knew her mama had wanted to shield her from their fate by pretending they were ready to embark on a new adventure. They'd had to leave the only home Kate had ever known. And for the past six years her mama had worked hard, using her business acumen to run a hotel in Los Angeles with dreams of coming back to Crystal Creek one day and reopening the saloon.

And the hard work had paid off. Louisa had managed to double the bustling hotel's profits, gaining the trust of her employer and earning big yearly bonuses. Kate, too, had worked at the hotel, helping with housework and cooking. Both of them had free room and board at the hotel, so they had saved every penny they'd earned.

But Mama's sudden death just months ago left Kate bereft and heartsick. She'd always expected they'd return home together. The only thing that mattered to Kate now was seeing her mama's dream come true. It had been Louisa's legacy, and now it was Kate's.

Lifting her valise, she left the depot and walked down the street toward the hotel. With head held high and never once glancing in the direction of the sheriff's office, Kate moved with efficient steps along the sidewalk. She wasn't ready to see Cole yet. She wasn't ready to feel the same sense of longing that struck her looking into his deep blue eyes. Nor was she ready to feel the gnawing ache in her belly that came about thinking she'd not been good enough for Cole Bradshaw.

The pain slashed through her like a knife at times. It was easier not to think about him. Not at all.

As she strode on, she noted Mrs. Whittaker's Millinery was now also part confectionery shop. One small window displayed her usual feathered frill hats in all colors of the rainbow while the other displayed platters of sugared delights.

Southby's Livery must have been sold, since the sign above the broad wooden doors, seemingly freshly painted, now read Cable Brothers Livery. The barbershop appeared the same, as did the telegraph office, but the floorboards beneath her feet squeaked with newness as she walked along the sidewalk.

She stopped short, bracing her free hand on a post, when she saw the Silver Saddle Saloon just twenty paces away. A slight tremor passed through her. She closed her eyes, momentarily blocking out the image. She'd hoped it wouldn't have looked so decrepit. She'd hoped it was just a young girl's vivid image of destruction that had plagued her mind all these years, but as she reopened her eyes, reality hit her. What was left of the once fine saloon was boarded up. The rectangular planks covering up the ashen skeleton of the building didn't hide the devastation. And it was clear as day that the Silver Saddle, as it stood, was the eyesore of this town.

Kate recalled all the happy times she'd shared there with her mama. And the tales her mama had told of how Grandpa turned a small wooden shack serving only one brand of whiskey into the grand palace the Silver Saddle had become.

Kate had always felt a sense of pride in the saloon, even though some of the townsfolk had scorned her and referred to her as "that saloon gal's daughter."

But Kate was here now, with a purse full of money, ready to rebuild her family legacy. She wasn't about to let melancholy feelings stop her. She turned and entered the lobby of the Crystal Hotel.

"Well, I'll be darned, if it ain't Miss Mary Kathryn Malone," Lou Bernard announced from behind the hotel lobby's desk. "And you're all grown-up, too."

She smiled, remembering the old friendly gent who ran the hotel. He'd been a regular at the Silver Saddle. "It's Kate, Lou. And it's good to see you."

"It's been, how many years?" he asked, coming around the counter to relieve her of the valise.

"Six years. I was fifteen when we left."

He nodded and set her valise down by the stairs. "You sure turned out pretty, Miss Kate. Image of your mama. Sorry to hear of her passing."

Kate had wired a few of Mama's friends in town when she passed. She wasn't surprised that people in Crystal Creek knew of her death. A sad smile pulled at the corners of her mouth, the loss too fresh and raw yet to speak of. "Thanks, Lou. I'll need a room."

"'Course, you will. How long will you be staying on in Crystal Creek?"

"I'll only need a room for a few nights, but I'm here to stay. I'm letting the Browns' house at the end of town."

"That place ain't seen the light of day for some time. It's gonna need a good polishing before it's fit to live in."

"I know," she said without regret, "but I'm not afraid to get my hands dirty."

Lou threw his head back and laughed. "You ain't changed a bit now, have you? You may look the lady in your fancy traveling suit, Miss Kate, but I got a feeling them are true words."

Kate couldn't keep a devilish smile hidden. "They are, Lou. And I hope you'll be glad to know I plan on opening the Silver Saddle again. That's why I'm here. And I'm inviting you in for the first drink."

Lou slapped his hand to his knee and let out a long, low whistle. "Well, I'll be darned. Glad to hear it, gal. I'll be there. This town's been dry for too long."

Kate agreed. She couldn't wait to get started.

Sheriff Cole Bradshaw stared out the window of the jail, keeping his gaze focused on the auburn-haired woman making her way down the street. Old and familiar yearnings settled in his gut. Kate was six years older and six times more beautiful than when she'd left Crystal Creek.

Cole winced at the pain he felt watching her move

with grace, head held high, those green eyes filled with determination. Same Kate he'd always known, just all grown-up.

They'd been the best of friends. As a boy, he'd always admired her untamed spirit. Many a night he'd wandered through his memories of her, oftentimes smiling at the silly games they'd played, the different competitions they'd entered into, and later on, the beckoning new sensations Kate had stirred in him.

He'd never told her how just the sight of her pretty smile could warm his heart, or how much he liked watching her cinnamon curls bounce against her shoulders. He'd never told her how much he'd wanted her to stay on, how much he would miss her once she'd left. And now that she was here, he wondered what other of her qualities he'd find admirable.

Too many to think about right now.

He knew why she'd come back. He knew how much that saloon meant to her. But the townsfolk, for the most part, didn't want the Silver Saddle to reopen. They enjoyed a quiet peace knowing the rowdies and cowpunchers with pay overflowing their pockets, moved on to the next town to get their liquor and cause a ruckus.

But Kate Malone wouldn't like what he'd have to tell her. She wouldn't cotton to being backed into a corner. Kate, he knew, would come out fighting. And it was up to Cole to see that she didn't.

Cole turned away from the window. With his hands

firmly planted in his back pockets, he called himself every kind of fool for caring so darn much.

Cole blinked away that thought when the door to his office opened suddenly.

"Look what we have here," his deputy, Johnny Martinez announced, "the prettiest *chica* this side of Rio Grande."

Cole watched a giggle escape, and the cherub-faced blond child ran straight into his arms. "Hi, Daddy."

Kate took a warm bath, happy to have washed all the grime and travel dust off her body and hair. The trip from Los Angeles wasn't overly long, but the Southern Pacific Railroad wasn't known for luxury, and with the cramped spaces and breeze of the day blowing in, a body hardly stood a chance at turning up at their destination unscathed.

After donning a white shirtwaist and a cream-colored skirt then brushing her wayward curls, she locked the hotel room door and ambled down the stairs. She wanted to see the saloon close up and make preliminary assessments, but as she headed in that direction, she noted two children rushing down the school steps, laughing their way down the street. She followed them with her eyes as they ran behind the livery stables, down a winding slope, and then she lost sight of them in the towering pines. Smiling, Kate picked up her skirts and headed in the same direction.

She'd raced down this path hundreds of times. She knew the way. When she finally reached the bank of the creek, a sweeping sigh escaped her throat. How she'd missed Crystal Creek. Nothing in her mind was more beautiful. Nothing compared to the cloudless blue sky, the gleam of golden sun on the water, the scent of fresh pine and earth. She loved this place.

Within minutes, Kate found the gray granite rock. The one she and Cole had named their finishing line. A small smile emerged. She brushed away some pebbles on the flattest part of the rock's surface and sat down, glancing out to the rushing creek waters.

She closed her eyes to enjoy the peace, but her mind flashed an image Kate had tried many a time to lock away.

Right before the fire at the saloon, when she was fifteen, Cole had asked to meet her here. She'd been thrilled and so sure he was finally going to ask her to Crystal Creek's Founder's Day celebration. It had been all she'd dreamed about, all she'd wanted. For Cole to see her as more than his best friend, to see her as the young woman she had become. To want her the powerful way she'd wanted him.

Her heart had leaped from her chest when he appeared behind this very rock. She'd stammered a quick hello. Cole had been quiet then, staring off in the distance. Kate waited for him to speak.

And when he had, Kate's heart broke in two. Cole had invited Patricia Wesley to the Founder's Day celebration. He explained that his older brother Jeb thought it a good idea, since Patricia was the banker's daughter and she'd taken a shine to Cole. Didn't hurt none getting friendly with Mr. Wesley, Jeb had said. He had influence in this town. He could help Cole get elected sheriff when the time came.

Cole hadn't looked her in the eye that day. She sensed he knew he'd disappointed her. But Cole was on the verge of manhood and wanted to be sheriff in the worst way. After all, Kate realized all too clearly, she was only the saloon gal's daughter.

Kate had cried useless tears for days and, shortly after, the saloon burned down. Cole had tried to console her. He'd done everything he knew to do to make her feel better, and when the time came for her to leave town, he'd taken her into his arms and hugged her tight, but never once had he asked her to stay.

She'd understood then, Cole didn't regard her as he did other women. He didn't think her good enough. Oh, she was fine to race down the path with and play silly games and even hold her hand on more than one occasion, but that's where it had all ended.

The saloon gal's daughter held no place with Crystal Creek's would-be sheriff.

Kate lifted herself off the rock, determined not to allow her one bad memory of this place to mar its own glorious perfection. When crackling leaves rustled from behind, she turned sharply around. Cole Bradshaw stood just a few feet away, his blue gaze burning directly into hers. "Hello, Kate."

Chapter Two

Kate stared into Cole's eyes, an unwelcome jolt of awareness passing through her. She'd hoped seeing him again wouldn't mean anything, that her feelings of wanting would have diminished, that Cole Bradshaw was only a young girl's fancy. But seeing him tall and sure, a man now, and even more handsome than she'd recalled, played havoc with her resolve to forget him.

"Cole," she said, her head held high. Sunlight flickered on the badge pinned onto his tanned leather vest, drawing her attention there. He was the sheriff now, a painful reminder of secret dreams they'd once shared. Cole had attained his dream. Kate had dreams of her own, but Cole didn't figure into them anymore. "Did you follow me here?"

He lifted his face to the sun for a moment then met her eyes. "I come here sometimes."

She nodded but couldn't respond. They stared at each other in silence.

Cole took off his well-worn Stetson and scratched his head. "Well, I did see you heading this way and thought to follow you."

"Why?" she asked.

"Do you have to ask? Lord above, Kate, you've been gone more than six years."

"So this is a welcome home?"

Cole tossed his hat down then jammed his hands on his hips. "No, well...yes. Welcome back," he said tersely. Then his voice softened. "I'm sorry about your mama, Kate. She was a special kind of woman."

Kate wondered what he meant by *special*. Different, an outcast, a woman who dared to do something outside what was considered proper and respectable? "Thank you."

"How did she die?" He stepped closer and Kate saw the compassion in his eyes.

"Her heart gave out. Least, that's what the doctor thinks. She just sort of slumped over in her chair and never woke up."

Cole nodded his understanding. "Must've been hard for you."

"It still is," she admitted, unable to keep the sadness from her voice. "We had so many plans."

Cole cleared his throat. "Uh, that's why I wanted to see you. To talk. Want to sit?" He pointed to the rock she'd just risen from, *their* rock.

"No, I'm fine." She turned her face to gaze out onto the creek waters. Absently she thought there must've been heavy snows here this winter for the creek to be this close to overflowing.

"Kate?" Cole's voice was closer now. She felt his hand on her shoulder, felt his breath on the back of her neck. She squeezed her eyes closed for one brief moment, relishing the feel of his hand on her, then stepped away and turned to face him.

"I'm going to open the Silver Saddle again, Cole. That's what you came to talk about, isn't it? You don't think I should do it."

The soft expression on his face evaporated. "Hell, Kate, you know the answer to that. You're heading for a barrel full of grief. Look what your mama went through in this town. You have a chance for a different kind of life. You're young…and beautiful." He stepped closer again. Kate stood her ground. "You should be thinking of marriage…starting a family."

"I might want that one day," she said defiantly, knowing the only man she'd ever wanted to marry was Cole. That dream had died long ago. "But the Silver Saddle comes first. It's all Mama and I dreamed about, all we worked so hard for these past years. Now, it's up to me."

"Well, the town doesn't want it rebuilt."

"We'll see about that."

"Kate, listen. The town council passed a new ordinance a short time ago prohibiting the start of any new establishments here in Crystal Creek without their approval. They'll never agree."

"Are you saying I can't open the saloon up again?"

He nodded firmly. "That's what I'm saying. Look, Kate, if you've got your hopes pinned on staying here, Mrs. Whittaker at the millinery is getting on in age. She'd been thinking of selling her—"

Laughter escaped, rushing out and relieving Kate of pent-up tension at seeing Cole again. "Cole Bradshaw! You can't be serious? You think I'd spend my days fashioning peacock-blue feathers onto silly strawberry-red bonnets?"

If he did think that, he truly didn't know Kate at all. Leastways, he didn't know her *anymore*. There was a time when they could pretty much read each other's thoughts.

Cole glared at her. "It's a suggestion."

"Well, I'm not taking it."

"Fine, Kate," he said in the infuriating way he had when he didn't get his way, "but you have limited choices. For your own good, maybe you'd be better off going back to Los Angeles."

Kate whirled around and stared blankly at the creek. She never once thought Cole would try to run her out of town. Tears stung her eyes, but she held them back. No more shed tears over Cole Bradshaw, she'd vowed. "Crystal Creek is my home. I'm staying."

Kate sat by the creek long after Cole left. *For your own good, maybe you'd be better off going back to Los Angeles.*

How could Cole possibly know what was good for her? He didn't know how it felt to be pushed out of your home, to move on to a new town and have to start all over again, when your heart and soul belonged only in one place. To only one man. So many times Kate had come here by herself as a young girl, filled with fanciful hopes of marrying Cole and making babies. Cole wanted a family. He'd always spoken of how he missed his own parents, losing them both at an early age. His older brother Jeb had raised him and the two young men had struggled hard to make their small farm profitable. They'd been poor, but they had their pride. Cole had always held his head high in town, and finally, Kate thought earnestly, he'd earned their respect. They'd honored him by electing him sheriff.

Kate didn't think anything was more important to Cole than being sheriff of Crystal Creek.

So why couldn't Cole understand her dream? He knew the history behind the Silver Saddle. He knew that saloon had sustained her family for three generations. She was the only one left now, to make the Silver Saddle what it once was.

No, better than what it once was.

Didn't Cole know that? Didn't he care? She hadn't been in town more than a day before Cole was asking her to leave.

Anger simmered on the surface and Kate asked herself when Cole had become so heartless. With a touch of sadness, she hated to see their friendship die. But in truth, she was now certain it had.

The boy Kate remembered as being her lifelong friend no longer existed. Still, she couldn't look to the past. She needed to live for today. That's what Mama had always told her.

Kate left the sanctity of the creek and walked back to town. She realized it had been nearly twelve hours since she'd had a meal.

And after she appeased her appetite, she'd have to see Cole Bradshaw once again. This time, she wouldn't let a pair of disconcerting blue eyes distract her from her goal.

Kate sat in the hotel restaurant alone, dining on a meal of boiled white potatoes, creamed corn and a medium-rare beefsteak. Her mouth watered from the aroma of a hot meal and she picked up her fork, diving into the food, trying hard to ignore the stares of some of the other patrons. Whispers of recognition filled the air, but no one came over to say hello, although she was sure about half a dozen people knew who she was. She'd never been granted the grace of the town's support when she lived here, except for a few friends like Lou, so Kate wasn't expecting their hearty welcome now.

Her mother had survived in this town and had turned a good profit running the saloon. Kate was determined to not only reopen the saloon, but gain the town's respect while doing so.

Give them what they want.

Louisa Malone's advice had stuck with Kate. She knew she could make a success of the Silver Saddle. She knew she could win over the town, if only they'd give her a chance. Then, she'd finally have the home she'd always wanted. She'd have her family's heritage back. She'd have a means of support. The only thing she wouldn't have…was Cole Bradshaw.

First things first, Kate cautioned herself, and realized she had to obtain a copy of the new town ordinance. She wasn't willing to go down without a good fight. And if that meant butting heads with the town sheriff, so be it.

Kate finished her meal and topped it off with a cup of coffee and a dish of tapioca pudding. She left the hotel dining room just as the sun was beginning to set on the horizon. The last blaze of California sunshine brought glimmers of golden settling light to the busy town. It was a quiet time, as if day was relinquishing peacefully into night. Kate enjoyed the calm as she strode toward the sheriff's office.

Once there, she jiggled the door to the jailhouse slightly, then peered inside. The office looked deserted.

"If you're lookin' for the sheriff, you ain't gonna find him there."

Kate swung around to find a fair-haired man standing on the other side of the walkway. "Name's Jethro

Cable.'' He pointed to the livery stable. ''Part owner of the livery.'' He smiled, bright and friendly. ''My brother Abe owns the other half.''

''Hello,'' she said, glad to have a smiling face greet her for a change. ''I'm Kate Malone.''

He whipped off his hat and bowed slightly. ''Pleased to meet you, Miss Malone. Are you new to these parts?''

''No, I…I used to live here when I was younger. I'm looking for Sheriff Bradshaw.''

''As I said, you won't find him here. He locks up in the afternoon unless he's got a prisoner in the jail. Ain't been a one, since I bought the livery, seems like. Been at least six months. It's sure a peaceable town.''

Kate nodded, wondering if Jethro Cable truly knew what he was talking about. When Kate had lived here, old Sheriff Cullen was busy throwing rowdies in jail, seemed like every other week.

''If it's important, miss, you can find the sheriff at home about now. See that house at the far edge of town, the one with the yellow curtains in the window? That's Sheriff Bradshaw's place.'' Kate followed the direction of Jethro's pointing finger. Cole's house was the most tended one on the street.

And it was only four houses down from the Browns' house, the one she would be moving into day after tomorrow. ''Yes, I see it. Thank you.''

''Pleased to meet you, miss. Maybe we'll get a chance to talk again soon.''

"Yes, I think I'd like that, Mr. Cable." Kate bid the mannerly man a farewell and started for Cole's house. Deep regret settled heavily in Kate's stomach as her gaze focused on the pretty little house at the end of town. Kate couldn't help wondering if she hadn't been the saloon gal's daughter, would she have been the one putting up pretty yellow curtains in Cole's house, making a home for him.

But it was too late for regrets. What's done was done and there was no going back. Kate had learned much from her mother about how a woman survives alone.

Kate's father had run out on them when she was only three and had broken her mother's heart. Kate had lived with that betrayal for all of her young years, hoping that one day, her daddy would show up, apologizing to his wife and daughter, pleading for forgiveness. That he hadn't tore at Kate's heart. She'd wanted to believe in him, believe she was worthy of his love, but each day he hadn't come home only reminded Kate that he hadn't really loved them, not at all.

Kate approached the picket fence leading to Cole's house, slowing her steps. With deliberate strides, she made her way to the gate, then took a deep breath before opening it and walking toward the stairs and his front door.

She knocked twice and waited, letting her breath out slowly, her heart thumping in her chest. Darn if she couldn't control her own emotions. She reminded herself she wouldn't be here if it hadn't been absolutely necessary.

The front door swung open wide with a quick thrust. A beautiful blonde child stood in the doorway, her smile beaming.

"Meggie, I told you not to run and open the door so quick. Daddy's got to be sure..." Cole came face-to-face with Kate and didn't finish his thought. He appeared as stunned as Kate.

"Daddy, who's the pretty lady?" The child tugged on Cole's trousers. He came out of his stupor to bend down and lift her up in his arms.

Kate's throat constricted. She tried swallowing, but the lump was lodged too tightly. Kate could only stare at Cole, then at the little girl who was wrapped rather snugly against him. Two pair of deep blue eyes stared back at her.

Kate slammed her eyes shut and whirled around, ready to make a hasty departure.

"Kate, wait!"

Kate stopped at Cole's rigid command, not because she'd intended to, but because of the force with which he'd spoken.

"I shouldn't have come," she said quietly, her back to them both.

"I'm glad you did." Cole's sweet declaration unnerved her.

"I have to go."

"Don't leave."

She turned to watch Cole lower his child to the

ground and whisper something to her. The child glanced curiously once more at Kate, then went back inside the house.

Cole straightened and directed his gaze back to her, his blue eyes warm with invitation. He stood by the opened door. "Come inside."

Kate was at a loss. She inhaled sharply and nodded, hesitating a moment before slipping past him quickly to enter his home.

"Would you like to sit down?" he asked, his tone conciliatory.

She shook her head and clutched her reticule tightly.

Cole blew out a breath. "I never got a chance to tell you about Jeb. I wanted to write, but at the time, it was hard for me to believe he was really gone. And well, you'd stopped sending me letters. I got the feeling you'd kinda moved on with your life."

Kate acknowledged that fact. She had stopped writing to Cole. It had been far too painful to hear how *he'd* moved on with his life. Last she'd heard from him, he'd just been elected sheriff. After that, she'd stopped their correspondence. "I—I didn't know he died. I'm sorry, Cole."

With a deep sadness in his eyes, Cole nodded. "Meggie is Jeb's child. I'm raising her as my own."

Selfishly Kate felt relieved that Cole hadn't fathered the child. "What about her mother?" she asked.

"She's gone, too. About two years ago a raiding

party swept through this area, robbing farms and ranches up past the north end of the creek. They hit Jeb's farm, killed his wife and took everything they could lay their hands on. Jeb went after them, shot one of them dead, but wound up with a bullet in his belly. I found him bleeding out on the range. There was nothing I could do to save him. We both knew he was dying. He made me promise to keep Meggie for him. Wouldn't have it any other way, anyhow, but Jeb had to hear me say it. I promised my brother I'd raise his young daughter all proper like, just the way he wanted. That's what I intend to do."

"Did you ever find the men who killed them?"

Cole nodded. "Turns out they were three brothers named Sloan. Jeb killed the one. We caught up with another a few days later. He was tried and convicted. We never found the third man, but I swear one day, I'll find him." A cold look stole over Cole's face then, making him appear older and more the man that he was now than the boy she'd once known so well.

Shivers ran down her spine. Cole sounded so determined. Suddenly the dangers of his vocation became clear. He was the sheriff, the person responsible for the safety of the town.

Violence hadn't hit Crystal Creek in such a way since the gold strike. Back then, she remembered many a story her mama told of people willing to stab their own kin in the back for an ounce of gold.

"It's been peaceable here ever since, Kate. Folks like it that way."

Kate ignored Cole's attempt at persuasion. "I'm truly sorry to hear about Jeb and his wife, Cole. Seems that we both lost someone close."

"That we did," he admitted, searching her eyes carefully.

He made her nervous with the way he was watching her. Kate turned away and walked about the room. Frilly yellow window curtains filtered the sunlight, embroidered pillows sat snugly on the sofa and a fine Irish lace tablecloth draping the dining table were among many feminine touches about the room. "How do you manage with the child?" she asked cautiously.

"I have a housekeeper. She comes during the day and watches Meggie for me."

Kate nodded, hating the relief she felt that Cole hadn't married. "Kate?"

She whirled around to face him. "I'm here to see a copy of the ordinance, Cole. You do have one, don't you?"

He was ready to answer when a soft knock at the door brought his head around. "Excuse me. I'll be right back."

A few seconds later, Kate came face-to-face with Patricia Wesley. She hadn't laid eyes on the banker's daughter in years, but the girl was now a lovely young woman. Dressed elegantly in a fine silk ivory gown, and with her dark hair pulled up into the latest fashionable style, Patricia Wesley spoke of refinement and taste. "Hello, Mary Kathryn. I'd heard you were back in town."

Kate peered at Patricia, then at Cole, who was steps behind her. Patricia sidled up closer to Cole once he'd finally made his way into the parlor. "Patricia returned to Crystal Creek a few months ago," Cole explained, his expression unreadable.

"Yes, I spent several years in Boston, visiting relatives and attending finishing school." She glanced at Cole then. "But I'm back to stay now. As a matter of fact, that's why I'm here, Cole." She turned her back on Kate and put a possessive hand on Cole's arm. "Father and I enjoyed having you to dinner so much last week, he's offering another invitation for tomorrow evening. He really enjoys your Meggie. He says she reminds him of me, when I was her age."

"Well," Kate said quickly, "I'd better let you two make your plans." Kate tightened her hold on her handbag and moved toward the front door.

"It was nice seeing you again," Patricia offered a bit too sweetly for Kate's liking. Patricia had always been one to turn her nose up at Kate in school.

"Goodbye, Patricia." Kate stopped right in front of Cole and looked straight into his eyes. "I'd like a copy of that ordinance, Cole."

Cole's expression changed, a hint of anger marring his handsome face. He followed her to the front door, a frown pulling at his lips. "You'll have it tomorrow."

"I'll be working on the Browns' place in the morning. Will you bring it by there?"

Cole nodded and opened the door for her. "Kate, listen," he began, but Kate dashed down the steps before he could finish his sentence.

"Tomorrow, Cole."

Chapter Three

Mrs. Gregory set a plate of eggs and bacon out for Cole and poured him a cup of coffee. Meggie sat at the kitchen table facing him, wearing a loose-fitting flowered nightdress, stabbing at her oatmeal with a frown.

"Eat up, little missy," Mrs. Gregory encouraged, bringing the bowl a bit closer to entice his daughter. Meggie was having no part of it.

"I don't like oatmeal," she announced solemnly.

"Meggie, take a bite or two—for Daddy?"

Cole witnessed the stark determination in his daughter's eyes. She might have Jeb's late wife's blond hair and coloring, but she certainly didn't have her accommodating qualities. That could only mean she had a streak of the infamous, stubborn Bradshaw nature.

"One bite, Daddy," she said, lifting the spoon up to her mouth. After that taste, she shoved the bowl away, causing Mrs. Gregory to pucker her wrinkled mouth. He knew Mrs. Gregory didn't rightly approve of Cole's indulgent ways with Meggie, but Cole felt somewhat justified. The child had lost a great deal already in her young years of life. She'd lost both of her parents and was subjected to being raised by a man who knew little about children. Cole knew no better way to make it up to the child than to let her have her way once in a while. Right or wrong, it was the way of it.

"Would you like me to bring the little miss down to the jail for lunch today, Sheriff?"

Often Cole enjoyed spending his afternoon meal with Meggie, but today he had too many things to do. "Not today, Mrs. Gregory." He turned his attention to Meggie, who was staring up at him with wide, expectant eyes. "But Daddy will come home extra early this afternoon and we'll do something fun."

Meggie's face beamed with delight and Cole was grateful his daughter hadn't been overly disappointed about not visiting him at the jailhouse. It was one of her favorite things to do. "Can we go to the creek?"

"That's a fine idea, darlin'."

Meggie jumped down from the ladder-back chair and ran over to him, lifting up her arms. Cole's heart swelled with pride and love and he reached down to deposit the child onto his lap. She hugged him tight around the neck. "I love you, Daddy."

He kissed her forehead, wiping wayward locks of wheat-gold hair off her face. She was born of Jeb's blood, but she was his daughter now, through and through. "Love you too, Megpie."

Meggie chuckled.

Cole set her down and swatted her bottom. "Off you go, now. Get dressed. Daddy's got to get on to the jail now."

Cole watched as his daughter left the kitchen, then stared up at Mrs. Gregory, who was tapping her foot at him. "That child has got to learn to mind. I love her dearly but I can see the writing on the wall, I can. She's not going to mind you or me at all when she gets a bit older."

Cole ran a hand down his face. He knew Mrs. Gregory was right, so he gave her the same answer he always did. "I'll work on it, Mrs. Gregory." With her staring down at him the way she often did, Cole felt as if he was back in Miss Ashmore's classroom, getting a stern talking-to. It didn't matter that he was sheriff of this town, that he'd become respected in the community or that he was raising a child now, her admonishments always managed to put him in his place.

"That child needs a mother," she muttered, removing the plates from the kitchen table and bringing them to the sink.

Kate's image pushed into his thoughts. She'd been all he could think about ever since he first caught sight of her walking down the streets of Crystal Creek. But Kate a mother for Meggie?

Cole shook his head. Doubts crept into his mind as

to whether the untamed, free-spirited Kate would make a good wife and mother. With being hell-bent on opening the saloon, what kind of mother would she make? Cole had promised Jeb he'd do right by his daughter. If Cole ever decided to marry, it'd have to be with someone who could teach Meggie proper. Someone like Patricia.

Why hadn't Patricia's image popped into his head at the thought of marriage? Why hadn't Cole taken her subtle hints and pledged himself to her? She'd be good for Meggie. She could teach her womanly skills, all the things a young, refined girl should know. Patricia would make a suitable wife and a good mother. Cole wanted a real family. He wanted a wife to come home to after a day of work and he wanted a house filled with children. He wanted his heart to thump like mad when his wife walked into his arms at night. But it wasn't Patricia entering his thoughts. It was Kate.

At one point, she was all Cole had wanted in a girl, but he hadn't realized it until it was too late. She'd already left Crystal Creek by the time he'd gotten it into his thick skull how much Kate meant to him.

But she was a woman now, and he was the sheriff—a man who should set a shining example for the townsfolk. People looked up to Cole. What kind of match could they make with him being the sheriff and her stirring up trouble, trying her damnedest to open a saloon?

Cole shook his head. There was no place in his life for Kate Malone. As much as he hated to admit that…after everything they shared in the past, Cole knew he was right in his thinking. He'd obtained a copy of the town ordinance she'd requested, promising to bring it over to her today. Maybe then, after reading the ordinance, she'd realize the futility in trying to open up the Silver Saddle again. And if she decided to take it to a vote, the town council would unanimously turn her down.

Cole would hate to see it come to that. Knowing Kate and the way the town had always treated her and her mother, Cole didn't want her to experience the unpleasant recollection again. If only she'd give up on the notion and either gain employment somewhere else in this town, or move on.

A sharp bolt of pain thundered in his chest at the prospect of her leaving. Yet, having her stay could only cause him a load of trouble.

Cole donned his tan vest, holstered his gun and slammed out the front door, heading straight for his office. Kate was expecting him this morning to give her a copy of the ordinance. He might as well get it over with.

A splash of water hit Kate's face. She swiped it away quickly, dipping the cloth into the bucket again and rinsing away another layer of dust from the kitchen counter. The cabinets were clean now, as were the table and cookstove. She'd swept the floor and brought in several rugs she'd bought at the general store to disperse around the house.

All in all, the house she'd let from the Browns was shaping up nicely. With a quick glance around the kitchen, Kate realized her work in here was done. She untied her apron, and with a clean burlap towel, she dabbed at the moisture on her brow.

Kate was pinning up strands of hair that had come loose from her bun, when she heard a knock at the door.

Cole.

It had to be him. She'd been expecting him all morning.

"I hope you have the town ordinance with you," she said quietly to herself as she headed for the front door, straightening her work dress. She knew she must look a mess, but there was really no help for it. Besides, her days of trying to impress Cole Bradshaw were long over.

When she swung open the door, she was surprised to find a young woman standing there wearing a tentative smile and holding a basket of baked goods. "H-hello," the woman said shyly.

Kate searched her mind. This woman looked vaguely familiar. "Good morning."

"Do you...remember me?"

Once again, Kate tried to recall the face as glimpses of a young girl flashed in her mind. "Are you...Nora? Nora Eldridge?"

The sandy-haired woman smiled, lighting up her entire face. "I'm Nora Cable now, but yes, it's me."

Nora Eldridge had been a shy girl who stammered

in class. She'd been the butt of many cruel jokes and as much an outcast in school as the saloon owner's daughter. Kate had always felt a great kinship with her and had never, ever, participated in the mean-spirited antics of her schoolmates.

And Kate had never seen the girl smile. "Did you say Cable?"

Still smiling, Nora nodded. "I married Abe Cable one month ago."

"Congratulations. I believe I met Jethro the other day. He must be your brother-in-law."

"Yes, Jethro's my relation now. That's how I knew you were in town. He came home sort of…well, you did make quite an impression on my brother-in-law." Nora blushed.

Kate chuckled. "Would you like to come in?"

"I don't want to intrude. I brought a basket of molasses cookies and corn muffins to welcome you back."

Kate took the proffered basket. "That was very sweet of you. Please, you're not intruding—come inside. I've been working since dawn and could use a bit of company. The house is beginning to take shape. I understand no one's lived in it for several years."

Nora entered the house and Kate guided her to the kitchen. "I hope you don't mind—I haven't cleaned up the parlor yet—but the kitchen is spotless. Would you care to have a seat?"

"Yes, thank you," Nora said, and Kate realized

that for the most part, her old schoolmate had lost her stutter.

Kate took out two plates from her newly polished cabinets and set them down. "I'm sorry I don't have coffee to offer you, but would you care for some lemonade?"

"Yes, that would be fine."

"So, you're married now. I understand that the Cables bought up Southby's Livery. Is that when you met your husband?"

Kate poured the lemonade, then set out some of Nora's cookies and muffins on a platter.

"Yes," she said with a joyful lilt in her tone. "I went with my father to rent a buggy just days after they had come to town. When I saw Abe for the first time, my heart kind of flipped over." Her eyes grew wide as she went on to explain, "I'd never felt anything so powerful in my life."

Kate knew something of powerful yearnings. At one time, she'd felt the very same way about Cole. But that all too potent jolt, she feared, came only once in a girl's lifetime.

And in a sense that was all right with Kate, because in the end, if it didn't work out, the pain the disappointment caused was brutally unbearable. Kate couldn't go through that sort of anguish again.

"And Abe surely felt the same way about you," Kate offered gaily, fending off her own personal heartache.

"He said he did. And it didn't matter to him that

I stuttered. He said it sort of made him like me even more.''

"You...stuttered then?''

"Yes, for all these years I have, but after being with Abe, well, I guess I just needed the right man to help me through it.''

"I'm happy for you and so glad you came to visit me.''

"You,'' she began, then paused. "You and Cole were the only ones who never...''

"I know. This town could use a dose of compassion. But you're happy now, and that's all that matters.''

"What about you, Kate?''

"Me?'' She sipped her lemonade, not knowing how to fill in the past six years of her life.

"What do you plan on doing?''

"I hope to reopen the Silver Saddle, Nora.''

"Oh. I thought it was because of Sheriff Bradshaw. I remember the two of you in school, the way you looked at each other.''

In a wistful tone, Kate recalled, "He'd spend his days trying to best me at everything.''

Nora smiled and shook her head. "No, I meant when you both were a bit older. I've never seen two people so suited for each other. I used to think if only I could find someone to put a glow in my eyes, the way Cole did for you.''

Kate squeezed her eyes shut briefly, blocking out the past. "It's not that way with us, Nora.''

"Oh, then I'm sorry for the presumption. I came here to welcome you back to Crystal Creek. I do hope you'll be successful with the saloon."

"You do?"

"Yes, I do. There's no shame in running a saloon. I never understood why folks treated your mama so mean. She was a good woman. And so are you."

Kate reached for Nora's hand. "Thank you," she said, touched by Nora's sincere declaration. "It means a lot."

"You're welcome. Abe and I and...of course, Jethro, we'd be pleased to have you over for supper sometime. Would you come?"

"I'd love to come. Thank you."

After eating muffins and cookies then finishing their lemonade, Kate saw Nora out, thanking her again for her kindness.

Kate resumed her work, tackling the large job in the parlor now, but this time with renewed eagerness. And she hoped that today, she'd made her first genuine female friend in Crystal Creek.

Cole stood outside Kate's door, ready to knock, when an all-too-familiar shriek had him bursting forth. Within the span of a second, Cole noted Kate on a stepladder, reaching up toward a candelabra, her arms flailing wildly as she lost her footing. He dashed to her side and caught her in his arms, just in time, as the stepladder fell away. "Damn it, Kate."

"Cole?"

She appeared dazed, looking up at him, confusion marring her expression.

He tightened his hold, the feel of her too good to abandon right now. "You shouldn't be up on that thing," he admonished, but there was no real effort in his command. He was too taken by the feel of her bosom crushing into his chest, the scent of her, not overwhelmingly sweet or flowery, just Kate, and the look of vulnerability in her eyes.

It was a look she'd only allowed at unguarded moments in her life. Right now, it was enough to make Cole lose all common sense. He pressed her closer, his gaze lowering to her lips. They were rosy pink and moist. Her body flowed into his. She felt so damn good in his arms. Yet, he wanted more. He wanted to kiss her for real this time, the way a man kisses a woman. As a young boy he'd never had the courage to kiss Kate that way.

"Kate," he said softly, then brought his lips down on hers. The sweet, giving way she returned his kiss wobbled his knees. Gently he pressed her mouth open and heard her tiny moan. He muffled that moan with a tender thrust of his tongue. She met his thrust with one of her own, bold yet innocent in the way she touched him. Cole drove his hands into soft clouds of coppery curls as pins fell away. He cupped her head gently and soft silky waves flowed over his hands. A whimper escaped Kate's throat then and Cole deepened their kiss. He had never known such powerful longings before. His heart thumped like mad. Lower regions tightened with fierce need and he pulled her closer into his arms. As he slanted his mouth over her lips again, he felt resistance. Something stopped him.

Kate.

She was pushing at him, struggling to get out of his arms.

"Kate," he rasped, his breaths coming in short bursts.

"Don't, Cole," she said, finally able to release herself from his iron-tight grip because he'd loosened it. "Don't," she said again, her face flush with color, her lips bruised from his kiss. She stepped back and put up her hand. Cole rubbed the back of his neck, staring at her.

Kate bore witness to gleaming passion in Cole's blue gaze. She wondered where it had come from. Why was he suddenly here, kissing her like there was no tomorrow?

Yesterday it had been more than clear to Kate that Cole had truly moved on with his life...with Patricia Wesley. How could he come in here and kiss her that way, making her heart nearly stop from wanting so, when he was most certainly courting Patricia? Land's sake, he was having dinner with the Wesleys on this very night!

She straightened her skirt and brushed aside the hair that had come undone from Cole's embrace. *She* had nearly come undone. But she'd not be a fool twice in one lifetime. Chin raised, she asked in a shaky voice, "D-did...you bring the ordinance?"

Dumbfounded, Cole nodded. There was turmoil in those confused, brilliant blue eyes. "What just happened between us—"

"It was a kiss, Cole. That's all."

She made a move to pass him, but he caught her arm, holding her firm. "That's *all?*"

She nodded, her eyes studying the floor.

He let out a string of curses. Kate flinched at hearing such language coming from Cole. He dropped her arm and she moved away, feeling his deep, penetrating gaze following her. When she had recovered from a kiss she'd only dreamed about, she turned to face him. "The ordinance?"

Anger lit his eyes, making them burn like blue embers. Kate was beyond caring about his sensibilities right now. She'd have enough of a time trying to forget the heart-robbing kiss they'd just shared.

Cole glanced around and found the papers on the floor. He must have tossed them the moment he had rushed to her aid. Retrieving them quickly, he arranged them in his hand before turning them over to her. "Here's the damn ordinance." Kate ignored his obvious irritation. She flipped through the pages, glancing at the signatures on the last one. "Your signature appears on the list." She sent him an accusing stare.

"I bore witness to the signing," he admitted. "It was designed to protect the town, Kate."

"From the likes of me?" she asked plainly.

"Hell, Kate. That's not what I meant. After what

happened with Jeb and some of the others, the town council thought it best to protect the citizens of this town."

"I'm hardly a threat," she said, tightening her grip on the papers.

"No, not you. But the saloon brings in rowdies and drunks. You have to remember what it was like before. Fights broke out, people got hurt. Sheriff Cullen was always tossing someone into a jail cell." He went on, "It ain't fitting for a woman, Kate. A woman's place is with her family, at home."

"I have no family, Cole."

"You could, Kate. One day, you could have a fine family. But not if you open that saloon."

Kate blinked at Cole's blunt declaration. He was telling her that no decent law-abiding man would want a woman who ran a saloon. Especially not Sheriff Cole Bradshaw. It wasn't proper, wasn't what women were expected to do. At times, Cole's rigid beliefs perplexed her so. "It was good enough for Mama. It's good enough for me."

"Kate, I'm warning you. The town doesn't want the Silver Saddle to open again."

"I believe you're wrong, Sheriff. And I intend to prove it."

"You'd best abide by the ordinance, Kate," Cole said, taking in a sharp breath. Kate didn't miss the threat in his tone.

"Or what?" She planted her hands firmly on her hips, her chin defiantly raised. She knew what he was about to say, but it still twisted a knot inside her stomach.

He hesitated a moment, peering into her eyes. Bringing his focus lower to her lips, she heard his slight, almost silent, sigh. She waited a moment, and when he finally spoke it was with deep regret. "Or I'll have to arrest you."

Chapter Four

Cole sat in the Wesley dining room, glancing at Patricia and nodding politely as Edward Wesley spouted his current assessment of President Hayes's recent win over his Democratic opponent, Tilden. "The country about came to blows over this. Goes to show you what happens when there's a direct loss of control. Compromise is what got Hayes elected, I say."

Cole listened with only half an ear. His mind was on Kate, and how it had felt holding her in his arms this morning. He couldn't quite get it out of his head, her body pressed against his, her lips warm and giving, as if she'd been born to kiss him. She'd grown up to become a beautiful woman. Strong willed and spirited, but beautiful just the same. Cole hoped he could talk her out of her fool notion to defy the town ordinance. But if it came right down to it, Cole knew he'd have to stop her. The law was the law. And he couldn't bend the rules, not even for Kate.

"Don't you agree, son?" Edward asked pointedly, driving thoughts of Kate from his head instantly.

Cole straightened in his seat. "What's that, Mr. Wesley?"

"That if the South hadn't wanted those Federal troops out of their cities, putting an end to Reconstruction, Hayes wouldn't have ever taken office?"

"Father," Patricia interrupted, "enough political talk for one evening, please. We don't want Meggie getting bored." Patricia smiled sweetly and reached over, adjusting the napkin on Meggie's lap. "How are you enjoying the meal, Meggie? You haven't touched your vegetables. Don't you like them?"

Meggie put her head down. "No, ma'am."

"They'll put a shine to your pretty hair. Just a bite or two each day will do."

"Yes, ma'am."

Patricia glanced at Cole. "Your daddy ate all of his vegetables," she said, her light brown eyes sparkling.

She did look pretty tonight, Cole thought, watching the candlelight put a glow onto her creamy complexion. And she sure knew her manners. A woman like that would be perfect to help him raise Meggie all proper-like.

"Won't you take one bite, Meggie, for me?"

Meggie shifted her attention to cast Cole an expectant look. He nodded, encouraging her. Where his daughter got her picky eating habits, he'd never know. The Bradshaws had all been healthy eaters. "Go on, Megpie, have a taste of the carrots."

His obstinate child twisted her lips into a pout. "Only if I hafta." Meggie took a tiny bite, chewed it quickly then put down her fork.

Edward let out a big belly laugh. "The child sure knows what she wants, doesn't she? I like her spirit, Cole."

"She's got the Bradshaw nature, that's for sure, Edward." Cole stroked Meggie's head, both amazed and grateful at the powerful feelings he had for the child. She filled a hole in his life left by Jeb's death. He and his wife, Lydia, had been Cole's only family.

"She just needs a woman's influence, Cole," Patricia said, rising from her chair. "A girl's got to understand the subtleties in life. There are certain things she can't learn from a man."

"I'm sure you're right, Patricia," Cole said, feeling himself being backed into a corner. He got enough lectures on the subject from Mrs. Gregory.

He rose slightly, the gentlemanly thing to do and watched Patricia come around the richly grained burlwood table to reach for Meggie's hand.

"Would you like to help me serve the dessert? We're having peach cobbler. I'll show you how to spoon on the cream."

Meggie nodded. "'Kay," she said, taking Patricia's hand and giving Cole a long sour look as she walked by. Cole silently chuckled at his daughter's behavior. Mrs. Gregory would have been appalled,

and although the elderly woman tried to teach Meggie
right from wrong, she had enough to do keeping the
house and tending to Meggie's needs. Cole couldn't
expect any more of her. Right now, Cole found Meggie's antics amusing, but he knew, eventually, he'd
have to do something about it. Meggie needed a full-
time mother. It was time Cole took a wife. He was
tired of sleeping in a cold, lonely bed.

"I hear that Malone woman is planning on opening
up the Silver Saddle again," Edward said, after Patricia and Meggie left the room.

"That seems to be her plan," Cole replied cautiously. He didn't like discussing Kate with anybody,
much less the man she blamed for pushing her out of
town.

"Well, I hope you know what your duty is, son.
She'd be going against the law. The town council—"

"She's aware of the ordinance." Cole leaned back
in his chair and stretched his legs in a casual gesture
he surely wasn't feeling right about now. "I think
she'll come around." He had to make sure of it. Cole
didn't need any trouble with the townsfolk. Not when
he was up for reelection next fall. Her defying the
ordinance would put him in a real uncomfortable spot.
And Kate too would get hurt. That was the very last
thing he wanted to have happen.

Edward narrowed his eyes and gestured with a finger. "See that she does, Cole. Compromise is for
weaklings."

Cole didn't like the way this conversation had turned. More than anyone else, Cole Bradshaw knew what his duty was. He took being sheriff of the county seriously. The only two things that really mattered to him were raising his daughter right and being the best damn sheriff the county had ever seen. He didn't need Edward Wesley dictating to him, bank president or not, no matter how much influence the older man had over the town. "I took an oath to uphold the law, Edward. It's what I plan to do."

Patricia entered then, holding a platter of large crystal bowls filled with peach cobbler and a generous dollop of cream on each one. "Here we go," she said cheerfully. "The coffee will be ready in one minute."

Cole rose to help, taking the platter from her hands. He set it down carefully on the table.

Patricia began serving the dessert. Coming up close to Cole, she spoke into his ear. "Meggie gave you the biggest scoop of cream. I think she likes her daddy...just as much as I do," she whispered.

Cole took the offered dish, casting Patricia a small smile. He waited for her to finish serving before taking his seat again, a gnawing ache growing in his gut. He liked Patricia, but hell, he wasn't...ready, to make her a commitment.

Thoughts of Kate Malone pushed into his head again. Would he ever get the feel of her body or the taste of her sweet lips off his mind? He wasn't going to allow her to run roughshod over his town, but damn it, the woman got his insides churning.

Cole forced himself to pay attention to Patricia. "Meggie was a big help in the kitchen, Cole," she said pleasantly. "Next time you bring her over, I'll show her how a lady sets a fine-looking table."

Cole told Patricia that was a good idea, but out of the corner of his eye, he could see his little scamp of a daughter making a face. He'd better get her home right quick, he thought wryly.

Cole finished the peach cobbler and took a last sip of coffee before pushing his dish aside. "That was delicious. Patricia, Mr. Wesley, thank you both for your hospitality. I sure do appreciate you having us over for dinner, but I'm afraid it's time for us to go." Cole stood and pulled out Meggie's chair. "Ready, Megpie?"

Meggie jumped down and took his hand. "Ready."

Patricia bit her lip, rising slowly from the table. "Cole, why don't you stay a little longer? Father wanted to show Meggie his checkerboard. And...and I thought you and I could take a little stroll."

"That's right. I learned to play checkers when I was just about Meggie's age. I bet she'd be good, too," Edward Wesley added.

"That's a very nice offer, but I've got to get Meggie to bed. It's getting late."

"Another time perhaps?" Patricia said, smiling graciously.

Cole nodded. "Another time."

Meggie yawned then, a big, wide opening of her little mouth. She rubbed her eyes too. His four-year-old daughter *never* tired this early. Most nights, she complained she didn't want to bed down at all.

Cole didn't know whether to laugh or sigh. There were too many doggone cunning females in the room for him. He thanked Edward and Patricia again for their hospitality and hightailed it out of the house.

Two days later, as Cole strode down the street heading for the jail, he noticed Kate, deep in concentration, muttering to herself as she worked on the weathered picket fence in her front yard. "Morning, Kate."

She whirled around, seemingly surprised to see him. He had to pass this way every morning on his way to his office, but this was the first time he'd come across her. "Good morning," she said without a smile.

"Working on the fence?"

"Trying to. The darn thing's so old and beaten that I don't know why I bother, but last night's winds nearly ripped the wood in two. I plan on strengthening it, then covering the ugly boards with a thick coat of whitewash."

Kate took the hammer and began to pound in a nail on the post nearest him. She missed and jammed her finger. "Ouch!" She jumped back and gripped her injured hand, tears misting in her eyes.

"You okay?"

She nodded, but he could see her frustration mounting. She'd been muttering when he'd come upon her.

Clearly she wasn't enjoying this chore. And now, she'd hurt herself.

Cole came around the inside of the fence where she stood and took the hammer out of her hand. He unbuckled his gun belt and threw it across the porch rail.

"What are you doing?" Kate asked. She was sucking on the finger that she'd nearly crushed.

Cole averted his eyes. His mouth had already gone dry, watching her move that finger over her lips. "Helping."

"But...I can do it."

He raised a brow. "I see how well you were doing."

"I didn't ask you...for help."

Cole pounded in a few long nails then glared at her. "If you want this fence steady by the time the winds come later on, move aside. It's going to take a while."

"But I said I could do it."

Cole set down the hammer and looked deep into her wintergreen eyes. "We aren't kids anymore, Kate. You don't always have to beat me at everything. There's no prize at the end, no finish line. I'm helping because you need it. Now, if you want to do something useful, bring me something cold to drink." Cole raked his gaze over her body and his gut tightened. She filled out a simple calico better than any woman Cole had ever known. She didn't need silk or lace; Kate was female enough without all the frills. Cole took a hard swallow and turned back to the task at hand. "My mouth's all but parched."

Twenty minutes later, and with nearly half the work accomplished, Cole took a break. He rubbed his sleeve across his forehead, wiping away sweat, then sat down on the grass near Kate and sipped his lemonade. "This half of the fence is good and tight now," he said, glancing at Kate. "Should hold up to the winds. Won't take me long to finish the rest."

Kate looked at his work and shrugged sheepishly. "You were right, Cole. I'd still be working on that first post if you hadn't come along."

He grinned like a devil. He knew he probably shouldn't tease her, but the temptation was too great. "You mean I bested you?"

Stunned by his remark, she flung the remaining drops of lemonade at him. "Cole Bradshaw!"

"Hey!" Good thing her glass was almost empty or he'd have had to go home to change a sticky shirt.

"You are such a, oh...never mind."

She folded her arms across her middle and lifted her chin in the air, just as she'd done countless times in their youth. This was the Kate that Cole remembered best. She gave as good as she got, but it had been a simpler time then. Now their different beliefs separated them like a towering sugar pine being split in two.

"What am I, Kate?"

"I can't tell you," she said impishly, "or you

won't finish my fence." She chuckled and stood up, her coppery waves bouncing against her shoulder.

Cole, too, stood and they stared at each other with smiles lifting their lips. Emotion rushed through him then, and strong familiar yearnings. "Don't build the saloon, Kate."

Her smile evaporated, like water on the desert sand. "I have to, Cole."

"And I have to stop you."

"I know," she whispered quietly, saying nothing else. She took his emptied glass into the house and never came back outside. It was better this way, he thought honestly. He'd finish her fence and be done with it. At least he didn't have to gaze into her beautiful eyes and ache from need when she got real close. He knew what he was up against. She wouldn't back down, and neither would he.

And in the end, no one would win.

Kate entered the Cable Brothers Livery later that afternoon with Cole's words still ringing in her ear. It was his duty as sheriff to uphold the law, she knew, but Kate couldn't see how opening the Silver Saddle would be breaking the law. As soon as she'd obtained the copy of the town ordinance, she'd sent it to a good friend of her mother's back in Los Angeles. Mr. Robert Pendicott was the finest attorney-at-law in the city. If anyone could find a way around the ordinance, Kate believed it would be him. She was placing all of her faith in him and holding back nothing. Time, money and energy would go into the rebuilding of the saloon and Kate was finally ready to begin.

Months ago, when her mama was alive, they'd placed an advance order for a long polished mahogany bar, two stained-glass windows with identical Silver Saddles etched in each and, as a safety precaution, an iron front door. Kate's mother insisted on spending the extra money for iron-shuttered doors as protection against fire. It was becoming a common but expensive practice of saloon owners, as added insurance against wayward flames. They'd also ordered shiny brass spittoons, a large gilded mirror and the piano, too, was coming from the East.

Kate heard voices in the back of the livery and, as she walked further inside, was surprised to find Patricia Wesley speaking with Jethro Cable. She stopped and stood by a post, allowing them to finish their conversation with privacy. "And next time I rent a horse, I'd like one that doesn't try to buck me every chance he got."

Kate noted Jethro's face flame with color. He yanked his hat off and ran a hand through his golden hair. "Miss Wesley, you've got to treat a horse with a certain respect. If you show him respect, he'll show you the same."

"Are you saying I don't know how to ride, Mr. Cable?"

"No, no. What I'm saying is that you...well, yes, I suppose I am. A riding lesson is just what you probably need."

"Ha!" Patricia's voice rose to an uneven pitch. "I'll have you know that I was trained by the most prestigious stable in all of Boston. The groomsman said I had a knack with horses."

Jethro laughed right in her face. "Is that so?"

"Yes, that is so." Patricia removed her fancy suede riding gloves and tapped them into her hand. "Don't you believe me?"

Jethro shook his head. "Don't rightly matter if I do or not. Truth is, those horses back East are most likely gentled to riders and they put fancy English saddles on them. I don't suppose you've ridden one of these here regular saddles since you were a girl."

Patricia's unyielding expression mellowed and she bit her lip. "Well, I suppose that could make a difference."

"It surely does."

Patricia filled her lungs with air and continued her admonishment. "Still, the horses you rent out should be more gentle."

Jethro didn't back down. He brought his face close so that he looked down his nose at her. "And the rider should treat the mare with more regard."

"Good day, Mr. Cable." Patricia turned abruptly, an exasperated look on her face, and began walking away.

"I'll put the charge on your father's bill, Miss Wesley," Jethro called out to her.

Kate hoped Patricia would continue on in a hurry to get away and pass her by, but instead she stopped when she noticed Kate just inside the livery. "Hello, Mary Kathryn," she said in greeting.

"Good afternoon, Patricia." Kate thought to tell her to call her "Kate," but decided she really didn't want Patricia using the name she preferred. To Patricia, she'd always be Mary Kathryn, the saloon gal's daughter, anyway.

"Are you planning on renting a horse from that rude man?"

"Jethro Cable? Rude? I've only met him once, but he seemed perfectly friendly. I plan on renting a wagon for tomorrow."

Patricia's eyebrows lifted. "Oh, going somewhere in particular?"

"Yes," Kate answered without elaborating. It was none of Patricia's business what she wanted with a wagon.

"I see, well, I do hope you have good weather for your ride. Cole and I were saying, last night over dinner, just how fair our weather has been lately. He hopes the good weather continues for the Founder's Day celebration coming up soon."

Kate's heart nearly plummeted to the ground. The Founder's Day celebration had caused her nothing but despair. She recalled all too vividly the past and how much she had wanted Cole's invitation to that particular celebration when she had been a love-struck girl of fifteen. But instead, he'd asked Patricia and he'd broken her young heart. Nothing seemed to have changed except that Kate had hardened her heart and her spirit to Cole. He was a different man than she remembered. But it still hurt when she looked into his eyes. It still hurt to see him about town, tall and proud, wearing his sheriff's badge like a shield of honor. It still hurt to know she wasn't good enough for him.

"I really have to see Jethro now, Patricia. Have a good day." Kate walked past Patricia without even a second glance. She had too much to do and couldn't spend any more time reliving the past.

She walked to a stall where she spotted Jethro combing down a bay mare.

"Hello, Mr. Cable."

He turned to face her, setting down his currycomb. "Why, Miss Malone, good afternoon." Kate watched as he swatted a fine layer of dust off his clothes and came out of the stall. "And it's Jethro, if you don't mind."

"Jethro," she said with a smile. "And I'm Kate."

"Kate," he repeated with a nod. "Nora told me she came by for a visit. She said you were working on fixing up the old Brown place."

"Yes, it's coming along nicely. I've actually gotten most of the cobwebs out," she said. "I'm so glad Nora came by. We had a good visit. She's a wonderful woman."

"She speaks highly of you, too." He grinned and white teeth flashed against a handsome face. "What can I do for you?"

"Well, I need to rent a wagon for tomorrow. Is that possible?"

"Sure thing. How long will you need it?"

"Not all that long. I have to drive over to the lumber camp on the other side of Crystal Creek."

Jethro scratched his head. "I see."

"Is there a problem?"

"No, ma'am, but a lady shouldn't be going into one of those lumber camps alone."

"I'm afraid I have no choice. I plan to order the wood to rebuild the exterior of the saloon. While I'm there, I also hoped to hire on a few men to do the building."

"Listen, Miss Kate, I have me an idea. Abe will be here all day tomorrow, working the livery. I'll be happy to drive the wagon and take you. No extra charge. It'll be my pleasure."

Kate debated about half a second. She had dreaded going into that camp alone. She'd heard stories about the women-starved men up there in the hills. Having Jethro by her side would certainly ease her mind. "Thank you, Jethro. I think I'll take you up on your offer, but only if you let me repay your kindness. I'd like to have the Cables to dinner one evening."

Jethro cast her a wide grin. "Just name the day, Miss Kate. I'll be there."

Chapter Five

Mrs. Gregory wiped her hands on her apron after breakfast and scooted Meggie out of the room, telling her to wash up and get dressed. Once Meggie had left the kitchen, Cole's housekeeper turned to him with a look of concern on her face. "I'll be needing to speak with you, Sheriff."

Usually the woman had a cheerful disposition, so Cole braced himself. He could see she had something serious to discuss with him. "Now's a good time, Mrs. Gregory. Why don't we sit in the parlor?"

"That'll be fine."

He followed her into the parlor and waited until she sat down on the horsehair sofa. He took a seat in his favorite chair and gave her his full attention. "What is it that you'd like to say?"

She heaved a heavy sigh and began with a small smile. "I love working here, Sheriff. It ain't that. And lord knows I love that little child with all my heart, but I'm afraid I'll be leaving you soon. You see, my youngest daughter Caroline is expecting her third child. She's asked me to come to live with them on their homestead after the baby is born.''

"Well, you can hardly refuse such an offer. I know you miss seeing your own grandchildren."

Mrs. Gregory truly looked regretful. Tears misted up in her eyes. "I've given this great thought. At times, it's perplexed me so. That little child of yours needs a woman about. I know that, but I am getting on in years and would like to spend my remaining days with my children."

Cole rubbed his jaw and furrowed his brows. He'd become accustomed to having Mrs. Gregory about the house. He had hired her just after Jeb's death, when Meggie was two and a half. They'd come a long way together, but he could understand her wanting to live with her children.

Family was everything.

"I understand. Meggie and I will surely miss you."

"I'm not rushing out on you, Sheriff. I'll agree to stay on for several months. Until you can find a replacement for me."

"Thank you. I don't know if anyone can replace you, but we'll try to find someone suitable."

Cole didn't know where. It had been a stroke of luck, like being dealt an ace-high straight, finding Mrs. Gregory when he did. He'd really come to rely on her.

"If I might add something. It's nothing you ain't heard me spouting about before, but you should find yourself a wife. A young man like yourself and that lovely child. I'm sure there's more than one lady who'd like to fill that position, if you get my meaning.''

Cole chuckled. Mrs. Gregory oftentimes surprised him with her blunt accounting of things.

''Meggie should have some brothers and sisters, don't you think?''

Cole's brief amusement vanished at the mention of his duty to his daughter. Yes, Meggie should have siblings to play with. He'd often thought her a lonely child, being raised by a father who struggled hard to make time for her. And how Meggie would love a little brother or sister in the house. Hell, he'd always wanted a house full of children. The woman he married would have to want the same. And not have ideas of building a saloon, he thought wryly. He'd find another housekeeper to help with Meggie before he made a mistake in marriage. ''I've given that some thought.''

''Well,'' she said, sitting straight up on the sofa and looking him dead in the eye, ''thinking isn't what's needed here. You got to listen to your heart. Why, before my dear husband Samuel passed at the age of sixty, I'd still get a warm feeling every time that man walked into the house. That's what I'm talking about…listening to your heart never steers you wrong.''

''I'll keep that in mind.''

''And I won't be abandoning you. I'll stay on

through the spring. I'm hoping you'll have found someone by then.''

Cole nodded. ''Me, too.''

''And if you don't mind, I'd like to be the one to tell the little miss about my plans, when the time is right.''

''That's fine by me.'' Cole had faith that Mrs. Gregory would know how best to tell Meggie of her leaving. Hell, he didn't relish the thought of taking yet another person away from the child. She'd already lost so much.

Kate hopped up into the wagon, ready for the trip back to town. She was thrilled with her success at the lumber camp. With Jethro by her side, she'd had no trouble in purchasing the materials needed for the Silver Saddle. Jethro was kind enough to seek out the men who would be building her saloon. He knew about fair wages and made the men an honest offer of employment.

The Silver Saddle was on its way!

Kate thought about her grandfather and the legend of how the Silver Saddle began with two empty barrels holding up a long plank that served as a bar. In those days, the prospectors didn't care where they got their beer, but having it cold was an added treat. With a good head for business, Grandpa John had found an easy way to keep the beer cold, by using big cisterns of readily available cool creek water to store the barrels in.

It had been a raw and humble beginning, but the Silver Saddle had thrived in those days and soon after, a building made of wood with a thick sod roof had been constructed. Kate's grandfather had seen the start of the saloon, but it was her mother who had added style and elegance to the decor. And Kate's ideas were even more elaborate. Oh, she had such grand plans for the Silver Saddle. She couldn't see how folks would stay away.

"Jethro, I can't imagine what my day would have been like without your aid. Thank you."

"My pleasure, Miss Kate. Let me know if there's anything else you'll be needing," he said as he worked the team down a steep hill. "I'm willing to help."

Kate appreciated Jethro's friendship. He was a man who wasn't stuck with an idea in his head about what a woman ought to and ought *not* to do in her life. Unlike a certain staunch and stubborn sheriff she knew. But thinking of Cole's views would only sour an otherwise glorious day.

Today Kate had taken the first official step in finally realizing her and Mama's dream. The Silver Saddle belonged in Crystal Creek. It had been one of the first gainful enterprises in a town filled with people coming and going. And it would stand again, as a loving legacy to her mama's family.

When Jethro pulled the team to a halt in front of the livery, Kate thanked him again. "I'll be checking with Nora to figure when all of you can come for supper. I thought, perhaps Sunday, after church?"

Jethro grinned heartily. "That's a fine time. Abe and me, well, we always take off a half a day for Sunday worship."

"Good, then I'll speak with Nora tomorrow and we'll settle it."

Jethro jumped down from the wagon and came around to her side. With a firm hand, he helped her down. Kate smiled warmly at her new friend but refused his offer to walk her home. She was too excited to go home just yet.

On impulse, she headed for the schoolhouse, located at the edge of town. She strolled leisurely, noting subtle changes to the town she'd grown up in. Many shops along the street had changed ownership, others had been torn down only to have been rebuilt into finer, larger structures. Crystal Creek was thriving, it seemed, but Kate stopped abruptly when the schoolhouse came into view. She hadn't recalled it looking so shabby before. The once-fine bright red-and-white schoolhouse now showed chipped and faded paint. Two of the side windows had been boarded up. Why, the very planks holding the structure together seemed to be hanging on by a thread. The schoolhouse was in desperate need of repair.

"Oh my," Kate muttered, saddened by the aged look of a place in which she had spent so much time. She had never really minded school so much. She and Cole had had many a good time here, eating lunch by the old swing, playing silly games in the yard, working on their lessons.

They had been good times, Kate had to admit. Back then, she and Cole saw eye to eye on most things. Now she feared they'd be nothing more than two people on the opposite side of the fence, looking for a way over but never once thinking to take one rung at a time until they reached the top at the same moment.

Kate walked away from the schoolhouse with sadness in her heart. She'd didn't know if seeing the schoolhouse in its run-down state had put her in such a melancholy mood, or whether it had been thinking about her past with Cole. Either way, there was no help for it. There were just some things a body couldn't change.

Cole stood in front of his office with hands on hips, staring at the supply wagons from Buckston Lumber Camp, watching as men unloaded large wooden beams in front of the saloon. Curiosity had many a shop owner coming out of their front doors to see to the goings-on. More than a few of them were darting glances his way, but there wasn't a darn thing he could do about it now. There was no law in building a new establishment, only in operating it. As soon as the saloon opened for business, Kate would be breaking the law.

Cole didn't know what irritated him more, having Kate openly defy the town ordinance, or seeing her riding into town yesterday with Jethro Cable. Cole had come out of his office to make his rounds on the street when he witnessed a smiling Kate being lifted down from the wagon by a clearly smitten young man. Cole's entire body stiffened when he saw Jethro's hands around her waist. He'd cursed up a streak and called himself every kind of fool for wanting her. He'd not be caught mooning over a woman he couldn't have.

He strode with purpose toward the saloon, a frown pulling at his lips, watching Kate's green eyes light with eager anticipation while the men unloaded the supplies.

"Good afternoon, Sheriff Bradshaw."

"Kate."

Kate bubbled over with excitement that he couldn't share. "The supplies are all here. Soon my orders will be arriving from the East and I'll be in business." Her smile rivaled the sun, and Cole got the feeling nothing would diminish her enthusiasm.

"Kate, I'm warning you one last time. You need to take this up with the town council. You need their approval. Let them put it to a vote."

"If you were on the town council, Cole, how would you vote?" she asked, her voice deceptively soft and sweet.

"You know the answer to that. The saloon's going to cause you nothing but trouble."

She ignored him and turned her gaze to the smoke-laden walls of the old structure. "Just picture it, Cole. It'll be the grandest building in town. Once folks see what a fine establishment it is, they'll come around. I'm sure of it."

"You're going to serve beer and whiskey, aren't you?"

Kate's eyes rounded. "Of course. I'm gonna use Grandpa John's method for cooling the beer. Cold beer is what I'll be serving."

"And there's going to be gambling?"

"Well, I chose not to put in gaming tables. But there's nothing to stop a man from sitting down for a hand or two of poker."

"What you'll get is drunken gamblers and a whole lot of grief."

Kate whirled around and scorched him with fire in her eyes. The rims sparked emerald flames. "Why are you so opposed, Cole? Don't you know how important this is to me? The saloon is my life. I don't know how to do anything else."

Cole raked a gaze over her body. She was all female, full-bodied and beautiful. He'd become painfully aware of that since she'd returned to Crystal Creek. Cole could think of a world of things Kate could do. Hell, she could pleasure a man with just one beautiful smile. He didn't allow his mind to wander to the other more exciting ways she could keep a man happy. "A woman needs to know how to keep a fine house and raise her babies, Kate."

The flame in her eyes died then. "I wanted that once," she said sadly. "But I'm the saloon gal's daughter, remember? It's what I was meant to do."

Anger began to mount and Cole had a time keeping his temper from flaring. "Fine, Kate, build your saloon. But mark my words, this town is gonna burn you down...*without* any flames."

Cole stared into her eyes for a long moment. He was through trying to protect her. He was through trying to change her mind. And he hoped to hell...he was through wanting her.

Kate sat in the Cable kitchen, sipping tea, enjoying Nora's company. "Honestly, Nora, I didn't come here to interrupt your day. I only wanted to extend an invitation for you, Abe and Jethro to dinner Sunday after church."

"Of course we'll come. Thank you. And nonsense, Kate," Nora said gaily, waving her off with a small gesture of her hand. "I'm happy as pie to have your company. There's not much for me to do around here with the men gone all day. Of course," she added with a sly smile, "in about six months, there's going to be plenty for me to do."

Kate glanced down at Nora's hand. She'd placed it on her stomach. "Are you...with child?"

Nora's face broke out into the happiest expression Kate had ever seen. Nora nearly squeaked her answer. "Yes."

Kate bounded out of her seat and so did Nora. They hugged each other tight, tears flowing freely down both of their cheeks. "Oh, Nora, how absolutely wonderful for you. When did you say the baby will come?"

Nora wiped away happy tears with the back of her hand. Her face positively glowed. "By the end of summer. I just found out. Abe doesn't know yet. I plan to tell him tonight, when we are alone."

Kate smiled, pledging, "I promise not to tell a soul."

"I'm so glad you came by today. I was nearly bursting with the news. I wanted to tell somebody. I'm glad it was you."

"Oh, Nora, so am I." Kate had never been privy to such special information, nor had she ever felt so close to another woman. "How are you feeling?"

"I'm...I'm fine, really. But in the morning sometimes, I get a little bit queasy."

"Hmm. I heard that's not at all unusual. Of course, I don't know much about babies." Kate urged Nora to sit and finish her blueberry muffin. "But I do know you've got to eat up real good. You're eating for two now."

"I'm so hungry all the time, Kate." Nora blushed, a red flush of color staining her tear-streaked cheeks. "I'm surprised Abe hasn't guessed. I'm eating more than he does now."

Kate laughed. "Well, after tonight, he'll understand what's gotten into his wife."

Nora sipped her tea and glanced at Kate. Her face still beamed with happiness, but she had a curious look about her.

"What?" Kate asked, aware that Nora had something on her mind.

"I was just thinking how nice it would be if I had a friend to share this feeling with. I was wishing that friend were you. Do you want to have children, Kate?"

"I...I don't know if that will ever happen." Kate smiled, attempting to keep the conversation gay.

"I know you're busy with the saloon and all, but...maybe someday?"

Nora sounded hopeful. Kate had just about given up all hope. The only man she'd want to share a family with was Cole. She'd put that notion into her head at such a young age that she didn't think she'd ever shake it loose. And Cole had made himself clear to her from the start, what he expected in a woman. He certainly didn't want someone like her to raise his daughter and have his babies. That was perfectly obvious to Kate. "Well, you're forgetting, I'd have to be married first. I don't see that happening anytime soon."

"Oh, I don't know about that," Nora replied, lowering her voice. "I think my brother-in-law is smitten."

"Jethro?" Kate was taken by surprise. She'd only just met him. "He's a nice young man, Nora. I think of him as a new friend."

"Being friends is a good way to begin." Once again Nora sounded hopeful. But Jethro Cable could never replace Cole in Kate's heart. She and Cole had started out as friends first, and through the years Kate's feelings for him had grown to something even more powerful than their pledged friendship. She wondered how the six-year separation had changed him so? Or perhaps, both of them had changed some.

"Nora, I'd like to keep Jethro as my friend. *Just* as my friend. No offense, because Jethro is a good man, but my—"

"Your heart belongs to the sheriff."

Kate hadn't planned on admitting that to Nora. She'd intended to say that her time and energy had to go into the saloon, but Nora had been so honest and forthright in sharing her good news that Kate wanted to reciprocate by confiding in her. Having a new female friend took some getting used to, Kate mused. "Yes, but Cole and I see things differently. We'll never have a real chance, Nora. I've come to understand that."

"But, you and Cole have been so close."

Kate shoved aside the remorse she felt at losing that one-time cherished closeness. "That was in the past. We were just children."

"And now?"

Kate closed her eyes momentarily. When she reopened them, she knew the truth and wouldn't hide it from her friend. Soon she and Cole would be on the opposite sides of the law. "Now, we're nearly enemies."

Chapter Six

$\mathcal{L}\!\!\mathcal{Q}\!\!\mathcal{Q}\!\!\mathcal{L}\!\!\mathcal{Q}\!\!\mathcal{Q}$

Kate took her seat on a pew in the First Presbyterian Church of Calaveras County, sitting next to the Cables. The men, Jethro and Abe, hugged the aisle seats, while Nora and Kate sat in the middle. Kate noted the many curious onlookers who kept turning their heads her way. They weren't being cordial in the least but rather hoping to gain a bit of local gossip about the saloon gal, she mused.

Kate was used to their scrutiny. It really didn't bother her and, when their eyes met with hers, she smiled, noting that some chose to smile back. It was a start and Kate appreciated any gift, small as it may be.

Not all the townsfolk were opposed to the opening of the saloon. But the ones who were primarily at odds with her had just walked through the wide double church doors.

Cole, with his daughter Meggie in hand, entered alongside Patricia and Edward Wesley. Kate's tender

heart skipped a beat seeing them together, *all of them.*
They appeared a united front, a family. It's what Cole
had always wanted.

Cole's gaze found hers and lingered a moment,
holding her hostage with the sharp blue of his probing
eyes until he noticed Jethro sitting to her left. A scowl
tightened the handsome features of Cole's face then
and he quickly looked away.

Kate couldn't help noticing Patricia. Schooled in
Boston, she appeared the picture of social grace,
dressed elegantly in a button-down light yellow gown
of silk. She had a proprietary hand on Cole's arm as
they walked down the aisle to the pew reserved ex-
pressly for Edward Wesley. Some things just never
changed.

"Snooty Miss Wesley has hired my services for
riding lessons," Jethro whispered near Kate's ear. "It
surely *won't* be a pleasure," he said adamantly.

Kate chuckled a bit too loudly, giving the church-
goers good reason to turn her way.

"Be nice, Jethro," Kate admonished without an
ounce of sincerity. "We are in the house of God."

Jethro pulled his lips down into a deep frown. "I
find it hard to remember my manners in Miss Wesley's presence."

The good Reverend Pritchard cleared his throat,
thus silencing the group. When he began his sermon
on the value of obeying the law, Kate had the distinct
feeling the entire service was intended for her sole

benefit. Kate listened politely despite the stares she felt at her back.

Dear sweet Nora caught on instantly and took hold of Kate's hand, giving her a squeeze of reassurance. Kate thanked her blessings for the gift of Nora's friendship. Although it wasn't quite the same as her longstanding friendship with Cole, at least now she didn't feel at such an utter loss.

How she missed the camaraderie she and Cole had always shared.

And all throughout the sermon, Kate's gaze kept drifting to Cole and his daughter, sitting several pews up on the other side of the aisle. The little child sat ever so close to her father, and when she'd become a bit too fidgety, incapable of sitting still during the reverend's monotone speech, Cole had lifted her onto his lap. There Kate witnessed Cole brush aside several strands of the child's golden hair absently and place a soft kiss on her forehead.

Cole was a good father.

He was a decent man, a man who deserved a family. Kate couldn't deny him that, but he was also rigid in his beliefs and as unbending as a one-hundred-year-old oak.

When the service ended, Jethro offered his arm and Kate joined Abe and Nora outside on the lawn.

"Well, that was some sermon," Nora whispered to the three of them.

Abe laughed and put his arm around his wife. "I just about nodded off to sleep."

"You'd best get all the sleep you can, brother," Jethro said on a teasing note, "'cause when that little babe comes, you won't be getting a whole lot of it."

Abe playfully jabbed Jethro on the shoulder. "What are you looking so smug about? Your room's next to the baby nursery."

Kate had only just met Abe Cable this morning before the service, but already she liked him. He had an easy manner, a good nature and he sure made Nora happy.

"I think I might take to sleeping in the livery. Then the only thing I'll be hearing is the snorting of the mares."

"And don't forget the hee-hawing of the mules," Abe added with a grin.

Kate enjoyed being included in their banter. Growing up with just her mama, she'd missed out on such things.

"What do you say, Miss Kate. Where do you suppose I should spend my nights?" Jethro asked innocently.

Kate was ready to answer when Cole suddenly appeared by her side. She froze when she glanced at his face. A tic worked out a beat in his jaw. He was fence-post stiff and eyeing Jethro with cold disdain. "Cole?"

Cole's attention didn't shift; he kept his gaze on Jethro. "If I didn't know you better, Cable, I'd say you ought to show the lady a bit more respect."

Chagrined, Jethro turned three shades of red. "No disrespect intended, Miss Kate. Honest."

"I know that, Jethro," Kate said softly, then turned to Cole with anger sizzling in her veins. She managed to keep her tone civil. They were, after all, still on the church grounds. "We were having a private conversation."

Cole's blue eyes blazed dark as midnight. He glared at Kate for a moment. Then he turned his attention to Nora and Abe and had the nerve to lift his lips in a genuine smile. "Sorry to interrupt. Just came by to congratulate you both. I understand you're in the family way, Miss Nora."

"Why yes, Sheriff. I am." Nora placed her hand on her tiny stomach and Kate assessed that gesture to be a purely maternal instinct. The babe couldn't be much bigger than a peppermint candy, yet Nora felt the need to protect and nurture the child already.

"I wish you both well. If the child's anything like my daughter, you'll know nothing but joy."

Abe and Nora looked at each other, their faces already filled with such elation they could barely hold back wide grins. "We think so too, Sheriff," Abe said. "We appreciate your good wishes."

The two men shook hands, then Cole tipped his hat to all of them and walked back to where the Wesleys were waiting with little Meggie. Kate let loose a long, tired sigh. She truly wished her path wouldn't cross Cole's so often. At times, the man infuriated her and made her wish for things she had no right wishing for.

She turned back to her friends and offered a smile. "Shall we go to supper?"

Kate had looked forward to having her new friends over for dinner. They'd be her first real guests in a house she'd labored vigorously to make livable. With a great deal of spit and shine, the once-neglected house had polished up rather nicely, faring far better than she'd ever have imagined. Kate was proud to show off her accomplishment to the Cables.

On the walk back to her house, Nora took hold of Kate's arm and steered her away from the men. "Kate, did you notice the way Cole was looking at you with Jethro?"

Kate frowned. "Cole shouldn't have said what he said, Nora. Jethro meant no harm." She'd felt immediate remorse the minute Cole stepped up and made his comment.

"No, I'm sure Jethro didn't, but there's something in the way the sheriff looks at you all the time. Something he can't hide. He's got feelings for you, Kate. I'm sure of it."

Kate let a chuckle escape. "I'm sure of it, too. He's *feeling* like stringing me up on a thick rope. He's not at all happy about me having the saloon built."

"Maybe, or perhaps, he's afraid of something."

Confused, Kate shook her head. "Afraid? What would Cole Bradshaw have to be afraid of?"

"Oh, plenty I'd say," she continued, as they neared

Kate's house. "Like losing his best friend, losing the woman he truly wants and fearing you'll get hurt when all is said and done."

"Nora, I'm convinced Cole doesn't want me. He's got Patricia Wesley. She's the perfect sort of woman for him. She's schooled and mannerly."

"And…spoiled," Nora added with a whisper. "Cole couldn't possibly enjoy her company. Why, I overheard the Wesleys inviting him and Méggie over for supper after church. Cole refused."

"That means nothing. Maybe he had other plans."

"Perhaps, Kate, but think about it."

"Oh Nora, you are so kind to worry about me. I'm fine, really. And there's nothing to think over. There's no room in Cole's heart for me. He's set on what he wants."

Nora smiled warmly as they climbed up the steps to Kate's house. "Hmm. I do believe I know another person with that very same quality."

"Be kinda quiet, Meggie, and ease up on them," Cole said, watching Meggie chase one butterfly after another in a field of new spring wildflowers. "You gotta wait until they settle, then sneak up on them."

Meggie lunged and scared half the butterflies away from all the noise and commotion she made. A fast and furious line of fleeting color rose up then parted, flying off in different directions. "I want that one!" she cried, pointing at a large, beautiful monarch. "It's so pretty, Daddy." She ran farther into the field, jumping from one plant to another, looking to Cole like a cute little jittery butterfly herself.

"The pretty ones are harder to catch," he offered, sitting down on the soft patch of grass and stretching out his legs. "They know you want them and they let you get real close, then poof! just like that, they're gone."

Meggie giggled and lunged again when the monarch landed on a golden-yellow poppy, but it lit off again as if on fire. Meggie followed it until the darn thing disappeared into the cloudless blue sky.

Meggie put her head down and walked toward him, disappointed.

Cole shook his head and smiled. There was such determination in her eyes, such want, and Cole was glad his daughter had a strong mind. Well, most times, he was glad of it. "Come here, Megpie. Daddy wants to talk to you."

"But I want to catch one," Meggie said, jutting out her chin.

"Well, we'll see what we can do about that later. We have to wait until the butterflies come back around."

Meggie plopped herself down next to him on the grass. "Will you help me catch one, Daddy?"

Her mind sure stayed on one track, Cole mused, just like another determined female he knew. "Sure will, sweet darlin'."

He picked a tall grass blade and tickled her under

the chin. Her frown lifted and she let out a giggle of joy. "It tickles," she said.

"I know. Feels sorta nice though, doesn't it?"

"Uh-huh." Meggie laid herself down on her stomach, bracing her head with her hands and swinging her legs up in the air.

"You're gonna get your pretty Sunday dress all dirty lying like that. Mrs. Gregory would pluck my whiskers if she saw you right now."

Meggie giggled again, bringing Cole a full measure of joy. "Daddy don't have any whiskers."

"Well, if I did, she sure would. Actually that's what I'd like to talk to you about, Meg. Mrs. Gregory spoke to you about her going to live with her daughter Caroline, didn't she?"

"Yep." Meggie nodded.

"She won't be leaving right away, but I suspect as soon as summer hits, she'll be moving on."

Meggie kept quiet.

"It ain't 'cause she doesn't love you, Meggie. 'Cause I know she does. She's getting old—but don't you tell her I said so—and she wants to spend more time with her family."

"I know…" she said.

"And…well, I'll be looking to find a nice lady to come help out at the house. It'll be someone new, Meggie, but I swear, she'll be nice and you'll like her."

Meggie plucked a blade of grass, but she didn't

tickle him with it. Instead, she swirled it around with her fingers, staring. "'Kay."

"Okay?" What did he expect her to say? This bit of news might be a tad overwhelming for a four-and-a-half-year-old. It nearly killed him to disappoint her again.

Hell, for two bits, he'd up and propose marriage to Patricia. She'd been hinting and Cole had been playing possum.

He'd been all over it in his mind a hundred times. His head told him Patricia would make a good wife and mother, but his heart said otherwise.

He'd been expected to dine with the Wesleys today after church, but at the last minute, Cole had changed his mind. He'd excused himself, claiming a need to spend the day with Meggie. That had been the truth. He didn't have enough time to devote solely to her and he knew that Meggie enjoyed their special "alone" time together.

But it had been more than that.

He didn't want to lead Patricia down a path he wouldn't take. Cole wasn't made that way. He had to be sure about his feelings.

And he was more confused than ever.

Damn, if only Kate Malone had been a different sort of woman, Cole would have her pregnant and tied to him with a lead rope. A devilish grin parted his lips, thinking about making Kate pregnant. And he'd keep her that way until their house was filled with children. But he recognized those thoughts as dangerous, so he banished them from his mind. Besides, something told him, if she were any other kind of woman, he wouldn't be thinking of her all the time. Plain and simple, Kate was Kate and he couldn't fathom her being any other way.

Cole lifted his face to the sun and took a breath of fresh spring air. Then he noticed a stream of bugs flitting by. "Looks like the butterflies are back. C'mon, Megpie, let's go catch us something elusive and beautiful."

At least he could do that for his daughter; he surely couldn't do it for himself.

Chapter Seven

Seated at the kitchen table, Kate poured a cup of hot tea and stared out the window, glancing at the bright night stars. Steam billowed up and warmed her face, but nothing much tonight could warm her heart. She'd been feeling uneasy lately and a bit edgy. She couldn't put her finger on the trouble, yet she was having difficulty getting a good night's rest.

The only thing that put her at ease was witnessing the progress of the Silver Saddle. It had been two weeks since the builders had begun, and they assured her each day that they were right on schedule with the construction. Knowing that all was going as planned calmed her like a salve over an old painful wound.

Kate sipped her tea, deep in thought, pondering all the improvements she intended to make on the interior of the saloon. She had everything sorted out in her mind about how grand the new changes would be. She'd commissioned a small stage to be built at the back of the establishment, one complete with drop curtains, which Nora had offered to help teach Kate how to stitch up. Nora assured Kate that, between the two of them, they could do just as fine a job as any professional seamstress and for minimal cost, as well.

Kate took Nora at her word and ordered three bolts of material in light crimson velvet. She'd also managed to procure golden tassels for the hems of the curtains from a San Francisco catalog. The material had arrived just this morning by rail.

The piano would go on the stage. Kate made inquiries about hiring a piano player. Of course, not a soul from Crystal Creek would apply for the position. She knew she'd have to go elsewhere to find both a piano player and a barkeep. She wanted to hire a real bartender, someone who knew how to prepare specialty drinks, and the old standards. Both would have to be willing to work for small wages and a free room at the back of the saloon.

Kate hoped the wires and handbills she'd sent to the surrounding towns, including those as near as San Francisco and as far south as Los Angeles would help her locate the right people for the jobs. But even if she couldn't immediately place someone in her employ, Kate knew enough about mixing the easier drinks to do the job herself. She didn't play the piano, but Kate could exercise her own brand of musical talent if need be. One way or another, the Silver Saddle would open up its wide iron doors right on schedule.

All was going terribly well, so why couldn't Kate shake off this unsettling feeling? The wall clock chimed midnight, startling Kate at the late-night hour. She stole a quick glance at her bedroom door, knowing full well that she ought to get back to bed and at least try to sleep. But that notion held no appeal.

She wasn't tired at all.

She'd probably lie there for hours, tossing and turning. It was times like these that loneliness consumed her. She had no one to turn to, no one to talk to during the night. Usually Kate was too tired to notice and she'd fall into bed, exhausted. But these starry evenings, when the night beckoned with air that cooled pleasantly as it blew by, Kate longed for something more, something that would make her feel alive, vital. Something unnamed and mysterious. Her body trembled in anticipation, and she didn't have a notion what it would take to stop the jittery sensation.

Oh, if only Mama was here. They'd stay up for hours, planning a future filled with promise. Kate knew her mama would be proud of her, building the saloon, standing up to the town. Louisa Malone had always instilled in Kate the power of her own potential. "You can do anything you set your mind to, Katie," her mother would say, when Kate began to feel defeated or discouraged as a young girl. "Just remember, you're as good as everyone else. I'd say even *better*." Then her mama would wink and grin.

Kate smiled, recalling that sound advice. And she believed her, for the most part. Kate had grown up to become a strong, determined woman, thanks to her mother. But Kate had a weak spot, one she had tried rubbing out of her mind now for weeks. She couldn't quite do it. She couldn't quite forget Cole Bradshaw and the kiss in this very house that made her heart pump like mad and her insides churn soft as butter.

"Enough of your whining, Katie Malone," she mumbled to herself. "You've not got a thing to be sorry about."

And that much was true. Everything was going Kate's way. The saloon would be finished soon, she'd made the nicest friends in the Cables and she had a comfortable place to live. She wouldn't allow losing Cole's friendship to play havoc with her heart any longer.

Kate finished her tea, then cleaned the teapot and tidied up the kitchen. Glancing out the window again, Kate lifted her eyes to the full and perfectly rounded moon. The stars above gleamed, their luster a welcome twinkle in the dark sky. The night seemed to call to her. She knew she wouldn't sleep for long hours to come.

On impulse, Kate moved down the hall to her bedroom and removed her nightclothes, tossing them onto her bed. She dressed quickly in a simple calico gown then threw a lacy ivory shawl around her shoulders. In the parlor, she picked up the kerosene lantern, turned up the light a bit then walked out the door. She moved briskly and with purpose. The only thing to put her at ease tonight was seeing the Silver Saddle, nearly completed.

Maybe then her restlessness would vanish and she'd be able to get some sleep.

Cole rubbed his sore eyes and glanced at his pocket watch. It was just after midnight and far too late for him to be poking about in the jailhouse, catching up on tedious paperwork. But Cole planned on spending the entire day away from the office tomorrow, checking out a claim of cattle rustling and robbery on a ranch at the far end of the county. He hoped to find it an isolated case and that the rustlers had moved on, out of his territory. Cole wanted Crystal Creek to continue as a peaceable town. He prided himself on keeping it so, and didn't want to see harm come to anyone else. It vexed him miserably that he'd lost Jeb and his wife to violence. And even more so, Cole hated that one of those marauders was still on the loose. Justice had come to two of the Sloan brothers, but there still was one killer who needed to pay for his crime.

Cole organized his files and piled them in stacks on his desk. There was only so much writing a man could do in one day, he mused. At least with Meggie gone tonight, he'd had a chance to finish the only part of his job he didn't enjoy doing. Mrs. Gregory had offered to take his daughter to Caroline's house to play with her children and spend the night. Meggie needed to be with children her own age now and again, Cole thought, but he sorely missed having her home at night. He liked thinking she was warm and cozy in her own bed, before turning down the lamps for the evening.

Cole rose from his desk and stretched his arms, letting go of a wide yawn. A flash of light caught his eye. He strode to the window and peered out, blinking back his surprise. He spotted a woman, striding with purpose down the darkened street. It didn't take long for Cole to recognize the swing of her hips, the soft curves of a woman he'd known all of his life. "Kate? What the devil are you up to now?" he grumbled.

Cole reached for his vest and strapped on his holster, buckling it tight. He was out the door both quickly and quietly, following the dim beam of yellow light. Fool woman, didn't even know she was being followed. She just moved along at a merry pace, unaware of the dangers. Didn't she know what could happen to an unchaperoned woman, walking the streets this late at night?

She stopped in front of the Silver Saddle, lifting her head to gaze at the nearly completed structure. Cole's anger abated some, watching as rays of moonlight cast a gentle radiance about her. She was encased by softness—a feminine glow that highlighted all that was truly beautiful about Kate Malone.

Cole squeezed his eyes shut, blocking out the image of Kate, the tightening need consuming his body and the heat that scorched him whenever she was near. He needed his anger. He summoned it like a dog to a bone and came up right behind her. "Damn it, Kate. What are you doing here all alone?"

Kate whirled around rapidly, her heart thumping hard against her chest. Utterly stunned, she couldn't believe she was staring into Cole Bradshaw's condemning blue eyes. "Cole! You scared me nearly half to death!"

"I'm not apologizing, woman. What in blazes do you think you're doing? It's past midnight."

After a long moment, Kate recovered from the shock of seeing Cole right smack behind her. She hadn't heard anyone else on the street. But seeing him now, his eyes blazing blue lightning, his stance sure and strong, Kate came to realize clearly, without doubt, that he, Cole Bradshaw, had been the source of her recent restlessness. Her once-best friend, the man she'd longed for since childhood still made her queasy with stomach flutters she so painfully tried to deny. He still made her ache with want. Nothing much had changed since the early years. He would always be the only man for her, but Cole would never accept her for the woman she was. She wasn't good enough for him. Chin up, Kate offered her only explanation,

"I...I couldn't sleep."

"So you thought you'd wander the night?" Cole made her sound foolish with his tone, the mocking way he had of peering at her.

She raised her voice. "No, I thought I'd come see my saloon."

"Shh." Cole took her by the arm and led her inside the newly built-up walls. The scent of freshly cut walnut hit her instantly as the lamp she held illuminated the hollowed-out structure, casting them in a bright glow. She could see Cole's face better now, his expression grim. But he stood so close with his body nearly pressed up to hers that Kate's traitorous insides trembled. "You didn't know I was behind you, did you?"

"No," she admitted. "I thought I was alone." She set the lantern down on a stack of lumber.

Exasperation contorted Cole's handsome face. "Exactly my point, Kate."

"Did you follow me?" she asked.

"Hell, yes, I followed you."

"Why?"

"You have to ask? Kate, it could have been anyone behind you. Someone without good intentions. A beautiful woman walking the streets at night…well, that's just plain asking for trouble."

He was angry with her, yet he said she was beautiful. Did he really believe her to be? "I can protect myself, Cole. Truly I can."

Cole's expression changed from grim to feigned amusement and he let out a dubious laugh. "I don't think so, Kate. A man could easily overtake you. Without much effort, I'd say."

"Not if I faced him with this," she said, reaching

into her pocket and coming out with her gun. She brought it up close, to give him a better look. Cole thought she'd been a fool, but Kate had just proved to him that she really did know a thing or two about protecting herself.

Surprise registered on his face and Kate knew a moment of pure, hard-earned satisfaction. He snatched the small gun from her hand and gave it a good looking over. "Nice," he said. "Pearl grips .22-caliber pocket revolver. Where'd you get this?"

"Los Angeles. Mama sort of had the same worry. She bought it for me and taught me how to use it."

Louisa had been proficient in wielding a revolver. Initially her expertise had amazed Kate, never having seen her mother draw a gun. Not once in all her years of running the saloon had Louisa had to resort to gunplay. But her mother's quiet acceptance of what was necessary and her uncanny ability with the gun only added to Kate's admiration of her.

Cole's brows lifted. "You good with this?"

On a slow nod, she answered, "If I have to be."

"And you think that's all that you need to keep you out of trouble?" he asked softly, taking a step closer and slipping the gun back into her pocket. She felt his hand brush her leg through the material of her dress. A shudder ran through her.

"It's...uh, it's a good start, Cole."

Cole moved closer and Kate backed up. "'Course, there's more than one kind of trouble."

"There is?" Her heart pumped and pumped, pounding hard against her ribs.

"Uh-huh," he replied, his hands bracing her hips and moving her back farther, until she was pinned against the new wall of the saloon. "There's all sorts of trouble a woman can get into."

Cole took the end of Kate's shawl and pulled it gently, until the lacy garment flowed around her shoulders and caressed her breast before coming completely undone. Her breath caught sharply at the subtle gesture.

"I...uh, I can handle myself," she breathed.

Cole touched the lacy threads of her shawl, fingering the ends and making her wish his hands were on her instead, caressing her in much the same way. Her breasts tingled at the very notion and filled her gown full, the tips going pebble hard. Oh!

"You think you can handle yourself?" he whispered, his face so near she felt his breath warm her cheek.

"I, uh...yes, yes, I can," she said, forgetting what she was agreeing to. She was at a loss, almost completely so.

Cole lifted one hand up and found her hair, weaving gently through the curly mass while the other held her firm. His intimate touch sent Kate's senses reeling. Her legs would surely have buckled if Cole hadn't been holding her, pressed so snugly up against her. She closed her eyes and rested her head back against the wall, relishing the feel of Cole's gentle stroking. His breaths came rapidly now, thrilling her so that her own breaths became equally labored. Softly he said, "You are more than beautiful, Kate."

Cole brought his mouth down onto hers with exquisite tenderness at first. She whimpered at the initial touch, but when Cole parted her lips and drove himself inside, a moan of pleasure escaped. Tremors racked her body with each thrust of his tongue, each murmured breathy word he spoke. She kissed him back fully, holding nothing back, giving to him what was in her heart—what had *always* been in her heart. She relished the feel of him, the taste of him. It was all she'd ever dreamed about, being in Cole's arms.

She felt a slight tug in her skirts then a yank and his hand once again brushed her leg. Abruptly he broke off the kiss.

Kate flashed her eyes open, confusion muddying her mind. She had just been in Cole's arms, but now he stood away, holding up her gun. "Looks like you can't protect yourself, after all."

Stunned, she blinked, then blinked again, awareness quickly dawning. It took only a second for Kate to realize what Cole had done. He'd seduced her to teach her a lesson…to prove his point. And she'd fallen right into his trap. Tears misted and anger surfaced. She shoved him away with all her might. "Get away from me, Cole."

Cole didn't appear remorseful at all. He stood his ground and glared at her. "If you plan on running a saloon, you're gonna have to learn something about protecting yourself.''

She flamed with anger now, burning hotter than a branding iron. "You're a snake, Cole Bradshaw.''

"True enough. But I bet you'll think twice now about that gun of yours. It's not the gun that keeps you safe. You've got to keep your wits about you, Kate. At all times…no matter what. That's your best protection.''

Kate braced both hands on her hips. She shouted with the fury she felt inside, "The only one I *need* protecting from…is you!'' She reached for the lantern and stormed out of the saloon, her pride hurt but her heart breaking. She had to get away from him, before he saw the devastating effect his little "lesson" had had on her.

She headed for home, hearing his footsteps from behind. Once she reached her doorstep, she whirled around. Cole stood at her gate, running a hand through his hair, watching her. There was no regret in his eyes, just a powerful glint that met her gaze candidly. He still had her shawl, absently wrapped up on one arm. He gestured with a brief nod toward her door.

Good Lord, he was seeing her home safely. The irony was laughable. He'd nearly destroyed her with his kiss and he worried about her safety? Didn't he know the best thing he could ever do for her was to leave her be?

Kate slammed the door as hard as she could and bolted it shut. Only then did she burst into tears.

Chapter Eight

Cole did a double check of his gun and rifle, making sure that both were loaded and ready, then mounted his mare. With a slight nudge of his spurs, his horse took off at a brisk walk heading for the far end of the county and Ely Morgan's spread.

He passed Kate's house on his way out of town and witnessed her in the front yard, tending to a rosebush. She bent her head to sniff a newly bloomed yellow rose and their eyes met. Cole tipped his hat in greeting. She turned away, giving him a fine view of the back of her pretty head.

Cole drew in a deep breath and returned his attention to the road. Damn, if Kate wasn't the most infuriating woman he'd ever encountered, jeopardizing her own safety on the street late at night. Why, if he'd been another sort, she might have found herself in a much worse predicament than meeting up with him. He'd been sworn in to protect the citizens of Crystal

Creek. Was it so bad if he saw fit to teach Kate a lesson about protecting herself?

Of course, he hadn't expected the *lesson* to go so far. Cole still smarted from holding her in his arms and sharing a kiss that had kept him awake most the night. He'd only meant to get close enough to whip the blasted gun out of her pocket, but being near Kate was intoxicating. The more he had of her, the more he wanted.

A scowl pushed the edges of Cole's mouth down. He rode on, deep in thought, pondering his future. He'd best decide what to do about Meggie's care mighty soon. Either he'd find another housekeeper, or he'd have to marry.

Fact is, Cole wanted to settle down. He wanted a family. Always had. But finding the right woman, now that took some doing. And having Mary Kathryn Malone come back to town when she did managed to make his decision all the more perplexing.

Twenty minutes later, Cole reined in his horse when he reached the Morgan house. He dismounted and ground-tied his mare. Ely came out onto his porch to greet him.

"Morning, Ely. Heard you had some trouble out here yesterday."

"That we did, Sheriff. Cattle rustlers. They ran off with fifty head, but it might have been plenty more if one of my men hadn't spotted them. He was going for help, but they caught up to him and one man knocked him out with his gun."

"He okay?"

Ely nodded. "Got a knot the size of Texas atop his head and they robbed him right down to his boots. But he's a lucky devil. They could've shot him, just as easy. He's resting up in the bunkhouse if you want to speak with him."

"I do."

Ely led him to the bunkhouse and introduced him to Tim O'Shay. "Hey, Tim, Sheriff Bradshaw has some questions for you. You feel like talking?"

The young cowhand sat up on his bunk and nodded. "Yeah, my head's clearing some now."

"Okay, I'll leave you folks alone. Stop back at the house later, Sheriff, and Rosa will fix you a cold drink."

"Thanks, Ely. Appreciate it."

Cole took the information from O'Shay. The man couldn't give him much. All the rustlers wore black and had on kerchiefs to disguise their faces.

"Can you recall anything else? Anything unusual about them or their horses?"

"No," Tim said, shaking his head. "Except I think one of the men had a scar on the side of his face. I couldn't see much of it though. The kerchief he wore covered up most of his face, but it sure looked like a slash mark from the eye down."

Air rushed through Cole's lungs, fast and deep. "Right side or left?"

O'Shay thought for a moment. "Looking at him, the scar was on his right side."

"Sloan." Cole's heart pumped fast now. His insides churned. If it was the same man, Cole would find him. He'd find the last man responsible for his brother's murder.

"What?" asked O'Shay.

"I can't be sure, but back a couple of years, three brothers named Sloan came riding through the farms outside of Crystal Creek. They killed my brother, his wife and others. We caught up with two. One was shot and the other hanged right after his trial. One of the brothers is still missing. According to the poster I got up on the wall at the jail, the man has a knife wound on the side of his face."

"That so?"

"If it's the same man, consider yourself real fortunate. He's a known killer."

O'Shay rubbed the back of his neck. "Yeah, guess getting a bump on my head ain't so bad then. 'Course, they took everything on me, right down to my high-stitched boots."

"I'm going to ride out with Ely and see where they ambushed you. I'm hoping someone else saw them. I'll do some investigating and see what I can turn up. You take care now."

"Right, Sheriff. I'll be right as rain by tomorrow."

Cole left the bunkhouse and marched up to the house. After sharing a tall glass of iced tea and some blueberry pie with Ely's family, both men rode out to the spot where the thievery was committed. They followed a trail up to the river. Cole's lead went cold from there, but he wasn't going to give up. He'd spend the rest of the afternoon riding to the surrounding ranches, investigating and warning the ranchers. The last thing he wanted in his county was more violence.

Cole knelt down beside his brother's grave, wiping away dry leaves that had accumulated there. He'd picked a batch of poppies from alongside the path leading back to town and set them between Jeb and Lydia's headstones. "Got me a lead today on the last rotten Sloan brother. I'm gonna find him, Jeb, I swear."

A soft wind blew by, lifting Cole's hat a bit, reminding him to take the dang thing off. "Okay, I got the message," he said, looking toward the heavens. He pulled his hat from his head and set it down near the flowers. "Didn't mean no disrespect."

Cole chuckled, more from bitter pain than amusement, the harsh sound echoing in the deserted cemetery. "You always were one for doing the smart thing, weren't you, Jeb?"

Cole sighed, thinking back on Jeb's influence over him when they'd been younger. He'd always looked out for Cole, always wanted what was best. Jeb didn't have it easy back then, being just four years older than Cole and assuming all the responsibility of raising him. He'd done right by him, guiding him the best way he could.

He'd convinced Cole in his teen years to get in

good and tight with Patricia Wesley, because he'd need every darn advantage he could get to make sheriff. And Jeb had been right. Edward Wesley had helped Cole get elected.

The man had great influence in Crystal Creek.

Cole knew what Jeb would say today. He'd encourage Cole to marry Patricia. It'd be the *smart* thing to do. "Hell, Jeb, I know it in my head. And I want to do right by Meggie, too. She needs a mother to raise her proper and all. Patricia's a fine woman, well mannered and schooled. But I've got to be sure. And right now, nothing's for sure. 'Cept, Meggie's a sweet young girl. I love her like my own. You and Lydia…well, you'd be proud. I won't let you down on this, Jeb. It's a promise."

Cole stayed a while longer, needing to somehow connect with his brother. They'd been more than brothers, they'd been friends. Being orphaned so early had brought them closer than most brothers. Cole never believed he'd lose Jeb at such a young age. His death still caused an ache in his heart.

At least he had Meggie.

Thank the dear Lord for Meggie.

Cole glanced at his pocket watch. It was time he headed to town. It'd been a long day and he still had to check in with his deputy before going home. Cole mounted his horse and left the cemetery in a cloud of dust, all the while wishing he had a wife waiting for him at home. He'd take her into his arms and she'd help ease the pain that life all too often offered up on a platter made of cold and hard stone.

That afternoon, Kate walked with Nora toward the livery after spending hours working on velvet curtains. It was good that Nora had come over this morning. Being with her and getting busy with the sewing had taken Kate's mind off Cole and the terrible way they'd parted last night. Kate hadn't slept a wink, but she'd stopped her crying quickly. One thing Kate knew without a doubt was that crying never solved anybody's problems. Her mama had taught her that at a very young age. "Fix what needs fixing," she would say. "And if it's not fixable, don't dwell, just move on."

That's what they'd done when the saloon had burned down. Louisa had tried her best to "fix" the problem, and when she had realized the futility in that, she'd packed up and moved on.

Well, Kate doubted she could fix her problems with Cole. But she could fix up the saloon. That's why Nora's generous offer to help with the curtains had come at just the right time. "Nora, thank you for all your help today. The curtains are going to be real pretty when we're through."

Nora agreed. "They are coming out so lovely. I can't wait to finish them off with those tassels."

"You've done nearly all the work. I wish I knew more about sewing."

"You'll catch on, Kate. And you did a fine job of stitching today."

"I poked a hole in my fingers three times."

Nora smiled. "I know. But it just takes practice. I'll come by again later in the week and we'll finish them."

"You practically did all the work yourself. I'm going to have to help more next time. How'd you learn so much about sewing anyway?"

"Oh, well, when I was a girl, we were very poor. My mother took in sewing to put food on our table. The farm wasn't doing too good, and then my father took sick. So, all of us girls helped with the sewing. With my mother, there were four of us helping out. We worked into the night sometimes and we'd often compete to see who'd get the surest, most straight stitching.

"I always made my own clothes. That's why, when I married Abe, he insisted on buying me new store-bought dresses." Nora's face beamed with happiness. "To own a ready-made dress had always been a dream of mine when I was young."

"And now, you have store-bought dresses, a wonderful man, a nice house to live in and a new little babe on the way. I can't think of another soul who deserves it more."

"I can. You do, Kate. You deserve all the happiness in the world." Nora cast sympathetic eyes her way. She bit her lip, before asking, "What's wrong? We haven't been friends all that long, but I believe I know you fairly well. You've been quiet and...sad today.''

Kate sighed and shook her head, taking her mother's advice. She couldn't fix what was wrong, so she wouldn't dwell. And she certainly didn't want to burden her new friend with her troubles. ''I'm a little anxious, is all. And I haven't been sleeping too well, lately. Don't worry, Nora. It'll pass.''

Nora took her hand and squeezed gently. ''I'm sure of it, too. But if you need a friend, you know where to find me.''

Kate nodded. ''I appreciate that, Nora.''

They had reached the livery and were ready to part when an amazing sight struck them. Jethro Cable rode up on his horse, wearing the biggest darn frown Kate had ever seen, and directly in front of him on the saddle in all of her riding finery sat Patricia Wesley. Her mood appeared equally sour.

Kate and Nora both giggled at the sight. ''I've never seen my brother-in-law looking so irritated,'' she whispered. ''If anyone can put Jethro in such a mood, it's that girl.''

Kate watched Jethro dismount then reach up to help Patricia down. She swatted his hands away as soon as her high-priced shiny leather boots hit the ground. ''Leave me be, Mr. Cable. Haven't you done enough damage for one day?''

Nora spoke up, stepping forward. ''What happened, Jethro? And where is Miss Wesley's horse?''

Jethro was collecting his thoughts, ready to answer

when Patricia ranted, "The horse is gone, thank goodness! He nearly killed me."

Jethro ignored Patricia and answered, "We were out for a riding lesson, when Miss Wesley's horse got spooked. It took off running and, well, Miss Wesley didn't know how to hold up on the reins—"

"I held up on the reins, Jethro. That horse wasn't about to stop, no matter what. I was lucky enough to hold on for dear life!"

Jethro's face contorted. "I caught up to you right quick, didn't I? Got you onto my horse safely. You didn't get so much as a speck of dirt on your fancy suede riding suit. And the horse will be back on his own accord. Right about feeding time."

"I certainly hope not."

"It ain't his fault, Patricia," Jethro said. "You panicked and the horse sensed it."

"Oh, that's ridiculous."

"It's not ridiculous. Ask Nora. She knows I'm talking the truth."

Nora's eyes went wide and her expression sobered. She clearly did not want to be thrust into this conversation. "Oh, well, Miss Wesley, if Jethro says so, I'd believe him. I've never known another man as knowledgeable about horses. Jethro's got a way with them, you see. And it was sure a good thing he was around. Sounds like he saved you a bumpy ride."

Kate chuckled silently. Nora had a way with words. She was so glad she had a friend in her. When Kate had woken up this morning, she didn't think she'd see a smile today, much less any laughter.

"Still, I don't believe these riding lessons are working out. I'd like a refund on the lessons I've paid for in advance."

Jethro's pride appeared bruised. Judging by the look that he shot Patricia, Kate couldn't tell which emotion he felt strongest—anger, irritation or a heavy dose of pure male stubbornness. He shook his head. "Sorry, we don't give refunds."

Patricia looked as though she'd burst a vein in her head. "What? Why father paid you handsomely for six lessons. The only one I had nearly killed me today."

"You were never in any real danger." Jethro wouldn't allow Patricia to disparage his good name. Kate knew him to be a fair and decent man who prided himself on his ability with animals. "I wouldn't let anything happen to you," he said softly.

Something flashed between the two then, when they looked at each other. "Oh," Patricia said quietly.

There was an awkward silence until Nora spoke up again. "Why don't you just try one more riding lesson, Patricia? If you're not satisfied, I'm *sure*—" she said, piercing Jethro with a sharp brown-eyed gaze "—Jethro will give you a refund. Doesn't that sound fair?"

Patricia glanced at Jethro again. She shrugged. "I suppose."

"Jethro?" Nora said, as though she were disciplining two five-year-olds.

He shrugged. "Okay by me."

"Fine, then it's settled. You'll meet one more time for a riding lesson."

Nora turned her back on the feuding couple and grinned like the cat who'd caught the canary. Kate grabbed her arm and walked them both away, stifling a hearty laugh.

"Nora, you're priceless."

With a modest lift of her shoulder, Nora smiled. "I'm learning how to speak my mind. Getting to know you, Kate, and all you've accomplished has helped me voice my opinion."

"Uh-oh. Abe's not going to like me much for that."

"Abe adores you. He likes me less shy."

"Oh, Nora, if you've learned a little from me, I've certainly learned so much more from you."

Kate left the livery with lifted spirits. And to think this morning she had been certain there wasn't one thing that could put her out of her melancholy mood.

Hours later and after a small meal, Kate readied for bed. Tonight she'd not have trouble sleeping. She was just plain exhausted. She poured a bit of rosewater into a deep cornflower-blue bowl and dabbed at her face and neck. The liquid refreshed and cooled her skin. She toweled off quickly and donned her favorite, most comfortable nightdress, then climbed into bed.

She hadn't been there more than three minutes

when she heard sharp knocking at her door. Kate bounded out of bed, more curious than concerned as to who would be calling on her so late in the evening. Slipping her arms through her robe, she tightened the sash and strode barefoot to the front door.

"Who is it?" she asked from behind the door.

"It's me, Kate." She immediately recognized Cole's voice. He was the last person she expected, and the one person she definitely didn't want to see tonight.

"It's late, Cole."

"I know. Kate, open up. I need you."

Chapter Nine

Kate unfastened the bolt and, with a quick thrust, opened the door. "Cole, if you came to apologize—"

She stopped when she caught sight of Cole. His face appeared pale and his eyes were laced with concern. She'd known Cole a lifetime and she couldn't recall seeing him so distraught. "What is it?"

"It's Meggie," he said with urgency.

"What about Meggie?" Kate's heart pumped faster.

"She's sick with fever. I can't seem to get it to break. She's thrashing around in the bed." Cole ran a hand through his hair. "Her mother, Lydia, would come down with fever often. One time she nearly died."

"Did you call for the doctor?"

"He's out delivering Mrs. Gregory's grandchild." Cole tried to keep desperation out of his voice, but Kate heard it. "They took off together as soon as I got back to town today. Caroline is known for having hard deliveries. Both are at her place right now.''

Kate nodded. ''What can I do?''

Cole didn't hesitate. He lifted his eyes and met hers directly. ''Will you come?''

It was plain to see Cole needed someone. And he'd come to her for help. He stood there on her porch, not as the sheriff, not as the man who'd nearly broken her heart in two, but as the young boy she'd grown up with. Her best friend. In the past, they'd always supported each other, in good times and bad. Kate wouldn't refuse Cole. Not when he came to her out of a friendship she cherished. She'd do what she could for his little daughter. Lord knows, the child could be in danger.

''Of course, I'll come. You go on, get back to her. I'll be dressed in a minute.''

''I'll wait for you, Kate. Johnny is sitting with her now.''

Kate wouldn't argue. She knew Cole's stubborn nature, and when his mind was set, nothing much could change it. ''I'll be just a moment.''

She dressed quickly and found Cole pacing in her parlor. ''Let's go.''

Cole took her hand and they walked at a fast pace to his house. Once inside, he led her to Meggie's bedroom. ''She's in here.''

Kate entered and Johnny Martinez rose from his chair. He nodded a greeting to Kate, then turned to

Cole. "She's still burning up. I've been putting the cold rag on her forehead like you said."

"Thanks, Johnny." Cole bent down to Meggie and brushed aside damp golden locks that had stuck to her moist forehead. The child looked so small, so fragile in the big bed. Her cherub face appeared flushed with color. "How's my little Megpie doing?"

The child opened her eyes and gave a little shrug.

Cole turned to Johnny. "Why don't you go on home, Johnny. I appreciate you coming over. Looks like it's going to be a long night. You'll need to open up the office in the morning."

"Right, boss. Don't you worry about a thing," his deputy said, then glanced at Kate. "I think our little *chica* will be in good hands now."

Kate cast him a small smile and hoped he was right. As soon as he left, she sat down on Meggie's bed. "Hi, Meggie. I'm a...friend of your daddy. My name is Kate. Do you remember meeting me?"

Meggie gave a little nod, her weary blue eyes rimmed with red. Poor child, Kate thought, and she was suddenly glad Cole had come for her. Meggie needed a woman's touch tonight. "I'm sorry you don't feel well, but your daddy and I are going to stay with you and make you feel better real soon."

Meggie closed her eyes then and Kate lifted hers to Cole. "Let's let her try to sleep. When she wakes later, I'll get her out of her sweaty nightclothes and give her a little bath. Then we'll try to give her some water or milk."

Kate stood and took Cole by the arm. He was stiff as a rod and immovable. "I'm staying," he said.

"We'll check on her in a few minutes. All this talk might wake her. C'mon, I'll fix us both some coffee. Like you said, it's going to be a long night."

Reluctantly Cole allowed Kate to lead him out of the bedroom. He showed her where the coffee was then sat down on a kitchen chair and ran his hands down his face. Kate began brewing the coffee. "She's going to be all right, Cole."

He blew out a breath and shook his head. "She's never been this sick before."

"When did she come down with it?"

"I'm not sure. I was out of town most of the day and when I came back, Mrs. Gregory said Meggie was tired from playing with Caroline's children this afternoon and I should put her down early for bed. Not long after that, Mrs. Gregory got word that Caroline was having the pains. She went for Dr. Royer and both went to see about Caroline. Meggie didn't eat her supper then she went to lie down on the sofa. That's when I noticed her body burning up."

"I once had a fever that lasted three full days," Kate said, bringing two cups to the table.

Cole shook his head, a look of complete fear crossing over his features. "I won't last three days. Not if Meggie is this sick."

Kate put her hand on his arm. "I'll be here as long as you need me, Cole."

Cole covered his hand over hers. "Thanks, Kate."

There was no need for thanks. No matter what had happened between them in the past, Kate wouldn't desert her friend. And right now, that's all she saw Cole as being. A friend who needed her.

She poured the coffee and set out biscuits and honey she'd found wrapped in a covered bowl on the counter. "Here you go. You should eat something. I bet you missed your supper too."

"I couldn't eat a thing once Meggie took sick."

"You're tired and hungry, Cole. Eat a biscuit and have some coffee." Kate shoved a plate under Cole's nose.

He cast her a sour look. "You've always been bossy."

"And you've always been stubborn," she said kindly. This was not the time to argue with him. She was here to lend support.

Kate smiled when Cole lifted the biscuit and bit into it.

She took a sip of coffee. "We should take turns with Meggie. I'll go in now and sit with her. When she wakes up, I'll undress and bathe her. Why don't you try to get some sleep?"

"No, Kate. I can't sleep."

"Okay," she said, softly blowing steam from her cup, "but at least rest on the sofa. I'll let you know if Meggie needs you."

Cole narrowed his eyes and grimaced. "You're gonna badger me until I do, aren't you?"

Kate grinned. "You asked for my help, didn't you?"

"I'll rest if you do, later on. I know I got you out of bed tonight."

"I don't mind," she said honestly. "I'd rather be here with...Meggie. And I'll close my eyes later on. I promise."

Cole finished the biscuit and followed Kate into Meggie's bedroom. He bent to give the child a soft kiss on her forehead, then turned to Kate. "Call me if you need anything."

"I will." Kate took up a spare blanket, pulled the chair closer to Meggie's bed and plopped herself down. "Meggie and I will be just fine."

But ten minutes later, Meggie began thrashing again in the bed. Kate rushed over to her, putting a hand on her forehead. She was hot with fever still. "Meggie, sweetie, wake up."

Cole sat down on the parlor sofa and closed his eyes. He wouldn't get a wink until Meggie was up and about, free of fever. She'd looked so miserable earlier, her usual bright eyes cast in a misty haze. Cole couldn't get her to eat or drink a thing. Maybe Kate could do a better job.

Kate.

Thank heavens, she'd been willing to come back with him tonight. She'd taken over the minute she walked through the door, grasping hold of the situation. Cole had been at his wits' end, trying to tend to

Meggie without much success. He didn't know about such things. Meggie had never taken sick like this. Sure, she'd had a case of the sniffles from time to time, but she'd never broken out with such a high fever before.

And just having Kate here made Cole feel better. He'd needed her desperately and she'd come, no questions, no qualms. It had been just like old times in their early years; when one had needed the other, they'd always come through. The friendship they'd shared over the years was rare and precious, but ever since Kate had come back to town, he'd considered it fragile at best. It would be a hard thing to lose a friend like Kate. Cole hoped it never came to that.

"Cole," Kate whispered in the darkened room.

He opened his eyes. She stood before him, a steady stream of light from behind casting her in a warm glow. It struck him like lightning—to open his eyes and have Kate there, with him, sharing this situation. "Kate?"

"Meggie woke up. I need you to bring in a tub and get some towels."

Cole bounded from the sofa. "Is the fever still raging?"

"Yes, she's uncomfortable, but the bath will cool her down considerably."

Instead of using the tub in the washroom, Cole fixed up a large metal bucket filled with warm water, as per Kate's instructions. Not cold, but not hot, either, she'd advised. The water should be a bit cooler than Meggie's body temperature. Cole brought the container in and set it down. Kate had Meggie partially undressed.

"Look, your daddy's here, Meggie," Kate said. "And you have my permission to splash him all you want."

Meggie smiled at Kate, then glanced at him. Her face was ashen, but her eyes lit a bit from Kate's remark.

"And you can soak Miss Kate with water all you want," Cole teased back.

Meggie giggled then, bringing a measure of joy to Cole's heart.

Kate lifted her from the bed, undressed her swiftly and Cole helped set her down into the tub. Meggie shivered a bit. "Is the water too cold?" Cole asked.

Kate rolled up her sleeve and stuck her elbow in. "No, just right."

Meggie shivered again. Her voice was a low, uncomfortable whine. "How long do I hafta be wet?"

Kate finger-combed Meggie's long, curly tresses, taking her time, speaking softly. "Not long, sweetie. Just close your eyes and lean back a bit. My mama used to tell me a story about the golden bear. Would you like to hear it?"

Meggie nodded and Kate began to weave a tall tale. "There was once a very small young bear cub whose coat was very silky. Why, Meggie, the bear's fur was nearly the same pretty yellow as your hair."

"Really?" Meggie asked.

"Yes, sweetie, now close your eyes and picture this little bear cub wandering away from his mama because, for such a small creature, this little fella had the most monstrous appetite. He went in search of…huckleberries.

Cole listened to Kate's tale, smiling at the creative way she told the story. With her eyes beaming wide, Kate's voice would lower then raise, her tone becoming either sullen or silly, according to how the adventure unfolded.

Within minutes, Meggie had dosed off, her head resting comfortably against Cole's arm. Kate stroked his daughter's head, a constant gliding of her hands, touching, caressing…caring. Sometimes her fingers would accidentally sweep over him as well and the hairs on the top of his arm would rise with awareness.

After finishing the story Cole was sure Meggie hadn't heard entirely, Kate whispered, "She's much cooler now. Let's let her sleep a little while longer in the tub, then I'll dress her in clean clothes and tuck her back into bed."

"Kate, you've done enough. You must be exhausted. Go rest on the sofa and I'll get her back to bed. Once she's asleep, I'll see you home."

"You don't have to see me home, Cole. It's not that far, but I will rest my eyes a bit before checking on Meggie again."

"You don't have to stay," he said, grateful for her help but even more grateful that she'd lent moral support. Cole didn't know enough about children's illnesses to face this situation alone.

"I want to...for a little while longer. I'll be in the parlor if you need me."

Cole nodded and Kate left the room.

Less than an hour later, after removing Meggie from the tub, dressing her in new nightclothes and tucking her back into bed, Cole went to check on Kate. She'd been quiet and he wondered if she had decided to go home after all.

Cole stood at the entrance of the parlor and smiled. Kate lay cuddled on the sofa, folded up in a quilt, resting her head back against the cushion, fast asleep. He watched her breaths come easily and decided not to disturb her. She deserved the rest she craved. Cole rubbed his neck then, and his sense of propriety knocked him upside the head.

She shouldn't be here overnight. It wouldn't be good for her reputation. She was already the subject of town gossip, with her free spirit and bold attitude defying the town ordinance, and Cole didn't want her helping him tonight to cause her any undue trouble. Not tonight. Besides, Kate had a way of getting into trouble all on her own, without his help.

Kate snuggled deeper into the quilt and made a slightly satisfied mewling sound. Cole smiled again. He'd let her sleep.

Wasn't much he could do about her reputation if anyone saw her leaving his house at this hour anyway.

Except maybe marry her.

Wouldn't that set the town on its ear? The sheriff and Miss Kate, the saloon gal.

Cole ran a hand down his face. It was an impossible dream, he and Kate. She wasn't backing down from building the saloon, and darn if Cole couldn't shuffle aside the notions in his head of what a wife and mother should be. What a real family should be. And he surely wouldn't break his promise to Jeb. Meggie's needs came first. Cole would never forget that.

He glanced once more at Kate, this time with regret. He left the room to check on his daughter, knowing full well he wasn't going to get a lick of sleep tonight in that chair beside Meggie's bed.

Perhaps he'd be better off not sleeping. Because he'd surely dream of Kate, in his bed, warming his lonely heart and flaming his needy body.

Yes sir, dreams would only cause him more regret. Cole sank down into the chair, propped his feet and watched his daughter take the first restful breaths she had all night.

Chapter Ten

"Hey! Lookee here, Miss Meggie, you can't just go throwing flour in anybody's face," Kate said, pinching up some of the white powder and flicking it onto Meggie's face.

She giggled. "Yes, I can." Meggie's chubby fingers took up a small batch of flour and missed Kate's face. Instead the flour landed on her throat and down the front of her dress.

"Okay, you got me!" Kate glanced at the rosy hue on Meggie's face. She'd made a full recovery from last night. Thank heavens.

When Kate had woken up on Cole's sofa early this morning, she'd risen quickly to check on Meggie. There she found both father and daughter in Meggie's bedroom, Cole draped rather uncomfortably in the chair, only partly awake, and Meggie sprawled out in her bed. But Cole had roused rapidly when Kate entered and she'd witnessed the lines of fatigue on Cole's face. She guessed he hadn't slept much last night and insisted that she take Meggie for the day so that he could get a bit more rest before going to the jail later that morning.

Cole had been too tired to argue. She could read the indecision on his face, but he'd relented, agreeing to let Meggie spend the day in Kate's care.

Now they sat in Kate's kitchen, baking cookies. Kate was sure to keep Meggie from too much activity, and baking was something that Meggie could do while resting.

"What kind of cookies?" Meggie asked.

"Oatmeal with raisin bits."

"Daddy's favorite."

Kate smiled. "Is it now? Well, we'll have to bring him a batch later. Some of the ones you baked, right, Meggie?"

She bobbed her head up and down. "Right."

After dumping the measured flour into a bowl, Kate instructed Meggie on how to crack eggs. The child did a pretty darn good job and, as a reward, Kate allowed Meggie to stir up the batter, then add the raisins. "Your daddy is going to love these. Especially since they're from you, Meggie."

"I got two daddies. One daddy is up in heaven. And I got one at home, too."

Kate's heart stirred. Meggie was such a sweet child. "I'd say you're a lucky girl."

"How many daddies do you got?"

Kate hesitated. She didn't enjoy speaking of her father, not even to Meggie, the pain of his betrayal always with her. She'd never gotten over his leaving. As a young girl, Kate had tried dismissing his abandonment with many reasons, but in the end she'd only come up with one. He hadn't loved her enough to stay. It had been a hard fight to regain her trust and believe she was worthy of love. Kate never quite knew if she'd accomplished that goal. "I have one daddy. But he's not at home." Meggie stopped licking batter off her fingers and looked up askance. "He left when I was very young."

"Is he in heaven?"

"Well, I'm not so sure."

Kate showed Meggie how to spoon the cookies on the pan and the subject was dropped, thankfully. Kate put the cookie pan in the cookstove and then fixed the lunch meal for Meggie. She warmed up barley soup and lathered biscuits with apple butter.

"Let's make a deal. We eat up all our soup then we get to have a cookie straight out of the oven," Kate coaxed. Cole had told her Meggie wasn't a good eater, being extremely particular in what suited her tastes, but Meggie didn't complain. She ate everything up, while Kate finished telling her the story of the golden bear.

After lunch, Kate put a hand to Meggie's forehead and was gratefully relieved to find the fever hadn't returned. Kate didn't mind that the child's blue pinafore was smudged with batter or that remnants of their little flour fight was evident on Meggie's hair and face. The child felt cool to the touch, and that was all that mattered. "I promised your daddy I'd take you home for an afternoon nap. We'd better get going."

Meggie frowned, a distinct downturn of her little lips. "I'm not tired."

Kate cast her an understanding smile. "I know, but you were very ill last night. It's best not to overdo."

"Can we go by the creek first? Daddy always takes me. He likes it there." Meggie's eyes lit. Her entire expression changed and Kate saw no harm in taking a slight detour by way of Crystal Creek.

"I like it there, too. Sure, we can walk down to the creek."

"Yippee!" Meggie jumped from her seat and wrapped her arms around Kate's middle. Kate hugged her back affectionately and tender feelings welled up inside her.

"I'll even show you how to skip rocks over the water."

"Daddy already teached me."

Of course, Cole would have taught his daughter one of their favorite pastimes.

"Well, good, then maybe you can show me a thing or two. It's been so long, I might have forgotten."

Meggie grasped Kate's hand and together they ambled pleasantly along to the creek.

Cole Bradshaw found himself just outside town in a field of wildflowers. He bent and picked a bouquet of pale pink primroses. The color suited Kate, matching the rosy hue of her cheeks. Cole frowned. What in hell was he doing? He wasn't courting Kate, yet he wanted to show his appreciation for her help last night and today. She'd given up an entire day to spend with Meggie.

"No harm in showing appreciation," he muttered. "They're just wildflowers." Kate's favorite.

Cole strode out of the field with the batch of flowers under his hat. No sense getting the entire town curious about his comings and goings. He walked along the sidewalk until he came up on the millinery. Mrs. Whittaker had the prettiest ribbons displayed in her window. Meggie would love a pair of colorful ribbons for her braids.

Cole entered the millinery and nearly did an about-face. But it was too late—he'd been caught. "Why, Cole, what are you doing in here?" Patricia Wesley walked over to him, Mrs. Whittaker just a step behind. "Not that I'm not tickled to see you."

"Good afternoon, Patricia," he managed cordially. "Mrs. Whittaker."

The ladies returned his greeting. "Were you looking for me, Cole?" Patricia asked coyly.

"Uh, well, actually," he began, glancing at Mrs. Whittaker then down at the hat he held in his hand. That had been his second mistake. The first was coming into the shop in the first place.

"What's that you're hiding under your hat?" Patricia asked with curiosity. She peered at his hat so hard that he thought she'd likely bore a hole straight through it.

Patricia gasped. "Flowers? How positively lovely."

Mrs. Whittaker cast Cole a look of approval. "The sheriff followed you in here to give you the flowers, Patricia. Isn't that nice?"

"Cole? Really? How very thoughtful."

Cole brought the flowers out from hiding. He stared at the primroses meant for Kate and, with great reluctance, presented Patricia with the bouquet. "Here you go."

"Why, thank you. What a pleasant surprise." Patricia brought the flowers up to her nose. "These are lovely."

Kate would have thought so, too.

Cole pointed to the ribbons in the window, explaining that Meggie had been sick last night and the ribbons would surely cheer her up. Both ladies agreed. He made his purchase then handed Mrs. Whittaker the money. She glanced outside toward the Silver Saddle, then captured Cole with a sharp gaze. "You know, that woman intends to ignore the ordinance and open up that saloon anyway, regardless of the law."

"I'm aware of the situation, Mrs. Whittaker."

The stout woman shook her head. "They've been working night and day, making a terrible racket, trying to hurry up the construction. Why? I'll never understand. You'll just have to arrest her soon as she opens her doors."

Cole grimaced, a knot twisting in his gut. "She knows the consequences."

"But do you?" Mrs. Whittaker leaned over her cash register and whispered, "We all know about your friendship with Miss Malone, Sheriff. But the town council is counting on you to do the right thing."

Cole didn't need to hear this right now. He'd spent the entire night awake, worrying over Meggie and thinking about kissing Kate again. Doing more than kissing Kate. Hell, how had things gotten so dang complicated? "I'll do my duty as a sworn officer of the law, Mrs. Whittaker. Like I always do."

The white-haired lady's eyes beamed with satisfaction. "Good. We didn't place our faith in you by electing you over that Sherman fella without knowing you'd do your duty. No matter what."

Cole nodded solemnly and turned to leave. Patricia waited for him by the front door. She smiled sweetly. "Would you walk me to the livery, Cole? I'm due to take another riding lesson today."

"Sure thing, Patricia. No problem."

Patricia took his arm as they headed down the sidewalk, her gay laughter floating through town. Cole didn't think anything he'd said was particularly clever, but Patricia surely did.

They'd almost reached the livery when Cole spotted Meggie. She ran straight into his arms. "Daddy!"

Cole bent down, studying his daughter. She appeared to be fine, all smiles and giggles, although she looked as dirty as a prairie dog who'd just tunneled his way to town. "Look at you, Megpie, what did you get yourself into?"

"We had a flour fight, Daddy, and we made cookies. Miss Kate letted me put the raisin bits in and I made up a batch just for you. Then we went down to the creek and skipped rocks on the water!"

"Did she now?" Cole brought himself up to full height as Kate came forward. She held a basket filled with cookies. Her smile was radiant and she, too, had flour on her clothes. A dusting of fine powder remained on her throat then dipped down lower to the hollow between the swell of her breasts. Cole fought off the temptation to stare, lifting his eyes to hers, but his wicked mind had already conjured up images of how he'd like to remove that flour from her chest.

Kate's gaze flowed over him, then to Patricia, who stood close holding those damn flowers. Kate revealed nothing in her expression, but Cole wondered what she was thinking.

Meggie grabbed the basket out of Kate's hands. "Here's the cookies, Daddy."

Cole peered into the cloth-trimmed basket. "Oatmeal with raisins. Thank you, sweet darlin'."

"Miss Kate didn't know they was your favorite," Meggie said innocently.

Cole pierced Kate with a knowing gaze. They'd grown up eating oatmeal cookies together, oftentimes fighting over who got the last one. "No, she probably didn't."

Kate shrugged and averted her eyes.

"Cole, this child is absolutely filthy!" Patricia reeled. "Why, she's full of flour. It's in her hair, on her clothes. What is that sticky stuff on you, child?"

Meggie looked down and with a finger swiped a bit of the sweet stuff from her dress then licked her finger. "Cookie dough."

Kate laughed.

Cole laughed.

Patricia gasped. "Oh dear!" Then she continued on with her softly spoken tirade. "Look at her legs, Cole. She's green with grass stains. It'll take a month of Sundays to clean this child up properly."

Meggie's mouth turned down and her happy expression vanished.

"No harm in a little dirt, Patricia." Cole needed to put the smile back on his daughter's face. "Meggie, why don't we go on home now and see about having some milk and cookies?"

"Cole," Patricia reprimanded quietly, "that's not the way to discipline her. She needs suitable tending. She needs to know about ladylike manners." Patricia darted her gaze over to Kate, a distasteful look on her face.

Cole swept Meggie up into his arms. His daughter had had a rough night and now she was the picture of pure joy. He saw no reason to discipline her. In truth, he hadn't seen Meggie so happy in a very long time. Cole knew Patricia had good intentions. She'd been schooled in the East. She knew about manners and such, so why did it rub at him crosswise when she tried to help out with his daughter? "Patricia, looks like Jethro is waiting for you." He gestured with a nod of his head.

All eyes turned back to the entrance of the livery. Jethro Cable stood wearing a frown and holding on to the reins of two mares.

"Oh, all right," she said quickly. "I don't want that man getting into one of his foul moods because I'm late."

"Have a good lesson, Patricia," Cole offered kindly.

Kate watched Patricia walk away in a huff swinging the bouquet of wildflowers like a weapon, as though she meant to do Jethro harm with them. Poor Jethro, Kate thought, then she turned to find Cole staring at her.

"Well, I'd better get home," Kate said, her heart still hurting from seeing Cole arm in arm with Patricia, holding that lovely batch of primroses just moments ago. It shouldn't shock her seeing them together. Kate had no claim on Cole.

It was clear what he wanted in a woman. Kate simply didn't measure up, but it still smarted like the dickens whenever she bumped into them together. She'd rather not be witness to their courtship.

"Goodbye, Meggie. You stay healthy, okay? And take that nap like you promised."

Meggie's big eyes rounded, a woeful expression on her cherubic face. "Do ya hafta go?"

On a regretful sigh, Kate offered, "I'm afraid I do."

"Wait, Kate," Cole said urgently. "I wanted to thank you for last night and for taking Meggie today." He grinned. "From the looks of her, she clearly had a great time."

Kate smiled at Meggie and stroked her floured hair. A sadness Kate wouldn't dare show consumed her now. At the moment, she had two Bradshaws in her heart. "We had fun, didn't we?"

Meggie bobbed her head up and down.

Cole held Meggie tight in his arms. There was such genuine love between them that it warmed Kate's heart, but it also reminded her of all she'd missed as a young girl, not having her father's love. She'd vowed to never again allow anyone to make her feel unworthy of love.

Cole flashed her a beautiful smile. He still had the power to make her insides tremble with a show of just a little Bradshaw charm. "Kate, you've been a good...friend. Let me show my appreciation by taking you ladies out for supper after Meggie's nap."

Kate didn't want to spend more time with either of them. It hurt too darn much. She looked into Meggie's hopeful eyes, hating to disappoint her. She couldn't bear to look at Cole, so she found the flour stains on her boots real interesting and shook her head. "I couldn't possibly. I, uh, lost a bit of time today. I really have a great deal of work to do at the saloon."

When she peered up, it was to find Cole once again staring at her. "Fine." Anger lit his eyes midnight-blue, but it was fleeting, because the light faded quickly. "I understand."

Kate wondered if Cole truly understood. Did he know how hard it was to refuse such an offer? It would be so easy for her to be with them, to enjoy Meggie's antics and have Cole's attention. But to what end? Kate had to protect herself from further pain. Cole wanted her friendship still, yet Kate wasn't sure how long they would be able to hold on. There was too much between them and too much that could tear them apart.

Cole spoke into Meggie's ear, whispering something, then the child turned to her. "Bye-bye, Miss Kate. Thank you…for…watching…me."

Kate brushed a soft kiss on Meggie's forehead. "Bye-bye, Meggie. And you're very welcome."

Kate walked away slowly, heading for home. How she hated leaving Meggie after the time they'd spent together today, but she knew it was for the best. No sense getting the child's hopes up, because there surely wasn't a place for Kate in Meggie's life. She'd only taken a few steps when she heard Cole call out, "I'm gonna love those cookies, Kate."

Kate squeezed her eyes shut and kept on walking.

Chapter Eleven

Cole sat at his desk, perplexed. He'd been sheriff of this town for nearly four years now, and this was the very first time he was at odds with the townsfolk. Not that he didn't agree with them about Kate going against the town ordinance and building up her establishment, but he didn't need every doggone member of the town council swarming around him to make certain he did his job.

He knew his responsibilities. He knew what he had to do.

And Kate.

He'd like to paddle her bottom until it turned as colorful as the rosy-pink dress she had worn the other day. That might just teach her a lesson about defying the law.

Hell, it'd been two weeks since they'd spoken. Two weeks since she'd helped him with Meggie and baked those damn delicious cookies. And in that time, word had it that she'd hired a barkeep. Big Josh, the Silver

Saddle's one-time employee, had seen her advertisement and ridden into town looking for work, and Kate had seen fit to hire him on the spot. He was rooming in the back of the saloon now. The saloon that was nearly finished.

Cole had stood outside his office just one week ago today and watched as the ornate mahogany back bar had been delivered to the saloon. The richly carved structure had most of the townsfolk stepping out of their shops to take a look.

Cole had watched Kate from a distance, her face flushed with excitement as she'd gone about issuing orders, gesturing to the freight operators where she wanted the bar to go. Shortly after, more items had arrived and been deposited inside the saloon. From what Cole could see, the Silver Saddle, with its etched glass windows and fancy iron door would rival some of the finest saloons Cole had ever seen. The transformation from burnt pillars to fresh whitewashed walls had been miraculous. Cole hated to admit that the saloon, as it stood, was the finest establishment on the street.

And he also hated to admit that very soon, his longstanding friendship with Kate, fragile as it was, would come to an end.

Cole groaned aloud when Edward Wesley entered his office. "Afternoon, Cole."

"Edward," Cole said, standing to shake his hand.

"We haven't seen much of you lately, son."

Cole scratched his head. He didn't know which was

worse, speaking to Edward about his daughter, or speaking to him regarding Kate. "No, sir. I've been real busy. Johnny took some time off last week. He's due back today and things should ease up a bit."

"Good. Well, we'll have to have you over again for dinner soon. But I'll let Patricia do the inviting." The man's smile faded and a fierce look stole over his round face. "Now, about that blasted woman and her saloon. Her mother only got the message when the saloon went up in smoke. I think Miss Malone might have even more gumption than her mother, if that's possible." The man's eyebrows twitched. "Real pretty women, those two...both mother and daughter. Kinda wild, if you know what I mean. That Louisa sure knew how to serve a man...a drink." Wesley chuckled at his own jest.

Cole flung his hat onto his desk, his insides rumbling. He braced his hands onto his desktop and leaned in. "Get to the point."

"The point is this," Edward said firmly, not backing down. He was a powerful man in town and was happy to remind people of it every chance he got. "We have to make an example of that woman for the whole town to see. What good are laws if they're abused? The town ordinance clearly states—"

"I'm aware of what the ordinance states, Edward. And I know the law. Until that saloon opens for business, Kate Malone is within her rights."

The man narrowed his eyes. "Patricia said you had

a soft spot for the woman. Is that what this is about? She keeping your nights from getting lonely?''

Cole balled his hands into fists, resisting the urge to hit the older man smack on his smug face. He clenched his teeth and spoke quietly. "I'm sure I'm not that lucky."

Edward's eyebrows rose. "Now, Cole, no sense getting riled."

"Trust me to do my job, Edward."

"The town council wants assurances."

Cole lifted his .45 from its holster, turning the shiny handle in his hand. He shot Edward Wesley a grim look. "Tell them they've got my assurance. And tell them I'll not listen to another one of their complaints on the matter. I've got everything under control."

At that moment, Cole wished he hadn't sought Edward Wesley's help in getting elected. Cole was his own man. As much as being sheriff suited him, he'd rather not have the position if it meant cowering to the likes of Wesley. He'd not ever do it again. He'd earned the town's respect. For the most part the town trusted him, placing their lives and safety in his hands. He'd have no trouble getting reelected without Wesley's help.

"I'll tell them, Cole."

Cole nodded and walked Wesley to the door. "See that you do." Cole slammed the door shut and cursed up a blue streak, because he knew that any day now, he'd have to destroy a friendship he'd thought would last a lifetime.

* * *

Kate's heart filled with joy as she entered the Silver Saddle. The saloon had turned out even better than she'd imagined. She walked slowly around, turning, gazing, filling her eyes up with every little detail, from the slightly used Conway piano she'd purchased to the sweeping velvet curtains above the stage that Nora designed. How grand, how stately, how positively perfect the saloon appeared. And how very proud Kate's mama would have been.

Kate leaned against the polished mahogany bar, studying her face in the gilded mirror over the back bar. "This is it," she said, smiling at her image. "Tomorrow, we open for business."

"Miss Kate, where do you want this sign to go?"

Josh McCabe, otherwise known around town as Big Josh for his brawny stature, came out of the back room, holding up a sign that read, No Gunfighting In This Establishment. It was one of many decorated signs Kate and her mama had ordered months ago. And thankfully for Kate, her mother's one-time employee had seen that advertisement and applied for the position of barkeep. His size alone had kept most of the patrons in line and no one could mix a better drink.

"Oh, Josh. Good morning. Let's see?" She rubbed her chin, giving the walls a good looking-over. "I'd say it should go on this side, opposite the bar. She gestured toward the wall directly over the round tables. "I expect a reminder wouldn't hurt when there's a game of poker or pike monte going on."

Josh nodded. "You got a head for business, just like your mama, Miss Kate. No doubt, the Silver Saddle will be as successful this time around."

With a rueful sigh, Kate shook her head. "You do know that we may run into trouble, Josh. The town council's opposed and...you might be out of a job before we even get started."

"I'll take my chances, Miss Kate. You went ahead and explained that to me already. I got a roof over my head right now, and I ain't a bit worried."

Kate's spirits lifted some. "Thanks, Josh."

Josh nodded. "I'll get the supplies I need to hang this sign and have it done quick."

"Oh, and Josh, while you're back there, would you bring out the Grand Opening signs. They're going outside first thing in the morning."

Kate pushed the food around on her plate, her excitement mingling with trepidation over the opening of the saloon. Dear Nora had noticed her mood and invited her to dinner.

"Jethro, would you pass Kate the peas and carrots?" Nora said brightly.

"Thanks, Jethro," Kate said, coming out of her haze to give him a smile. "This is a wonderful meal, Nora."

"Kate, you haven't taken two bites yet," Nora pointed out with a chuckle.

Kate looked down at her plate. Braised beef, potatoes, biscuits and gravy and now vegetables filled up her dish, but she hadn't made much of an effort to eat. She couldn't be rude to her friends, especially Nora, who'd gone to all this trouble, just to make certain that she had a decent meal before tomorrow.

Kate dipped her fork into the creamed potatoes and took a bite. "It's delicious, Nora."

Abe poured Kate some lemonade. "Now, you just relax and have a good time tonight."

Kate groaned. "Why do I feel as if it's my last supper?"

"You're just fussing about tomorrow, Kate. Don't worry about a thing. Abe and I plan to be your first customers," Jethro said assuredly.

"Really?" Kate darted a look to both men.

They nodded.

"Of course they'll be there," Nora said.

"And I know a few others, too, have expressed interest," Kate said, feeling better now. She dug into her food.

"I can't wait to see these curtains Nora's been bragging over," Abe teased.

"I haven't been bragging, Abe." Nora's face colored.

"She has a right to brag. A professional seamstress couldn't have done better. They turned out beautiful," Kate offered honestly.

"My Nora is a talented woman," Abe said, glancing at her growing belly. "Can't wait to see what else she's created beautifully."

"Abe Cable!" Nora blushed full out this time.

Kate and Jethro both laughed, along with Abe.

"Last I remember," Jethro said, grinning, "it takes two to make...uh, things beautiful."

Abe cleared his throat and directed a sharp gaze at his brother, but his eyes fairly twinkled. "I think a change of subject is in order. How're the riding lessons going with Patricia Wesley?"

Jethro's face contorted unbecomingly. "Ah, Abe, why'd you have to go and spoil things. Just when I was having a good laugh."

"That well?" Abe said dryly.

Jethro scratched his head. "That woman...uh, pardon me for saying...she's too snooty for her own good. Always talking about my manners not being worth a damn...uh, darn. Sorry, ladies."

Nora glanced at Kate with a smile.

Jethro continued. "She's forever talking about the sheriff. Seems she thinks she's gonna end up with him. Least that's the point she's always pressing. But I say it ain't so. That woman wouldn't recognize a man's interest if it hauled up and hit her. She's too busy jabbering all the time about what's proper, what's right, what she learned at that fancy school in Boston."

Abe eyed his brother intently. "I only asked about the lessons. Didn't expect to get such an earful."

Kate giggled at the sour expression Jethro presented to his brother. The banter between the two helped ease some of her tension whenever Cole's name came up. It had been weeks since she'd seen him, and that suited her fine. He was always in her thoughts, but at least, she didn't have to put those thoughts together with seeing the actual living, breathing man.

After the meal, Nora served apple cobbler with coffee then they sat outside on the porch to enjoy the night air. Kate felt better, more relaxed as the Cables, all of them, managed to put her at ease. She treasured their friendship. At least Kate knew she had allies in them when the entire town, it seemed, was going against her. Cole included.

"Well, I'd better go home. It's getting late," she said, after helping Nora with the cleanup. She thanked all of her friends, giving each one a hug.

Jethro seemed to hold on to her embrace a bit longer than the others and Kate cringed inwardly. She didn't want to injure his feelings. According to Nora, Jethro held some hopes about courting her. Kate truly liked Jethro as a friend, but it ended there. Fool that she was, she knew there was no room in her heart for anyone but Cole.

"I'll walk you home, Miss Kate. Unless you'd rather ride in the buggy?" Jethro offered.

"Oh Jethro, a walk is just what I need. Thank you."

The evening breeze blew Kate's curls into her face as they walked the short distance to town. She shoved aside the unruly strands, enjoying the quiet calm. Tomorrow night if all went well, she'd be in business and her life from then on would be entirely different.

"Miss Kate?"

"Mmm?"

"Do you think you'd like…uh, would you enjoy going on a picnic with me after church on Sunday?"

Kate slowed her steps and chose her words carefully. Jethro was a dear man who would make some deserving woman very happy. She only wished it could be her. "You know I'll be busy when the saloon opens, Jethro. I don't expect to have much free time. And, well, in all honesty—"

"You got feelings for someone else," he interrupted with a knowing nod.

"Well, I, uh—"

"It's okay. Nora hinted that you did, but I had to know for myself." His shrug came with a big smile. "Can't blame a man for trying."

"Oh, Jethro. I want us to be friends." Kate stared into his eyes so he could see the depth of her sincerity. She truly cared for him and couldn't bear hurting him.

Jethro claimed her hand then, squeezing with gentle pressure. "I'll always be your friend, Miss Kate. You don't have to worry."

They strolled down the street, hand in hand, an overwhelming sense of relief swamping her.

Johnny Martinez let loose a long, low whistle when he entered the sheriff's office. "The Grand Opening sign at the saloon has got the whole town buzzing, boss. It went up just a few minutes ago and I couldn't get a mouthful of coffee down my throat at the diner before I was hit with a load of questions.''

On a weary sigh, Cole raked a hand through his hair. He'd noticed the sign as he walked to work. Acid churned around in his gut and he cursed. He'd weighed his options in his head this week when he noticed the saloon nearly completed. He cursed again. What options? He was out of time…and so was Kate. He got up from his desk, put on his vest and holstered his gun. "Okay," he said, pushing the air from his lungs, "I'll go talk to Kate."

"Do you think it'll do any good?"

Cole strode to the door. Before shutting it, he answered grimly, "Not one damn bit."

Cole ignored the stares of the shop owners and walked briskly toward the Silver Saddle. Once there, he gazed at the signs decking the sidewalk, pursed his lips and walked through the iron doors of the saloon.

Cole was struck by the elegance of the saloon. He'd not ventured inside since the night he'd taught Kate a "lesson" about protecting herself. A lesson he'd take to his grave, he was sure, since he'd never forget the heady excitement of her kiss, the lush feel of her skin.

He studied the interior, from the polished carved-wood bar to the flocked paper on the walls. The stage, the piano, the cane-backed chairs, everything spoke of refinement and taste. An unwelcome sense of admiration for Kate and her accomplishment washed over him like a sudden blast of rain. It was momentary, fleeting and just plain stupid. How could he admire something yet hate its very existence?

Kate came out of the back room then, her face brimming with joy. She stopped short when she spotted him just inside the saloon doors. "Oh, Cole."

It wasn't much of a greeting. What did he expect—her eyes to light when she first saw him? Her face not to lose that incredible glow? "Morning, Kate."

She stared at the gun he had holstered, his badge, then focused her green eyes directly at him. Chin up, she went behind the bar. "What would you like?"

He gritted his teeth. "What I would like is for you to take down those damn signs out front. What I would like is for you to see reason."

"Cole, I'm not going to take down those signs. And as far as seeing reason, if that low-down snake of a banker, Mr. High-and-Mighty Wesley hadn't refused my mama a loan, the Silver Saddle would've never shut down for good. I'm within my rights here. The signs stay." She came around the bar to face him head-on.

"I'm asking you, Kate, for all that we've meant to each other through the years, take them down."

"And I'm asking you, Cole, for all that we've meant to each other, let them stay."

Cole's temper flared and his voice rose. "You know I can't do that."

"Well, I can't, either." Kate folded her arms across her middle. Her face held an expression of resistance, defiance and sheer stubborn will.

"You're asking for trouble."

"I want what's right."

"You're gonna keep the saloon open?"

"Yes."

"And defy the town ordinance?"

"That ordinance isn't fair."

"You're breaking the law, Kate."

She stared into his eyes, hers shining bright with green fire.

He returned her gaze, burning into her with myriad emotions packed tight and ready to explode. "Then I'm placing you under arrest for violating Crystal Creek Town Ordinance Number 735."

She gasped. An expression of sheer astonishment crossed her features and Cole's gut clenched. "F-fine," she said bravely.

"Let's go." He took her by the arm, just under the elbow, as though he was escorting her to a grand ball.

Kate didn't fuss but insisted on locking up the saloon. Cole allowed that and, once again, took her by the arm. They strode in silence, passing the shops and the curious onlookers along the way. Thankfully, the jail wasn't a far walk. Cole stopped just outside his office and glanced around once. He released a breath, pushed open the door and led Kate inside.

Johnny Martinez rose from the desk and stared first at Kate, then at him.

"Not a soul comes in here today, you got that?" Cole commanded. He pointed to the front door. "That door stays locked."

"I got it," the deputy replied.

Kate began walking toward one of the cells. "Where in hell do you think you're going?" Cole snapped.

"I'm under arrest, aren't I?"

He glanced at the dingy cell Kate had headed toward. "Get back over here, Kate."

"But...I thought," she began, then hesitated and peered into one of the cells.

No way in hell was he going to lock Kate up. He'd never had a woman prisoner before and he damn well wasn't going to start now. Whether she deserved it or not, Cole wouldn't subject Kate to such humiliation. "Do you *want* to spend the night in that filthy cell?"

"Of course not!"

"Then sit down and let me think on it."

Kate took a seat across from his desk and sat quietly, which was unlike her. He'd expected anger. He'd expected retaliation. He'd expected anything but a subdued Kate. Placing her under arrest had really rattled her today. He'd seen it on her astonished expression when he'd taken her into custody. He supposed Kate never thought he'd really do it. Hell, he'd been dreading this moment since the woman had walked back into his life, weeks ago.

Cole paced the floor, the silence in the small outer office stifling. After long moments he came up with the only solution that made any sense. "Johnny, watch the pris—uh, lady for me. I'll be right back. And remember, don't open this door to anyone."

Johnny nodded.

Cole was back at the jail in less than ten minutes. He found Johnny sitting on the edge of his desk and Kate in her seat, weaving a tall tale about the beginnings of her grandfather's saloon. Their smiles brought an unbidden twist in his gut.

"Having a good time?" he asked, slamming the door.

Johnny bounded up from the desk. "Just, uh, passing the time."

"Is that also a crime in this town, Cole?" Fire sparked in Kate's eyes and Cole knew the old Kate was back and ready to give him hell.

He ignored her irritating question and turned to his deputy. "I'm taking Kate out of here, the back way. She'll be in my custody until this thing gets resolved. I'm counting on you to see that no one comes inside this jail for any reason. Keep the front door locked at all times. Make your rounds as usual. The whole darn town knows by now that I arrested Kate, so I doubt you'll have too much explaining to do. But just in case, keep it simple, Johnny. And don't give away anything."

"Where are you taking her?" Johnny asked.

"She'll be staying at my house."

Johnny's dark eyebrows rose.

"Don't I have anything to say about this?" Kate asked, a sour expression on her face.

He pinned her with a glare. "No."

"Cole, you can't just sneak me out—"

"Do you have a better solution, Kate? 'Cause I'm listening."

"You could let me go," she replied haughtily.

"I could chop my head off, too, but I'm not gonna do it."

Johnny chuckled, then coughed to cover up his mirth, but his eyes twinkled with mischief. "Ah, what a job I have, boss. I stay here, locked up like a prisoner myself, while you take a beautiful woman to your house."

Cole didn't see humor in any of this. He didn't want to take Kate home with him, but he couldn't fathom tossing her into one of his jail cells.

And why did she have to look so pretty today? She'd dressed up real fancy for her grand opening, wearing a shimmering satin dress that matched the meadow-green of her eyes. Her hair was trussed up, all curly, with coppery ringlets caressing her throat. His gaze drifted down a ways to the hollow between her breasts and Cole swallowed hard. A soft, lacy fringe teasing the skin there set off lust-filled thoughts in his head. How he'd like to play a bit with that lace, stroke her flesh with it, put his mouth there.

Cole cleared his throat and took the lead. "Let's get going, Kate. We'll head for the trees back behind the jail, then follow the path to the edge of town and enter the house through the back door. You ready?'' he asked, reaching back to slip her hand in his.

They had run like this a hundred times over in their youth, with Cole taking Kate's hand. It felt familiar, it felt right, but Cole knew this wasn't childhood play. This was a far more dangerous game.

And Cole wondered grimly who would come out the winner this time.

Chapter Twelve

Meggie ran straight into Kate's arms when she entered the kitchen. "Miss Kate!" Kate lifted the child up and hugged her tight. She'd missed seeing the little girl all these weeks, forcing herself to stay away from Cole and his daughter. Kate didn't think any good would come of getting too attached to Cole's child, but as she held her in her arms, smelled the sugary sweet scent of apple pie on her mouth, and touched the soft curls of her golden hair, Kate's heart tumbled with love.

"Hello, Meggie. How's my favorite little baker today?"

"'Kay."

"Have you been practicing skipping, like I showed you?"

Meggie bobbed her head up and down. "Mrs. Gregory says you're gonna sleep in her room tonight."

"Oh, uh—" Kate glanced at Cole, uncertain how to respond.

"That's right. I gave Mrs. Gregory the day off to spend with Caroline and the new baby," Cole added.

"What did she have?" Kate's curiosity overrode her anger with Cole.

"A boy," Cole answered. "It was a long labor, but the child is healthy."

Kate nodded, then asked, "Mrs. Gregory has a room here?"

"It's a small room off the parlor. Sometimes I need her to stay overnight."

Kate's insides churned, and she wondered if Cole had a woman somewhere. Did he visit her during the evenings when his housekeeper could stay over? Or did he spend nights with Patricia? Kate shook that thought clear, doubting the very proper Patricia Wesley would ever do anything remotely scandalous. Kate peered deeply into Cole's eyes and he looked away. She set Meggie down and glanced around the kitchen, wondering what to do next.

"Meggie, sweetheart, Daddy needs to speak with Miss Kate for a few minutes. You go and finish your pie and we'll be back in just a short while."

"'Kay," Meggie said, climbing up into her chair.

Kate followed Cole into the parlor. He turned when they were out of earshot of Meggie. "Listen, Kate. I spoke with Mrs. Gregory. She knows the situation, but Meggie doesn't. I'd appreciate keeping it that way. You're a guest in my house. When I'm gone during the day, I need your word that you'll stay put and not cause a bit of trouble. Besides, Meggie can't be left alone.''

''I wouldn't leave her,'' Kate said in a huff. Did Cole think she had no motherly qualities? She knew enough not to leave the child alone in the house. What did Cole think she'd do, try to escape?

Cole paced the floor. ''I know, I know.'' He pursed his lips and rubbed the backside of his neck. ''It's just that this is such an unusual situation.''

''At last we agree on something,'' Kate said in earnest.

Cole snapped his head up and stared deeply with the penetrating blue eyes that reminded Kate so much of the boy she'd grown up with. Their gazes locked and, after a long, quiet moment, Cole asked, ''You hungry?''

''A little.''

''Let's join Meggie and have some of Mrs. Gregory's apple pie.''

Cole returned home as the sun was setting. He'd had better days, he thought wryly, what with arresting Kate then having to face the three men he'd met up with at the office. Both Cable brothers and Big Josh had been waiting outside the jail when Cole had arrived back to work.

News traveled faster than lightning in his town, and arresting Kate had been the biggest doings this town had seen in years. He'd stood just beyond the locked doors of the office, listening to the three men rant about his tossing Kate in jail.

The woman had broken the law, Cole thought bitterly, and though he hadn't let on that even he couldn't abide making her serve real jail time, he also couldn't very well admit that he was housing Kate in his home. He couldn't tell Kate's friends that she was in his custody, that she'd be safe and warm throughout the night.

He'd managed to assure them all that Kate wouldn't be left alone and that he'd make a personal effort to see to her comfort. The three men scoffed at that notion as they walked away, but it was Jethro Cable who'd glared at him with cold disdain and obvious disgust, muttering about the indecency of throwing a woman like Kate in jail.

Cole walked into the parlor and poured himself a whiskey. He didn't often drink, but today's events had tried his patience. The amber liquid went down smoothly, caressing his throat before burning his gut. He closed his eyes, relishing the taste, the feel, the soothing effect the alcohol had on his nerves.

Giggles broke out from the kitchen and Cole went to investigate. He stood in the doorway, sipping his drink, watching Kate and Meggie splatter cake batter all over the counter and table.

Meggie looked up. "D-Daddy," she said, chuckling, "we was making a cake and lookee what happened!"

"I can see that, sweet darlin'."

"We scooped most the batter back into the bowl, Daddy. Miss Kate says it don't matter. The cake's gonna taste even better now."

Kate smiled as she continued to mix up the batter. Cole took another swallow of whiskey, leaning against the wall, telling himself to walk out and let them finish without him intruding. Telling himself to leave things be. He didn't want to spoil their fun. Hell, Kate wouldn't even look him in the eye.

"I'll make fried chicken for dinner," she said, handing Meggie the wooden spoon for the stirring. When she finally glanced up, Cole noticed a dollop of batter in Kate's hair.

"That's fine," he answered, walking into the room to face her. She looked away, pretending to busy herself with the cake. Cole took her chin in hand, gently turned her to face him then gazed into her curls. He wound a finger into one coppery lock to remove the batter, twirling it onto his own finger and wiping it clean. "Sticky stuff," he said softly, looking into her green eyes before backing away. He took his daughter into his arms. "Looks like you need a bath before we eat, Megpie."

"I gotta help Miss Kate with supper first, Daddy."

"Meggie, your daddy is right. You can help me put the cake in the cookstove, then off you go. When you're all cleaned up, the cake will be ready."

"But I don't want no bath."

Kate bent to Meggie's level. "If you go, I promise to cut you the biggest piece of cake because you've been such a big help. And you can help me set the table.''

"Mrs. Gregory puts flowers on the table sometimes. Can we have some?"

Kate glanced at Cole then shook her head. "I don't think—''

"I'll go out and pick some before supper, Meggie.''

An hour later, Cole returned from the meadow and handed Kate a huge bouquet of light lavender primroses. Her eyes lit with joy as she admired the flowers. Cole took his seat at the table, watching Kate bustle about his kitchen, setting the flowers into vases, turning the fried chicken and stirring the potatoes. Meggie dashed about, setting out dishes and glasses, then carefully and with her full attention, she centered one vase overflowing with flowers onto the table.

"Looks pretty, Daddy.''

"Uh-huh,'' Cole agreed, his gaze fastened on Kate. Her hair had come loose, the curls falling onto her forehead, her cheeks, and down about her neck. She moved with grace around his kitchen, and with each swish of her satin skirts, each shift of her sleek curves, Cole's body grew tight.

He didn't want her here, yet it was where she seemed to belong. Cole cursed silently and tore his gaze away from the woman wreaking havoc with his mind.

She was his *prisoner*, he reminded himself. This was supposed to be her punishment. But just who was being punished the most? he asked himself, catching a whiff of her scent as she leaned over to adjust the flowers in the vase.

He groaned aloud when he glimpsed sight of Kate nearly spilling out of her gown.

"Did you say something?" she asked, fingering the petals of a flower.

"Nope." What in blazes was wrong with him, lusting after Kate when he knew darn well that she wasn't the right woman for him? He needed a wife. He wanted a family.

Kate ran a saloon.

Maybe it was the ease with which she accepted her fate and took over the household duties like a wife…and mother that had him thinking crazy thoughts. Maybe Cole liked her being here a bit too much.

"Cole, would you like to say grace?" Kate asked.

He'd been so deep in thought he hadn't realized Meggie and Kate had sat down at the table.

"Yeah," he answered, staring at the food Kate had prepared, then staring into her expectant eyes. He reminded himself once again that Kate Malone was in his custody for breaking the law. She wouldn't be here, offering up a delicious meal, caring for his daughter, delighting in a simple bouquet of primroses if he hadn't arrested her.

Cole cleared his throat and began, "Heavenly Father, let us give thanks for the bounty before us…"

* * *

Kate sat in the parlor, staring at the hearth, a shiver creeping up her spine. She huddled her arms about her, closing her eyes, wondering what tomorrow would bring.

"Cold?" Cole asked, coming into the room and startling her.

She opened her eyes and nodded. "Maybe a little."

"I'll start a fire." She watched him set wood into the fireplace and spark the kindling until a low, glowing blaze cast the room in dim evening light.

He stood and stretched, then sat down next to her. "Meggie's asleep."

She nodded. "When I kissed her good-night, she barely knew I was there."

"She's a sound sleeper. Always has been, ever since she was a tot." Cole's chest swelled with pride.

"You're a good father, Cole." Kate didn't mind offering up the truth. As angry as she was with him, she couldn't deny him the praise he deserved when it came to Meggie.

He seemed taken by her compliment. "Thank you. I don't know if I'm always doing right by her, but I try. Made a promise to Jeb that I intend to keep."

"You are…keeping it, I mean. She's a wonderful child."

His face broke out into a grin. "She is, isn't she?" Then his expression turned somber. "But she needs…more. Mrs. Gregory isn't going be with us much longer. She's planning on moving in with Caroline and helping out with the grandchildren."

"Then what will you do?"

"Hire someone, I suppose." Cole stared into the flames, his voice low and deep with regret. "Or get married."

"Patricia?" Kate asked, dreading his reply.

Cole didn't hesitate. It was as if he'd thought on the subject many a time. "She's suitable, but I don't..."

"You don't...what?" Kate's heart hammered fiercely. And she wondered if Cole would ever describe her as "suitable."

"...know," he said. "I don't know. What about you and Jethro?"

"Jethro Cable?" Surprise elevated her voice. "He's a friend, Cole. A dear friend."

Cole nodded, but a deep frown marred his handsome face. "Like we were friends?"

"No." Kate wouldn't lie. Nothing and no one would ever compare to her one-time treasured friendship with Cole.

"Are we still friends, Kate?" he asked, taking her hand. He turned it over and traced a finger over the scar she'd had since childhood. It was a mark, a brand on her palm that symbolized both the pain and joy of her youth. Cole pressed his palm to hers, entwining their fingers, joining their mutual wounds.

Kate closed her eyes and answered truthfully. "I don't know, Cole."

Several silent minutes passed with both watching flames snap and spark in the fireplace. When Kate yawned, rather indelicately, Cole took note. Heaving a heavy sigh, he rose from the sofa, lifting her with him. "It's time for bed. I'll show you to your room."

With hands entwined, Cole led the way to a small alcove behind the main room. Kate's rapid heartbeats thumped hard in her chest from the possessive way Cole held her hand. "It's not fancy, but it's clean."

Kate did a cursory glance around the small room. "It's fine, Cole. I'll be okay."

He applied light pressure on her hand before releasing her. "The meal was delicious."

"Thank you. Just fried chicken and fixings."

"Cake, too."

She bit her lip and stared into his eyes.

He stared back, burning her with scorching blue heat.

"Well, good night." Her insides nearly turned to tapioca just looking at him. He was so handsome, so enticing, the most appealing man she'd ever known. They were on opposite sides of the law, but that didn't matter right now. He still made her queasy with want.

Cole hesitated, then brought his body up close so that her shoes touched the tips of his snakeskin boots. His gaze focused on her mouth and he leaned in, his warm breath fanning her skin.

"Kate?"

Her breath caught. She couldn't speak, so she mumbled, "Hmm?"

"I'm still your friend."

Kate's knees buckled when his lips touched hers briefly, tenderly, exquisitely. But he broke the kiss off too soon, looking into her eyes, searching, probing. When he seemed to have his answer, he wrapped her closely into his arms, the extent of his desire clear and potent as their lower bodies brushed. He spoke quietly into her ear. "All those years ago, I wanted you, Kate. I never told you. I should have, but I didn't. It nearly killed me when you left town. You were my best friend, but you were so much more. And I didn't realize it fully until you were gone."

"I'm here now, Cole," she offered bravely.

A slow, sexy smile stole over his face. "I know, darlin'." He took claim to her lips again, kissing her deeply, stroking her with his tongue, creating a rhythm, a cadence that Kate found easy to follow. He streamed kisses onto her hair, the crest of her cheeks, the hollow of her throat and lower still. She arched and allowed him free rein over her body, moving with him, flowing into him. It was natural and true.

"Kate," he said, breaking away to gaze intently into her eyes, his voice ragged with need. "You're the only woman I want. Lord help me, but I need you."

Intense heat flamed her body, a quick blazing spark that only Cole could extinguish. She knew that she needed him, too, and she wanted him as badly as he did her.

Her nod of affirmation was all he needed to see. Cole lifted her up into his arms and carried her out of the small room, past the low-burning fire in the hearth until they reached his room. He kicked open his bedroom door and set her down, holding her snugly about her waist. "Are you sure, Kate?" he rasped.

Kate smiled into his eyes. "Yes, I'm sure. I've been sure for nearly ten years, Cole."

Chapter Twelve

....
....
....
....

....
....
....

Chapter Thirteen

Cole gazed into Kate's eyes, the gleam of desire burning bright with blazing heat. Cole warned himself to take it slow, to make love to her the way he'd always envisioned, pleasuring her, tutoring her, loving her completely. He'd not rush this moment, no matter the look in her eyes telling him to hurry.

He smiled at Kate's guileless innocence. She didn't know what that look did to him. She didn't know of his restraint, how difficult it was for him to simply stand there, giving her time to adjust to her decision, while all he wanted was to take her to his bed and bury himself within her.

"Come over by the window, Kate. It's a beautiful starry night."

Cole walked over to the window, parted the curtain and leaned on the windowsill. He looked out at the dark night lit by what seemed like thousands of silver lights. He waited for Kate to join him. When more than a few moments passed, the silence in the room called his attention to the fact that Kate hadn't moved from the doorway.

With a sigh of regret that she'd changed her mind, Cole turned slowly. His heart nearly dropped to his boots and his groin tightened painfully with need when he viewed her. A steady stream of incandescent light poured in and bathed Kate in a radiant glow. She stood before him with hair down, bared of all clothing, completely, beautifully, deliciously naked.

He blinked back his surprise and met her eyes. "Good Lord, you're perfect, Kate."

"Cole, I'm not a frightened young girl. I'm a woman," she said huskily, her voice taking on a tone Cole would dream about later. She lifted her arms to him with unabashed invitation. "And I'm giving myself to you."

Cole's strides ate up the distance in the room, bringing himself to face her. He touched her cheek tenderly, running his fingers down the line of her jaw. Her eyes spoke of many things—vulnerability, passion, trust. He knew how difficult this was for her. She'd been let down by the only other man in her life—her father. Kate's pain at having been abandoned, of feeling unworthy of love, of being cast out as the saloon gal's daughter, had festered through the years. And now, she'd not only given him the gift of her body, but she offered the gift of her trust.

Cole's chest swelled with pride. He'd not let her down. "Mary Kathryn Malone, you do know how to humble a man."

"Humble?" she asked with an adorable pout. "Cole Bradshaw, if you don't touch me soon, I swear I'm gonna die from want."

Cole grinned. "Oh, there's gonna be touching, sweetheart. Lots of touching. And you'll not be complaining anymore."

Kate wrapped her arms around his neck, the movement causing a gentle heaving of her full breasts. Cole groaned aloud, letting Kate see fully how she affected him. "You have entirely too many clothes on, Sheriff."

Cole chuckled, berating himself for expecting a timid, shy, backward girl in his bed. This was Kate. She never did anything halfhearted. Lord above, the woman drove him crazy.

There was a frenzy of movement as his clothes were scattered hastily about the room. Within a minute, Cole stood bared to her, his manhood undisguised now and fully erect. Kate's gaze fluttered over him first with wide shock-filled eyes, then her expression changed to brazen admiration. He took Kate's hand and led her to his bed. Together they sank down, with limbs entwined, their warm skin touching.

"You're perfect too, Cole," she whispered into his ear. Cole's body went a notch tighter, if that were possible. Kate stirred him in ways he'd not ever known before.

"Ah Kate," he said, taking her in an all-consuming, intoxicating kiss. He stroked her delicately, running a finger down her throat, cupping her breast then bringing his mouth there to suckle. Kate's body arched and he moistened the pebble-hard tip with his tongue, giving her pleasure, relishing the soft, muted sounds of her ecstatic moans.

Cole had never wanted more to please a woman, to give her all she deserved, to show her the ways between a man and a woman. That Kate greedily accepted all that he could give warmed his heart and fueled his too-hot body.

When he slipped his hand down farther, past her belly to cup her feminine mound, Kate's body jerked. "Cole!"

He kissed her lips. "I said there'd be touching, sweetheart…everywhere." He stroked her tenderly with an expert hand, caressing her softness, gliding through her coppery curls until she made a low, sensual, mewling sound. "'Course, if you want me to stop…?"

Kate ran a hand through his hair and tugged gently, bringing his head up so that their gazes met. "You do and I'll shoot you with your own gun."

Laughter erupted and Cole kissed her hard this time, pushing her down farther onto the bed, covering her body with his. He rubbed up against her, feeling one with this woman who was his best friend, his lover. He stared into the brilliant green of her eyes, clouded only with the haze of arousal. All amusement left him for a more serious, more somber sensation.

He needed to take claim to her body, to make her his in the most elemental way.

Now.

The urgency that he felt shocked him in its intensity. "Open for me, sweet Kate," he said, his voice deep with desire.

Kate parted her legs, her heart hammering hard. This was the moment she'd dreamed about. This was the dream she'd never believed would come true. This was where she belonged, with Cole, always with Cole.

He moved his body over hers and she witnessed great restraint on his face as he positioned himself. He thrust into her, once, breaking the barrier of her womanhood. Kate bit down hard on her lip, taking the pain with the pleasure. But the ache she felt ebbed quickly with Cole's next words. "You're mine now, Kate."

"Yes," she breathed, relinquishing herself fully to him. He moved inside her now, slowly as she adjusted to his size and, seemingly on instinct when he knew she was ready, his movements intensified.

She matched him thrust for thrust, raising her hips, arching, giving to him everything she had in her heart, as the searing ache of the past melted away. She was Cole's and he was hers. There wasn't any better or more certain truth than that.

Kate flowed with him now, meeting his powerful strides until finally, and all too soon, their erotic ride reached a towering peak. Kate cried out his name, the shudders of passion erupting uncontrollably. Kate's body tingled. Cole's face twisted with pleasure and he too shuddered his release.

They came tumbling down together, arms entwined, hearts forged. Kate lay there in breathtaking awe, wrapped tenderly in Cole's embrace. He had his eyes closed, his face a picture of contentment, and for Kate, her heart filled with joy.

"I never knew it would be so wonderful."

Cole tightened his hold on her. "It was, wasn't it, sweetheart?"

"Is it always...like that?"

Cole blew out a breath and hesitated before answering. "No. If your heart isn't involved, then it's just your body taking release."

Brazenly Kate played with the hairs on his chest, curling a finger around them and tugging. "And so, your heart was involved this time?"

Cole put his hand over hers, halting her playful game. He stared deeply into her eyes. "You know it was, Kate."

She flung her arms back over her head, feeling free, elated. "Mine too, Cole Bradshaw, mine too."

Smiling, Cole kissed her leisurely then wrapped her into his arms and tossed the sheet over them both. "Better get some rest now."

"Oh, I'm not a bit tired, Cole."

"You will be, sweetheart, if you don't sleep now. Trust me, or we won't make it through the night."

Kate closed her eyes, her lips curving up, welcoming his subtle invitation.

And just hours later, Kate woke to Cole's sensual caresses. They lay spooned together, coiled closely, his tongue making erotic, lazy circles upon her throat. She smiled in her daze of awareness, the night still bright with stars. And an urgent tingle, more like a bolt of heat coursed down her body.

Kate turned to him then, opening her eyes wide to gaze into his handsome face. "Cole," she whispered softly.

He fell back upon the bed. "Hmm?"

She leaned in, crushing her breasts to his chest. He held her there with a gentle hand, amid the tangle of sheets. "I want to touch you…everywhere."

Cole closed his eyes slowly but didn't respond.

"Cole?" she whispered again, desperately.

He opened one eye. "Have I died and gone to heaven?"

Baffled, Kate shook her head. "I haven't shot you with your own gun yet, but you're in danger of—"

"Don't keep a man waiting, Kate." He grabbed hold of her hand and placed it on his chest. "It's not polite." He scorched her with a look so full of heat, she nearly felt the burn on her cheeks.

Kate moved her hand slowly, searing a path from his taut muscular chest, down farther to his torso. She stroked his tight belly and heard his deep inhalation of breath. And finally her hand found what it sought, the thick arousal that surprised her in its silky texture. She wound her hand around him and he cursed softly, moving into her until she understood what he wanted.

She slid her fingers up and down, creating heat and friction. Heat and friction, until Cole stopped her from going further with words of caution. "No more, sweetheart, or the night will come to a quick end."

He brought her up to kiss her soundly on the mouth, then set her atop him, so that she straddled his thighs.

Kate shifted a bit, rose up and took Cole in, using her knees to brace herself along his side. She settled herself down, filling herself full. He groaned with pleasure as she moved on him. Kate too let out a tiny whimper, the feeling powerful and potent.

She rode him slowly, throwing her head back, letting her hair fall down to tickle his legs. He arched and lowered with each one of her movements, creating more and more heat, stirring her senses until she needed more. Quickly now, desperately, she rode him faster, harder. Her pulse rate matched the rapid thrusts until suddenly Cole arched, calling her name out raggedly, and Kate shuddered from the shared release, her body collapsing onto his.

He wound his arms around her, planting small kisses onto her throat, and whispered sweetly, "Like I said, you're mine now, Kate."

Exhausted, Kate rolled onto her side and fell asleep wearing a blissful smile.

Golden sunlight poured into the room, arousing Kate from a sound sleep. She stretched and twisted her body right smack into Cole's. The man needed no stream of nature's light to waken him. She felt his desire pressing against her belly. "Good morning, darlin'," he said wickedly, taking her in a heady kiss that she greedily returned.

And that was all the encouragement Cole needed as he shed the sheets and began to make love to Kate once again. His touch sent her spiraling headlong into an unknown world of newfound desire. The sensations he evoked caused Kate nothing but sheer pleasure. She relished the brawny feel of him, breathed in his male scent and savored each minute of their lovemaking.

He took it slow, easy, making sure he'd touched every inch of her, making sure he'd caressed every part of her. Kate had never felt so treasured, so adored. And when he mounted her and brought them both to the brink of ecstasy, Kate's heart soared with love.

They fell slowly back down to earth. Cole kissed her softly with an apology on his lips. "I'm sorry, but I've got work to do at the jail today. I'm asking you to stay here and watch Meggie for me."

"I'll stay." Kate didn't want to remind him that he'd placed her under arrest yesterday and she couldn't leave. But none of that mattered now. Cole had finally accepted her for who she was. The saloon gal's daughter and the sheriff had finally come to terms. They'd shared their bodies, but they'd also shared their hearts. For the very first time, Kate felt that a future filled with promise awaited them.

"Thank you, sweetheart," he said, rising and splashing his body with water from a bowl on the table. "I like knowing you'll be here when I get home tonight." Kate couldn't think of any place she'd rather be than here, waiting for Cole. She watched him wash, then throw on clean clothes. Once he buttoned up his shirt, he turned to her. "Meggie sleeps late. Why don't you go back to sleep for a while and get some rest?"

Cole bent to cover her up with the sheets then he tossed a blanket over her. Without him there, she'd need the warmth. "I think I will, Cole."

"That's my girl," he said with a big smile.

His girl.

Kate's throat went dry. Kate Malone was Cole Bradshaw's girl. Finally and forever.

He threw on his vest, holstered his gun and put on his hat. He bent again, this time to kiss her goodbye. "Soon as you shut down that saloon, every morning can be like this."

He brushed a quick kiss onto her lips and hustled out the door.

Kate bolted upright on the bed, clutching the sheet to her chest, her mouth gaping open, completely and utterly stunned.

Chapter Fourteen

Kate opened the door to the jail and stepped inside, unmindful of the stares of curious shop owners on the main street of town. Johnny Martinez had rescued her by agreeing to take Meggie for a walk down by the creek, after unlocking the jailhouse door.

The entire town thought she'd been holed up in that jail cell overnight, but Kate couldn't worry over that now. She had to see Cole and she couldn't wait until he came home this evening.

Her appearance startled him. He rose from the desk with a questioning gaze. "Kate, honey, is something wrong? Where's Meggie?"

"I left her with Johnny. They're headed down to the creek for a while. I had to see you."

His blue gaze softened on her, melting her bones like hot sugar over a fire. "I'm glad you came then," he said in a husky voice. "I was missing you already."

Kate's heart tripped over itself. And when he

opened his arms, she walked into them, certain she'd heard him wrong this morning. Certain that Cole didn't mean for her to give up on her dream.

With a finger, he lifted her chin and bent his head to take her in a long, lingering kiss. "Can't hardly wait for tonight," he said softly, bringing her against his chest. She squeezed her eyes shut. Images of their lovemaking, of all they'd shared last night, came crashing into her mind. She'd been so happy before Cole had shocked her with his declaration.

"Cole, what you said this morning…about me shutting down the saloon…you didn't really mean it, did you?"

Lightly amused, he spoke calmly. "'Course I did, honey. Can't rightly have you running a saloon if we're gonna be together."

Kate pushed herself out of his embrace. "Why not?"

"Now, Kate. Don't go getting stubborn. I thought that it's all settled between us. You and me and Meggie, we'll be a family."

Kate shook her head. "Only if I close down the saloon?"

Cole nodded. "That's right."

"I'm not closing the saloon, Cole."

He gestured with his hands, palms up. "Okay, then sell it."

She gasped and wondered if Cole knew her at all. It seemed as though nothing had changed regardless of the night they'd just shared. "I'd never sell the Silver Saddle."

Cole grimaced and set his hands on his hips. "What are you saying, Kate?"

"I can't close the Silver Saddle. And I won't sell."

"It can't be any other way, Kate. You have to know that." Cole walked over to his desk, shaking his head, running a hand through his hair.

"Cole, please listen to reason…"

"What reason is that, Kate? That you'll spend your days and nights in that saloon serving up whiskey to rowdies who'd just as soon shoot up the place as have a peaceful drink? It's not a woman's place, Kate. It's just not."

"Cole, we've always disagreed on this."

"Yep," he said, nodding his head. "That's not about to change."

"No," she agreed, "so there's not much use talking it to death, is there?" And she knew right then what was about to happen, that there was no hope of being with Cole again. Ever.

Cole pierced her with a dark look. "You won't change your mind?"

"No," she offered adamantly, "I can't."

"Damn it, Kate! Don't do this. Don't put that saloon between us."

"There's a river between us. There's no crossing it and there's no bridge. We're on opposing sides, looking for a way over but there is no way, Cole."

Cole frowned and shook his head slowly, his eyes filled with regret. "Kate."

Kate's heart split in two. She'd been foolish to think Cole had accepted her for who she was. His expectations for the future didn't include a woman who ran a saloon. But Kate hadn't changed. She was the same woman she'd always been, with the same wants and dreams. Why couldn't Cole abide by that? She couldn't give up the Silver Saddle, so that meant giving up on Cole. He wouldn't have her any way but on his own terms, and the price of his love was far too high. Sometimes Kate hated the strength her mama had instilled in her. A weaker woman would have surrendered her dream for the man she wanted. But Kate couldn't do that. It was more than the saloon now—it was about Cole's regard of her.

With chin held high, she announced. "Arrest me for real if you have to, but I'm not going back to your house and I'm not closing up the saloon."

"That won't be necessary," he said firmly, picking up a paper from his desk. He walked over to hand her a telegraph wire. "Perry from the telegraph office figured you'd be here, so he left it with me to give you."

She lifted her eyes to his. "You read this?"

He nodded without apology. "After last night, I thought I had the right."

Kate read the wire quickly, realizing that Robert had come through for her in Los Angeles. She was free to operate the saloon without hesitation. It seemed the town ordinance was clearly written for new establishments coming into the area and since the Silver Saddle was "existing," only in need of repairs, it didn't fall under the jurisdiction of that law. Small consolation, Kate thought. She had the law on her side now, but not the lawman. He'd always needed a different kind of woman. Hurt and angered that he wouldn't give them a chance, Kate clutched the paper to her chest. "You have no rights where I'm concerned. Not anymore," she said quietly, watching Cole blink back the pain her words had caused.

His expression turned as cold as Crystal Creek waters. "You're free to go, Kate." He turned his back on her and sat down at his desk, dismissing her.

Kate's eyes misted, but the real tears would come later on, in the privacy of her own room. She turned and grabbed the knob of the door, twisting it open. "Goodbye, Cole," she said softly, and walked out of the jail.

Kate entered the Silver Saddle shortly after her confrontation with Cole. She glanced around at the elegant saloon she'd rebuilt with a deep sense of pride, but no joy filled her heart. Instead, heavy sadness swept through her. She pulled out a cane-backed chair and slumped down, feeling like a young child again, the one her father had abandoned. The one the schoolchildren had taunted for having a mama who ran a saloon. She closed her eyes, weary from the highs and lows of the past day, unable to come to grips with Cole's blatant rejection. She'd always known of his strong convictions regarding family life. But after the night of passion they'd shared, Kate had assured herself that he would see things differently, see that they could make it work if they cared enough for each other. She'd showed him how much she cared by willingly giving him her innocence. Kate didn't believe it was too much to ask him to understand her reluctance in giving up her family's legacy. It was something he could do for her. But his mind was set and Kate wondered if it was more than wanting a proper wife and mother for Meggie.

He'd earned the town's respect and accomplished his goal of becoming sheriff, but did he fear losing ground if he got involved with her? The doubts clouding her mind and instilled since childhood had come back full force now. When would Kate Malone be good enough for Sheriff Bradshaw? When would she be worthy of love?

"Miss Kate?" Josh came out of the back room and grinned, distracting Kate from her disturbing musings. "You're a sight for my sore eyes. Did that sheriff finally come to his senses?"

"He had to let me go," Kate said, then related the reasons for her release.

After her explanation, Josh poured them both a glass of their best whiskey in celebration. "To the Silver Saddle," he said, raising his glass in a toast.

Kate smiled and sipped, the liquid burning her

throat. She wasn't one to drink normally, but she couldn't refuse a toast with Josh. He was one of the few who'd stuck by her in all this. "To the Silver Saddle," she repeated.

"What are your plans now, Miss Kate?"

"We reopen the Silver Saddle tomorrow. The Grand Opening signs go back up outside. And I'd like to hire on a piano player."

Josh rubbed his chin, scratching at the dark beard concealing most of his face. "I might be of help there. I know a man who played all the honky-tonks in Charleston before the war. He's living outside the lumber mills not far from here now. He's getting on in age, but I've heard him play. He's real good. He might be interested in some work."

"Oh, Josh! That sounds perfect. Will you go talk to him? Tell him I can't pay much, but that's bound to change soon. See if he can work three or four nights a week."

"I'll check on it first thing, Miss Kate. Soon as I change the date on those Grand Opening signs. We'll put them out first thing tomorrow morning."

"Thanks, Josh."

Kate sighed deeply after Josh had left the room to see to the signs. Her body ached some from her long night of loving with Cole, but it was her heart that hurt the most.

Don't dwell, she reminded herself. She had work to do and plans to make. She'd not wallow in misery.

Kate had an establishment to operate—a *legitimate* establishment. And no one was going to stop her now.

In the privacy of her bedroom, Kate changed out of the clothes she'd worn for two straight days, gladly peeling them away. She poured water from the corn- flower-blue pitcher and washed up, splashing her face and letting the water trickle down her throat. The cool liquid refreshed and cooled her skin. She changed into a simple cotton calico, devoid of petticoats and headed for the kitchen, ready to prepare herself an easy meal of bread and cheese. She was just too darn tired to fix anything substantial.

A soft knocking at her door startled her and she jumped, letting go an unladylike curse and blaming her reaction more on raw nerves than surprise. She walked to the door. "Who's there?"

"It's us, Kate. Nora, Abe and Jethro. We brought you supper."

Kate grinned, happy to hear Nora's voice. Quickly she thrust the door open. "Oh, Nora! This is just what I need. Come in, everyone, come in."

Kate ushered her friends inside. Nora set down a platter of food on her kitchen table. "After what you went through in that jail, we figured you'd need a decent meal. I hope we aren't intruding. How are you, Kate?"

Guilt assailed her instantly at having her friends worry about her, when in truth, she'd spent the night in a warm bed at Cole's house. Heavens, she'd spent the night in *his* bed, with his arms wound tightly around her most of the night.

But she couldn't rightly admit that to them now. Perhaps, one day, she'd speak of it to Nora, her most trusted friend, but not tonight. "No, of course, you're not intruding, Nora. And I'd never turn down a hot meal." Kate laughed, but all eyes were upon her, seemingly waiting for her description of her supposed jail time. She cleared her throat. "I, uh, it wasn't so bad, really. I'm fine, truly I am. And did you hear the good news? I got the wire I'd been hoping for from Los Angeles. The town ordinance has no jurisdiction over the Silver Saddle. We're opening for real tomorrow. And it's all within the law."

"We heard!" Nora said.

"The whole town's buzzing about your night in jail and about the saloon being legal and all. Seems Big Josh told Mr. Becker at the general store and, well, now the entire town knows the way of it," Abe offered.

"I sure gave the sheriff a piece of my mind," Jethro said sourly, "arresting a woman like you."

"It's okay, Jethro," Kate said softly, patting his arm. "It all worked out for the best now." She wished she felt that way in her heart, but at least she still had the Silver Saddle, and nobody could take that away from her.

Her friends sat down to eat the meal with her, boosting her sagging spirit by making jovial conversation. Abe and Jethro bantered back and forth with customary brotherly affection, each one trying hard to best the other with verbal play. It warmed Kate's heart to listen to them, to simply sit back and enjoy their teasing. When the meal was finished and the men agreed to a smoke outside, the women collected the dishes. "How's the baby?" Kate asked, happy to have a pleasing subject to speak about.

Nora's face split into a big smile. "I felt him move today, Kate. It was the first time."

"Oh, Nora!" Kate's elation matched Nora's. "Can I feel him, too?"

Nora took hold of Kate's hand and guided it to her expanding belly. "Here," she said hopefully, "but he doesn't always move when I want him to. Abe hasn't felt him yet, either."

Kate waited patiently, but she didn't feel any baby movements. "Well, he's just a stubborn one, isn't he?"

Nora chuckled. "Probably, if he takes after his mama."

Kate peered at Nora's stomach and her mind filled with wondrous thoughts. "What's it like, Nora? To know you've created a life?"

"Oh," Nora said, a wistful expression taking shape on her face, "it's like nothing I've ever felt before. It's…a miracle, Kate. I can't really explain it. You'll just have to find out for yourself one day."

Kate turned away from Nora to wash a dish, fighting a battle against her sentimental tears.

Nora, darn her sweet soul, wouldn't let the subject

drop as it should have. "Kate, you *will* find out one day, I'm sure of it."

"I don't think so, Nora. It...it doesn't matter, anyway. I have what I want. A girl can't be too greedy now, can she?" Kate attempted a smile.

"You're not greedy, Kate. And you deserve nothing but good things in your life."

"Thank you, Nora. That means a lot, but I'm satisfied with just running the saloon, now that it's legal and all."

Nora handed her another dish to wash, then took up a cloth to wipe the clean ones dry. "You seem different tonight, Kate. Is there something you're not saying?"

Kate needed to keep her night with Cole close to her heart where she could look back on it and know that for a short time she'd had the "good things" that Nora had spoken about. She wasn't ready to divulge her secret, not even to Nora. It was almost as though if she spoke of it aloud, some of the enchantment of their time together would be lost. Silly as it seemed since she'd pretty much been discarded by Cole, Kate still needed to embrace the special feeling from the night they'd shared—the only night she'd ever have with Cole.

"It's been a trying few days, Nora."

"Of course," Nora said sympathetically, "I understand. It couldn't have been too comfortable for you in that jail cell, all night." Nora lifted her brow and Kate wondered if she knew. Could her best friend tell that Kate was keeping something private and special all to herself? "Oh!" Nora's eyes went wide. "Here, quick, Kate. Feel the baby, he's moving."

Kate placed her hand on Nora's abdomen just in time to feel the life stirring around. "Oh…my," she breathed. She'd never in her life felt anything quite so mystical, so magical. The slight movements brought with it a sense of awe. Kate smiled warmly at Nora. "It's wonderful, isn't it?"

Nora nodded.

Kate kept her hand there, hoping to feel life again. She was truly pleased for her friend, and Kate knew deep down in her heart, she'd never, ever, experience this feeling for herself. She'd never give herself to anyone but Cole, and that wasn't likely to happen again. They'd never have a "heap" of babies together. They'd never be a family.

A hollow ache buried itself deep inside where she could conceal it from her friends' good intentions.

"He moved again," Kate said eagerly, when the baby kicked.

Nora's gaze flowed onto hers and Kate had the profound sense that Nora had guessed everything.

"It *will* happen for you, Kate."

Kate removed her hand and shook her head, laughing with a lightness she didn't really feel. "My *baby* is sitting on Main Street, ready to be delivered at first light. There'll be some joy in that, Nora. Don't you worry."

But Nora only pursed her lips, a wise light sparkling in her eyes. "I'm not worried, Kate, just wondering when two stubborn people I know are going to stop butting heads."

Sadly Kate knew the answer to Nora's pondering. And that answer was...never.

Chapter Fifteen

A thin whiskered man sat at the Silver Saddle's piano, wearing an insightful smile and playing a lively tune that lifted Kate's spirits instantly. Kate stepped closer, glancing at Big Josh, who stood beside the piano. She silently thanked him with a grateful smile. He made short work of introducing her to Shady Rawlings. The man nodded his greeting, his fingers sweeping over the keys fluidly, not missing a note and Kate knew without a doubt he was right for the job.

"That was lovely," she said when he'd hit the last key.

"Thank ya, miss. It's been a while, but it's amazin' how it all comes back." He tapped a slim agile finger to his head. "Music's all up here," he said, gray eyes twinkling. "Has been ever since I can recall. Feels good to get these hands back on the keys."

Kate spoke with Shady for several minutes, offering him the job and finalizing details of his employment. Shady agreed to her terms, happy to have the chance to play his music again. He was an odd man, she mused, living on his own for years, never having a family. He'd said he lived for his music for most of his days but had hit upon hard times recently. He moved north to a small shanty outside the lumber mills and hadn't touched a piano for two years, although Kate thought he'd played expertly, as though the music lived within him.

He'd had his music all of his life, which clearly brought him joy, yet Kate sensed in him something deeper, a fragile loneliness that called to her.

Was that how Kate would end up? Sacrificing everything for her dream, only to grow into a lonely old woman?

Kate pushed the melancholy thoughts far from her mind. She should be thankful that everything was running smoothly. She had a beautiful saloon that would be opening in a few hours, a barkeep who was becoming a dear friend and she'd just hired on a piano player. Now all she needed was customers.

The saloon door opened and Kate immediately turned. Cole stood just inside the door, his heart revealed in his eyes as he glanced around the saloon, taking in the two men at the piano and then finally resting his gaze on her. Kate's breath caught, seeing that look in his eyes. It dawned on her then that she hadn't been the only one to lose something special yet fleeting. Cole had lost, too, and defeat didn't sit well with him.

Big Josh took a step forward. "If he's here to arrest you again," he muttered, alarming Kate.

"No, he's not," Kate said, putting a stopping hand on Josh's arm. "I'll take care of it. Why don't you show Shady his room in the back and have something to eat? We'll be opening just after noon."

Josh shot Cole one more condemning look then ushered Shady into the back. Kate lifted her skirts, moving toward Cole. She stopped three feet away, abhorring her fear of getting too close to him, taking in his scent, letting his breath touch her cheek.

She waited for him to speak.

"Who's that man with Josh?" Cole demanded.

"My new piano player."

Cole inhaled sharply and stared into her eyes, the silence echoing off the walls. There was a time when they could read each other's thoughts, but Kate didn't know Cole that way anymore. Instead deadly quiet surrounded them like a cloak. Finally Kate found her voice. "What do you want, Cole?"

Cole raked her over thoroughly, his gaze touching every part of her intimately, speaking of his physical want. Kate's body responded instantly, the pull of his gaze, the desire in his eyes too profound to ignore. But seducing her wasn't the reason he'd come to the Silver Saddle.

Cole was a man of his convictions. Kate had always admired that trait in him, but those very convictions were keeping them apart.

"I came to tell you not to expect much today. I've

heard talk, Kate, and it's not likely you're going to have too many customers. Your grand opening might not be so grand.''

Kate's temper flared and she wondered again when Cole had acquired such a mean streak. ''You must find great joy in telling me that. Did you come here to gloat?''

''No.'' He glared at her.

''I'll thank you to leave.'' She folded her arms and spun around, unable to look at Cole another second.

She felt him come up from behind, standing inches away. His breath caressed the back of her neck and he spoke softly into her ear. ''I find no joy in hurting you, Kate. Consider it a warning, from a friend.''

The door slammed shut and Kate whirled around to find Cole gone. She stared at the thick, protective iron door and wished she could shore up her heart just as powerfully.

That afternoon, Kate counted five customers at the bar. Jethro, Abe, Lou from the hotel and two drifters she'd never seen before had come in a short time ago. She hadn't expected much since Cole's warning, but the showing was even more dismal than she'd imagined.

''It'll take a while for word to spread,'' Abe said cordially, sipping his beer and winking at her.

''We'll be sure to remind folks at the livery. I bet you'll have more than a handful by nightfall tomorrow,'' Jethro offered.

Kate smiled graciously. She wouldn't let the poor showing get her down. Surrounded by friends at the saloon, she could only rejoice that she'd made it this far. But Kate was even more determined to make her saloon a success now and she had a plan. Her mama had taught her early on that a woman surviving alone in the world always had to have a plan.

"Thank you all for coming. It means a great deal to me, having my friends here. Enjoy the music and eat up!" She gestured to the dishes of cold meats, fresh peach cobbler and breads she'd prepared earlier in the day and had laid out on a table. Shady's tunes filled the air, lending a jovial atmosphere to the near-empty saloon. "And, Abe, take a plate to Nora."

Kate began fixing up a dish for Abe to take home.

He nodded. "I think she'll like that. Thanks, Miss Kate."

Two hours later, the sun set to a night absent of many stars. A few customers wandered in and out, to see what all the fuss was about, Kate surmised. Mostly they stayed for just one drink then left quickly, with gossip ready on their lips to spout out to the small crowd of men who'd gathered outside.

Kate nodded to Shady and leaned against the piano. Once his fingers hit the keys, Kate began singing. She'd heard her mama sing these tunes before, and many a time, Kate would join in. Her mama had always complimented Kate on her melodious voice. She was about to find out if that were true.

Big Josh opened the saloon doors and let the music

drift outside. "Drinks on the house tonight. Come in, gents. Hear the lady sing."

Slowly and with sheepish expressions, several of the townsfolk made their way inside. Kate recognized many shop owners and workers. There were more men than Kate had originally thought, but she didn't mind giving out free drinks tonight. It gave her a measure of pride to see the saloon fill up with patrons.

As the night wore on, melancholy feelings assailed her. She no longer felt like singing boisterous tunes like "The Blue Tail Fly" or "Oh, Dem Golden Slippers." The late-night hour called for more soulful ballads—songs that spoke to the heart. And she sang them deep into the night.

Cole was late getting back to town. He'd been gone the better part of the afternoon and into the night, riding hard to the far end of the county on another lead regarding Sloan. The lead had proved false, leaving Cole with a bitter taste in his mouth. He'd sworn on Jeb's grave that he'd avenge his death. It was something Cole intended to do before he left this life, yet finding the man wasn't an easy task.

Cole slowed his mare to an easy gait as they headed for the jail. A honeyed, sweet voice floating out from the saloon knocked into him like a herd of wild mustangs. He knew that voice. Kate. A smile lifted the corners of his mouth as he thought back on the silly songs they used to sing years ago, about leapfrogs and prairie dogs and flapjacks that wouldn't rise. But this voice was more compelling, more satisfying, coming from a woman ripe with heartache in her young life.

Cole reined in his mare near the saloon and dismounted, tying up the horse at a post nearby. The doors to the saloon were open, but Cole wouldn't go inside. Seeing Kate by the piano, dressed in her finest and singing her heart out, would only stir in him emotions he couldn't afford.

Hell, listening to her outside would do the same, but at least Cole wouldn't have to look into her eyes, see the beauty there and the pain. He wouldn't have to doubt his own convictions or battle to keep from going against all his beliefs and surrender his heart to her. He leaned back, bracing one boot up against the wall and listened.

Songs poured out of Kate with lilting harmony. Her voice called to him, singing of loves lost, of hearts broken, of sad and lonely souls. The music, the poignant, powerful lyrics touched him deep down inside.

Cole didn't have to close his eyes to envision Kate in his arms, in his bed. He'd had that dream once. He'd made love to her. Felt her body close, felt her heart beat in tune to his. He'd made her breathless, she'd nearly destroyed him. They'd been together, body and soul.

But it wasn't enough.

Mounting frustration met with anger. Cole let out a string of oaths, pushing away from the wall of the Silver Saddle. He was dog tired but too riled to sleep.

He walked through the door of the saloon, ordered a bottle of whiskey from Big Josh and paid for it quickly. He left the saloon so damn fast he hadn't even caught a glimpse of Kate.

Which was good, he thought wryly.

Darn woman drove a man to drink.

Kate sat down in church next to Nora and the Cables, wearing a big grin. She knew she should be listening to the sermon, but her mind kept wandering to her newfound success, small as it was. For the past week, Kate had enlisted the aid of Big Josh and Shady to drive her to the outlying ranches, farms and lumber mills in the mornings to deliver handbills she'd had printed up special. They'd even gone into Grass Valley seven miles north and posted some handbills there as well.

Her advertisements, an offer for the lowest prices west of the Rockies and an invitation for a free drink of choice to any man bringing in a new patron to the Silver Saddle, had worked! Each night more and more customers filtered in. The Silver Saddle wasn't boasting crowds, but at least Kate was seeing a small profit.

The townsfolk of Crystal Creek weren't shedding their bias and coming in, but Kate knew that too would change soon.

With the sermon finally over, Kate and Nora walked out of the church and into the yard. There, Jethro and Abe excused themselves to get back to work at the livery. Nora and Kate walked arm in arm toward the gate. "What's got you grinning from ear to ear?" Nora asked.

"Nothing much," Kate answered, "just glad to see Mama's advice really works. After the first night at the Silver Saddle I was afraid I'd be run out of town, just like Mama had been. But she always said, 'Give them what they want' and, you know, it's working. I'm not getting rich by any means, but the saloon is picking up business, Nora. I think we're going to make it."

"I never had a doubt," Nora encouraged.

"You have so much faith in me." Kate cast her friend a grateful smile.

"Miss Kate!" Meggie came running at her full speed and wrapped her arms around Kate's legs.

Kate's heart nearly burst seeing Meggie again. It had been far too long, and she'd missed the tiny imp. She bent down to give Meggie a tight squeeze. "Hello, my little friend. How are you?"

"'Kay," Meggie said in her sweet voice then announced, "Daddy's sick. Mrs. Gregory is taking me to Aunt Caroline's today to play."

"Oh, I see," Kate said, straightening. When she reached full height, she met with Mrs. Gregory's soft brown eyes.

"Good afternoon, ladies," the older woman offered cordially.

Kate and Nora both greeted the woman.

"Meggie and I were just about to leave for my daughter's house. She'll spend the night with us. Allow her father some peace to recuperate," Mrs. Gregory confided.

"What's wrong with Sheriff Bradshaw?" Nora asked. Kate hadn't wanted to pry, but she was dying to know, also.

"He's been under the weather for a few days. Sneezing and coughing. That man's caught himself a germ, I'd say. It's best that Meggie isn't around him. The little miss shouldn't get sick again so soon after her fever."

"It's good that you're taking her," Kate said, concerned for both Meggie and her father. "I know Meggie loves playing at Caroline's. How's the new baby?"

"That child is round as a melon already," Mrs. Gregory declared proudly, her face lighting up.

The women all laughed and Mrs. Gregory took Meggie's hand. "Well, we'd better be off. Say goodbye to Miss Kate and Miss Nora."

Meggie gazed up at Kate with wide blue eyes. Bradshaw eyes. "I want Miss Kate to come, too."

"Oh, uh," Kate said, glancing at Mrs. Gregory then down at Meggie. "I'd really like that, too, but I...can't, Meggie." Kate bent down to her level and looked directly into her eyes. "I promise that we'll go down by the creek again real soon. We can practice skipping. And I have a new game to teach you called Run Sheepie Run, okay?"

"'Kay." Meggie smiled, warming Kate's heart.

"Will you teached me how to cook my Daddy a cake, like before?"

Kate blushed straight down to her white button-up shoes. "Sure," she said quietly, "we can do that too."

Meggie hugged Kate around the neck and Kate placed a soft kiss upon her forehead. "Bye-bye, Meg-pie. Have a fun time."

Meggie giggled when Kate used her father's favorite nickname for her.

Nora patted Meggie's head and said goodbye also. "Sweet child," she said wistfully, once the two had turned to leave.

"Yes, Cole's done a good job with her."

Nora took her arm as they headed out the gate. "Why don't you see if you can help an ailing man this afternoon, Kate?"

Kate shuddered. She wasn't going to go anywhere near Cole Bradshaw, today or any day. "Oh, no! I couldn't."

"Bet he'd be glad to see a friendly face."

"It wouldn't be mine, Nora," Kate said woefully. "I'd only add to his illness. He and I, we don't…get along anymore."

"Hmm," Nora said as they neared the main street of town, "seems to me, there's been a whole lot of 'getting along' between the two of you."

"Nora!"

"Am I wrong?"

Kate tilted her head coyly. "I'm not saying."

"Go see him, Kate."

"I have to get back to the saloon," Kate declared adamantly.

"It's Sunday. You said earlier you don't expect much business today. I'm sure Big Josh can handle it."

Kate chuckled. "There's not much that man *can't* handle."

"There, you see. You have time. You want to. Just go and see if you can help him."

"No, Nora. You don't understand the situation fully." She wasn't ready to tell Nora details of her brief time with Cole although Kate was sure she'd already guessed.

"Okay." Nora finally relented. "But if he were my man, I'd go see him."

"That's just it, Nora. Cole's not my man."

Twenty minutes later, Kate found herself in her kitchen cutting up chicken, dicing carrots, peeling onions and throwing them all together in a big pot.

Cole's not my man.

But he was an old friend. And what harm could come from bringing a sick man a pot of soup? She'd leave it with him and hurry on home.

Cole closed his eyes as hot water swirled around him, soothing his bones, bringing life back to his limbs. He'd been down and out for days, but he was finally beginning to feel human again. Even his head began to clear from the cloudy haze he'd been in the last part of the week. He washed his hair, soaped himself from top to bottom, scrubbing away heat and sweat.

It felt so good to lie here peacefully and enjoy the quiet solitude, his house absent of sound, perfectly silent. Ah, Cole closed his eyes. No reason why a man couldn't enjoy a good nap while soaking in the tub.

The back door creaked. Cole immediately snapped his eyes open and listened intently. He heard noise, the back door closed. Quiet footsteps. It wasn't Mrs. Gregory and Meggie. Those two made an awful racket when they entered the house. No, someone was stealing into his home.

Cole lifted himself silently from the tub and wrapped a large towel about his waist. He moved cautiously, quietly swearing that he'd left his gun holstered in his bedroom. He headed with slow deliberate steps toward the kitchen and dropped his jaw open when he saw her from behind.

"Kate?"

Her body jerked and the lid to a pot crashed to the ground. It rattled around on the floor in a spiraling motion, making tinny sounds, until finally, it stopped.

She whirled around with surprise in her eyes. "Cole, you about scared me half to death!"

Cole nearly laughed aloud. Kate had sneaked into his kitchen, for heaven only knows why, and she was admonishing him? "What are you doing here?"

"I'd heard you were sick." Her gaze traveled over the length of him and a spark of desire she couldn't conceal crossed over her lovely face. "I, uh, made you a pot of soup. I'll just leave it here and go," she said hurriedly, and began walking toward the back door.

"You broke into my house," he stated evenly.

"I knocked, but you obviously didn't hear me."

"As you can see, I was bathing." Cole tightened the towel about his waist, drawing her attention there.

She cleared her throat and lifted her gaze to meet his. "Don't let me disturb you."

"You always disturb me, Kate." And pretty soon, Kate would see just how much. If only she'd stop looking at him as though she'd like to dry him off with a female talent only Cole knew she possessed.

"I don't mean to."

Cole ignored her. The woman got under his skin and there was no denying it. "You made me soup?" He peered at the cookstove and the large pot she'd set there.

"Yes."

How could she look so damn innocent, wearing a Sunday-finest yellow dress with pretty white lace and fancy high-top boots when every flash of her eyes, every flutter of her lashes, every breath she took said she wanted him? "Why?"

"Why did I make you soup?"

"Uh-huh."

"Mrs. Gregory said that you'd caught a germ. When you didn't answer the front door, I thought I'd come the back way and leave the pot for you."

"Why?"

"Because you were sick, Cole." She stared at him, her lips parting. A droplet of water fell from his damp hair onto his chest. Kate followed its path along his chest, sweeping down his torso until it disappeared beneath his towel. "You don't look...sick."

He watched her take a deep swallow. "I'm better today."

"Good." She had trouble meeting his eyes.

"Why did you really come, Kate?"

Her head snapped up. "We were good friends once, Cole. Isn't that reason enough?"

Cole smiled. "I could drop this towel and show you that we're more than friends, Kate."

Kate's breath caught. Her eyebrows lifted and her bright green gaze flew to the towel wrapped around his waist. There was no concealing his desire now. Lord, he wanted her. And Kate wanted him too. He gauged it by the warm gleam in her eyes and the way her body trembled. "You should go."

She nodded then said softly, "I know."

"Thanks for sparing me your time."

"Cole?" Puzzled, Kate bit down on her lip.

"Go on back to your saloon, Kate."

She left then as quietly as she'd come. Cole fought the urge to call her back, to strip her of her proper Sunday clothes, to lay her down atop the table and ease the ache hidden beneath his towel. He fought the urge with every ounce of willpower he possessed. And when the back door shut, Cole closed his eyes as well, letting go a string of profound oaths entirely indecent for a Sunday afternoon.

Chapter Sixteen

The next day Kate walked into the general store and didn't hesitate to approach the proprietor. "Good morning, Mr. Becker."

"Hello, Miss Malone." Mr. Becker was cordial to his customers, but Kate knew she wasn't his favorite person. He wiped his hands on his apron and leaned in against the counter. "What can I get for you today?"

"Actually, I came here with a proposition for you. As you know, the Silver Saddle opened a short while ago. Business is fairly good, but I think I know a way both of us can prosper even more."

The tall, lanky man scratched his head. "I don't know, miss. Folks around here don't much approve of your saloon."

"This is business, Mr. Becker. And it's between you and me." Kate pressed her point by lowering her voice. "I have a glass case by the bar ready to sell items from your store. If we can agree on terms, both of us stand to benefit.''

His eyebrows lifted and Kate knew she had his attention. ''Hmm, what kind of items?''

''I'd like to sell pickles, tobacco, candies. Those sorts of things. If you supply them for me, we'll share in the profits.''

''I don't know...''

''Well, take some time to decide, but I've already spoken with the mercantile owner, a Mr. Whitmore in Grass Valley. He's willing if you're not. Of course, I'd rather give you the first opportunity since you're local and all. It'd be a good way to increase your business here in Crystal Creek. I'll come back later on if you'd like?''

The man did quick calculations in his head, Kate surmised, watching myriad emotions cross over his face. It was clear he was a businessman first, as Kate had hoped, knowing that if he didn't take her up on her offer, another competitor would benefit. ''No, no. That's not necessary. I think we might agree on terms.''

Twenty minutes later, Kate walked out of Mr. Becker's general store with a smile and a handwritten contract of terms. Once she closed the door, she bumped directly into Miss Ashmore, her old schoolteacher. ''Miss Ashmore! I'm sorry.''

Miss Ashmore steadied herself then glanced at Kate. ''Mary Kathryn?''

Kate grinned. She'd know her schoolteacher anywhere. The brown-haired woman always wore the same kind of drab-colored clothes, a black bonnet with cream lace and the same black crocheted handbag. "It's me."

"Hello."

"It's good to see you," Kate said, noting that Miss Ashmore wasn't as old as she'd once thought. Perceptions often changed as one grew older and wiser. Kate had once thought the woman ancient, but as she gazed upon her with adult eyes, she looked beyond the dreary tones she wore and knew her teacher couldn't be more than thirty-five.

"I wish I could say the same." Her lips pinched together and she frowned. "Oh dear! I don't mean to be cruel. It is good to see *you*, but it's your saloon I'm not all that happy about."

"I knew you were against it from the start."

"And with good reason."

"I don't understand what the town has against the Silver Saddle, but it's operating legally now."

"Yes, I'd heard you were taken into custody for a time."

Kate shifted uncomfortably, pressing a crease out of her skirt. She chose not to lie to her teacher, but Kate had become rather proficient in evading a subject. "It all worked out. Actually, I'd planned to come see you one day after school let out."

"Really? Well, it's always nice visiting with my older students. So many have left the area that I don't get the opportunity to see how they've fared."

Kate nodded and smiled. It was obvious Miss Ashmore didn't approve of the way Kate had fared, being arrested then opening a saloon most of the town didn't want. "Many have done well for themselves."

"Yes, that's true."

"Nora is a good friend of mine now."

"Ah, Nora. She was a bright child. Pity the children taunted her. I tried my best not to allow that to happen."

"She's going to be a mother soon." Kate couldn't help boasting. "And she's very happy. She's married to Abe Cable."

"I don't believe I've met him yet, but I'm very glad to hear she's doing well. I like to know my students are making their way in life."

"You were a good teacher, Miss Ashmore," Kate said sincerely.

The woman seemed surprised by Kate's blunt pronouncement. "Why, thank you."

"I know you probably thought me a bit on the wild side, but I did learn quite a great deal from your lessons. I *was* paying attention."

Miss Ashmore laughed, something she did seldom. "I was never really sure."

"Well, I'm confirming it now. I didn't always want to be in school, but I did learn," Kate said. "I walked by the schoolhouse the other day and noticed how different it appeared. Are my recollections wrong or is the school in shabby condition?"

Miss Ashmore let go a wearisome sigh. "No, your

recollections are correct. When you attended school, things were different. We had supplies and money to do repairs. I'm afraid we've hit a bad time. The schoolboard promised us money for reparations, but we're still waiting. And a few months back, our new shipment of McGuffey Readers, the dictionary and almanac I'd ordered, as well as chalk and boards were lost when the train bringing them here caught fire. I'm told there's no money available to replace them.''

"How are you managing?"

"The children must bring in their own supplies. Some can afford to, others can't. I have half-a-dozen readers. We share. We make do. What's important is that the children have a chance to learn."

"Mmm." Kate's mind began spinning with thoughts of how she could help. Frankly, she was surprised the townsfolk hadn't done anything to remedy the situation. "I agree. The children must learn."

Kate hadn't always liked going to school. At times, she hadn't liked Miss Ashmore, plain and simple, but she'd always respected her and knew her to be an excellent teacher.

Miss Ashmore looked at her then, a light of admiration shining in her eyes. "You do surprise me, Mary Kathryn."

Kate laughed and nodded. "I'm all grown-up now, Miss Ashmore."

"Yes, I see that. I believe I may have misjudged you. If that's the case, I apologize. I still can't abide the saloon, but I do admire your persistence and determination. I understand the Silver Saddle is quite elegant.''

''Thank you for saying,'' she said. It was the greatest compliment Kate had ever received from her.

''Well, I'd better tend to my chores. I've got a list for Mr. Becker to fill.'' Miss Ashmore patted Kate's arm and looked warmly into her eyes. ''It was good seeing you, dear. Good day.''

Kate beamed with joy all the way back to the Silver Saddle. It was years late in coming, but she did believe now that she'd truly earned Miss Ashmore's respect.

Kate tossed and turned that night, unable to sleep. She'd been having many restless nights of late. Bone weary from running the saloon most of the day, Kate didn't understand why, when she collapsed into bed at night, sleep didn't overtake her.

An image of Cole popped into her head. Again. She'd been trying hard to forget about their encounter in his kitchen, without much success. She kept seeing him, dripping wet, with hair slicked back, eyes dark with desire and…and his chest covered with moisture. Heavens. Her throat had constricted, going dry. She'd swallowed back her longing, fearing he would witness it in her eyes.

Cole hadn't expected her in his home and she surely hadn't expected to find him near naked. She'd known him once that way. She'd never forget the night of passion they'd shared, but that night would have to remain a cherished memory. That's all they'd ever have. And, oddly, Kate felt no shame in their joining, only considered it a shame that they couldn't find their way back to each other.

Kate faced the truth without hesitation, although the pain of losing Cole would be permanently etched in her heart.

She tossed a coverlet aside and groaned. "Stop thinking, Kate. Stop *thinking*."

She needed sleep. The saloon was bound to be busier than usual tomorrow. While making her visits to ranches last week, she'd learned that spring roundup was just about over. And tomorrow was payday. Cowpunchers with cash overflowing their pockets would be filling up her saloon. At least, she hoped they would be. She'd done everything within her power to offer her patrons the best deal around. The saloon was something new to try and that always seemed to attract business.

Kate nestled down further into her bed. This time, when she closed her eyes, it wasn't Cole's image popping into her head. It was Miss Ashmore's. And she was standing on the steps of the run-down schoolhouse.

Kate thought about that situation long and hard before finally, long sought after sleep claimed her.

"Here's your next round," Kate said to a group of cowboys from the Bar T Ranch. She set their glasses down and took up the empty ones placing them on the tray she held. A deep sense of accomplishment settled inside, watching the Silver Saddle prosper. For the first time since she had opened her doors, the saloon was entirely full with customers. She'd counted at least forty men, some standing at the bar, others sitting at the tables playing pike monte, while the rest were happy just to have a seat for their behinds and drinks in their hands.

Her notices throughout the county had panned out nicely. Most of her customers were from five sizable ranches in the area. Some patrons came from Grass Valley and Kate was happy to see a few locals in her saloon tonight. All seemed to be enjoying themselves. The place hadn't been so lively since the old days when her mama had run the saloon.

Shady began playing the piano, the tunes barely heard over the boisterous crowd. Kate walked up to the bar. "Two more beers, Josh. And two cigars."

Josh poured the drinks and set the cigars on the tray. "Here you go, Miss Kate. Sure you don't want me to serve these up?"

"I don't mind. You're too busy behind the bar."

Josh smiled. "You're just like your mama, Kate. Smart as a whip and a hard worker." He winked and she laughed, taking up the tray.

"Flattery might just get you a raise in pay, Josh," Kate said gaily.

"Did I mention that you're pretty and kind and sweet natured, and talented to boot?"

Kate rolled her eyes. "My, my, a girl's mind might

turn to molasses for all that sugary talk you're pouring on.''

Josh smiled as he wiped some glasses clean.

Kate took up the tray again and headed for a table near the stage. She bent to serve the drinks to a table of five when a handsome cowboy put his hand on her wrist. ''Didn't get a chance to meet you when you came out to the ranch the other morning. The boys here said I missed out. Said you was real pretty. For once they didn't fracture the truth.''

''Oh, well, thank you,'' Kate said, pulling her wrist from his grasp.

''My name's Cody. Head wrangler at the Randolph spread.'' He took in the bodice of her satin dress before lifting his eyes and granting her a seductive smile.

''I'm Kate Malone,'' she offered tentatively. Kate knew enough not to encourage a man who'd been drinking. ''Nice to meet you.'' She finished setting the glasses down and scurried back to the bar.

''He giving you trouble?'' Josh asked, eyeing the wrangler intently.

''Nothing I can't handle, Josh.'' Kate shot him a reassuring smile.

''Good, because you might not like what you see when you turn around.''

Instantly Kate whirled around to find Cole Bradshaw making his way through the front door.

Chapter Seventeen

Cole entered the Silver Saddle with trepidation. He'd warned himself to stay away from Kate, but he couldn't allow his personal feelings to interfere with his duty as sheriff. Making nightly rounds was part of the job, seeing that there was no trouble brewing in town. And just a short while ago, Cole had spied a rowdy bunch of cowpunchers entering the saloon.

The smoke-filled saloon, crowded and noisy with mingled sounds of piano tunes, husky voices and an occasional burst of laughter struck him hard like a swift punch to his insides. Kate's business was succeeding. He glanced around and found her smiling and serving up drinks to a table of men.

Cole strode over to the bar and leaned in, his back to Kate. Josh noticed him, frowned and managed to fill his time serving all the others at the bar first before coming his way. "What'll it be, Sheriff?"

"Beer." Cole had to look up to meet Josh's eyes. "She always serve the drinks?" he asked.

Josh lifted a brow, glanced at Kate then shook his head. "No, I usually do, when it's slow. As you can see, business is booming tonight. Kate is pitching in."

A tic worked at Cole's jaw. Hell, she shouldn't be serving the drinks. She owned the saloon—couldn't she hire someone else to do that? She was the only woman amid a congested roomful of men and she was waiting on them. Cole didn't know what he'd find when he came in here, but now he regretted his decision. It was a brutal reminder of the differences between him and free-spirited Kate.

Cole gritted his teeth.

Kate came up to the end of the bar, her face flushed, her smile bright. "Two more whiskeys, one beer and throw in a dish of candies, Josh. We've got a table full of men with a sweet tooth."

Cole glanced at the glass case behind the bar, filled with items usually sold at the general store. A deep scowl pulled his lips down. Pretty soon, she'd be selling Mrs. Whittaker's lace and bonnets in here, too.

Cole sipped his beer, his stomach churning.

When she didn't acknowledge him, he knew it was for the best. He'd finish his drink and walk out. He'd seen what he'd come here to see.

Kate had what she wanted. There was no doubt the Silver Saddle would profit now. There was no doubt she'd live her life running this saloon. And there was no doubt that he and Kate had no future together. The burn of truth went deep and scorched him unmercifully.

Cole turned to lean his back against the bar, getting a last glimpse at Kate. She looked so darn pretty tonight, with her hair pinned up in curls, shining coppery red from the overhead lights. She wore a gown of green satin that fit her curves snugly and shimmered when she walked. He took another gulp of beer and watched her smile and greet her customers. Men gawked and flirted. Cole had set his mug down, fixing to leave, when he noted a young randy cowboy manhandling Kate. She pushed at him to move away, but he gripped her waist and tried bringing her down onto his lap.

Fury unleashed, Cole strode quickly to the table, the man's loud, indecent proposal flaming his temper. "Aw, come on, we can just go on into one of them back rooms and—"

Cole gripped Kate's shoulders, moving her aside, then reached down, hoisted the man up to full height and landed a solid, hard jab to the man's jaw. The cowboy reeled back, shook his head then lunged for Cole. He was only too glad to punch him again, this time in the gut. The man groaned then went down, collapsing onto the floor. Cole stared at him, waiting. He didn't get up. Half a dozen of his friends clustered around him. One man tapped his face, trying to revive him. Finally the man came to.

Cole steadied his breaths. "Get him out of here," he ordered. "And don't any of you come back. Ever."

"Cole!"

Kate's angry voice startled him. He looked at her once, noting her irate expression and not caring one damn bit, then surveyed the room. Everyone fell silent.

"If anyone shows this lady an ounce of disrespect, they'll have to answer to me. No one touches her. No one says an unkind word. No one makes any sort of indecent remark. You all got that? 'Cause if not, I'd be more than willing to toss them into my jail and forget where I stored the key."

A voice from the far corner of the crowded room shouted out, "She your woman, Sheriff?"

Cole didn't hesitate, the truth dawning on him faster than a wild prairie fire. "She's my woman."

Kate stood next to him, dumbfounded. Cole had never seen her speechless before. Heat rose up her cheeks and colored her skin rosy pink.

Cole turned his attention to the cowboys filtering out and taking their bloodied friend with them. Once satisfied that he'd gotten everything under control, Cole made his way to the door. As he was leaving, he heard Kate say, "Start up the music again, Shady."

Cole slammed the door and headed for home, the din of the saloon muted clamor to his ears now.

Once Kate found her voice and gathered her anger, she followed Cole outside. Without a word to her, he'd left. Just like that, he'd made a humiliating declaration, nearly destroyed her business and then, without so much as a tip of his hat, he'd left. She spotted him heading toward home.

"Cole Bradshaw, you had no right," she called out.

He kept walking.

"I had that situation under control."

He kept walking.

Kate picked up her pace and followed him.

"He was a drunken cowboy. I knew how to handle him."

The jingle of Cole's spurs was the only sound on the street. He kept walking.

"You chased men out of my saloon!" Infuriated, Kate lifted her skirts and nearly caught up to him. He kept walking.

"Damn it, Cole. I am *not* your woman."

Cole stopped then, turned and, within two large strides, faced her. His arm snaked around her waist, pulling her up, crushing her to his chest. "Oh," she gasped. Their bodies meshed, hip to hip as his lips crashed down on hers.

Heat consumed her, a searing potent flame of desire that swept all rational sense from her head. Cole's lips pressed down hard, demanding and intoxicating her with his familiar expert mouth. He kissed her again and again, drawing her up, rubbing their bodies, growling into her mouth. Their tongues mated fiercely as though they'd been starved and sought sustenance and solace from the heady union.

Kate's bones melted, her insides shredding to nothing but Cole—the taste of him, the all-powerful feel of his hardened body ready to take release. He touched her everywhere with hands that knew her so well. She moaned and fell into him, clinging for her life.

His heartbeats, rapid and strong, pounded in rhythm with hers. They kissed on the darkened street until kissing wasn't enough. Cole pulled away first, his body trembling. His hot gaze probed hers. "Tell me now you're not my woman."

Kate couldn't respond, the truth, the pain of it, too difficult to bear. She bit down hard on lips bruised from his kisses.

"Good night, Kate."

Cole turned and left her standing alone in the street, wanting him with a fierceness she'd only just begun to understand.

Three days later Kate stood on the steps of the schoolhouse waiting for the day's session to end. She heard noises, children's animated voices then witnessed a rush of students descend the stairs and head toward the gate. Nothing much had changed, yet everything seemed to have. Kate didn't have time to ponder that thought. She entered the school to find Miss Ashmore straightening out the benches and stools that served as seats for her students. "Good afternoon, Miss Ashmore."

She looked up, clearly amazed to see Kate standing

at the threshold. "Why, Mary Kathryn, come in. This is certainly a surprise."

Kate stepped inside and noted that the inside of the schoolhouse didn't appear to be in any better condition than the outside. "I was hoping you'd have time to speak with me. Are you in a hurry to get on home?"

"No, no. I usually stay a while and plan my next lesson. This is no interruption. Come and have a seat."

Kate chuckled when she sat down on a small upturned pickle barrel that served as a seat. "I'd forgotten how tiny everything is."

"Everything is small, including most of my students. The oldest child I have in class is only eleven right now." Miss Ashmore sat down on the only real chair in the room. She cast Kate a genuine smile and waited.

"I, uh, came here to give you something. Remember the other day when we discussed the condition of the school and that the children don't have enough readers."

"Yes, I certainly do remember that conversation," Miss Ashmore said, nodding patiently.

"Well, I want to help." Kate handed a small tin box to the teacher. "There's enough in there to buy some books and maybe as time goes on, I can help with repairs, too."

Miss Ashmore opened the box. "I don't understand?"

"It's to buy books the children need," Kate repeated.

"Where did you get this money?"

"It's a percentage of profits from the saloon. We're doing steady business now, I'm happy to say. I don't need much for myself right now and, well, I want the money to do some good."

Miss Ashmore shook her head and handed her back the box. "It's a generous offer, Mary Kathryn, but I can't accept this."

Kate looked her dead in the eyes. "Because it's saloon money?"

"You know I've been opposed to that saloon."

"But it's a legitimate business now. You wouldn't refuse money from Mr. Becker or anyone else who offered."

"Mary Kathryn, this is gambling and drinking money."

"No, it's profit from an establishment in Crystal Creek. Take it and let some good come of the money. Please, Miss Ashmore, the children will benefit and that's what's really important." Kate pushed the box full of money back into her hands. "Readers, chalkboards, new chairs and desks. Spend it any way you see fit."

Miss Ashmore stared at the box in her hand, tears misting in her eyes. "This is so generous."

"It's not all that much. I hope to do more."

"Thank you."

Kate beamed with joy. "Then you'll use the money?"

"Yes, dear, I will. The children deserve it. I don't know what to say. No one's come forth like this before."

Kate stood and smiled. "I hope to change that."

Miss Ashmore rose from her seat and took Kate's hand. "I'll be sure to let the children know that a former student donated money so that they may learn. I'll be sure to let them know it was you, Kate."

"Kate?" Puzzled, Kate stared at Miss Ashmore. She'd never once called her by her preferred name.

"Yes, *Kate*." Miss Ashmore laughed heartily. "I don't know why I insisted on calling you by your given name. From now on, I'll call you Kate. And you may call me—"

"Miss Ashmore," Kate answered all too quickly. She couldn't fathom using her teacher's first name. "That's who you are to me. Miss Ashmore, my schoolteacher."

"Yes, your schoolteacher and your...friend."

Cole stood just inside the church entrance, leaning leisurely against the door, watching the five men who made up the town council discuss the upcoming Founder's Day celebration. Edward Wesley, the more vocal of members planned most of the activities, advising that Patricia be put in charge of securing the entertainment.

Cole had forgotten about Founder's Day. He supposed Patricia would expect an invitation from him. Cole winced, recalling the last time he'd spoken with her, a few days ago when they'd accidentally met up just outside the diner. She'd been overly sweet, hinting about the celebration, and Cole knew he'd have to come to terms with her sometime soon. He felt his life was stalled at a fork in the road, knowing which way he ought to head yet wanting so badly to go in the other direction.

Mr. Becker cleared his throat, calling Cole's attention to him. "I, uh, have here a note sent to us by Miss Ashmore." All heads shot up and he began reading.

Dear members of our town council,

As you very well know, I have been recently and actively in support of the town ordinance prohibiting the construction of the saloon owned by Miss Malone. While I agree that sometimes saloons bring in an element we don't enjoy seeing on the streets of Crystal Creek, I do have to uphold Miss Malone's right to operate the saloon now legally. She has proved to be a friend of our local town and most especially a friend of our school. Because of her charitable efforts, the school now has enough cash to purchase much needed supplies. This is a generous act on Miss Malone's part and I wish that she be acknowledged for contributing to our school. I am very proud to call her a former student of Crystal Creek School.

Sincerely,

Miss Eleanor Ashmore

"Well, don't that beat all," Mr. Teasdale, the town barber called out.

Cole noted Mr. Becker nodding in agreement. "I've had some dealings with the woman myself. She seems to be fair and honest."

Edward Wesley stood up, decidedly irritated. "It's a ploy, men. Don't you see? A little goodwill and she's got all of you under her thumb."

"Ploy or not," Mr. Becker announced, "it's about time someone did something about the state of our school. Mrs. Johannson came into the store the other day, complaining that her little Ingrid had sores on her...uh, well, she came in for a salve. The stools those children sit on are all splintered and broken down."

"I heard Miss Ashmore say that Miss Malone gave her a portion of the saloon's profits to buy new readers for the children." Mr. Teasdale and the others muttered in hushed tones after that, and Cole couldn't hear much else that was said.

Dumbfounded by Kate's generosity to a town that had rebuffed her time and again, Cole felt his admiration for her grow. Kate never ceased to surprise him. She was a woman who'd definitely keep a man on the tips of his boots.

* * *

Kate planted her bottom down on one of her cane-backed chairs and took in a deep breath of air. She'd just finished cleaning up the bar from last night and washing down the floor. The Silver Saddle sparkled with a freshly polished glow.

When the iron door opened then closed, Kate spun her head around. The Silver Saddle didn't open for business for two more hours. She stood immediately when she realized who had entered her establishment. "What are you doing here?"

Edward Wesley approached her, his thick belly nearly busting open the buttons on his fancy tailored shirt. "I came to talk, Miss Malone."

Kate put distance between them by walking behind the bar. Not only distance, but also a wide mahogany counter separated them now. And it wasn't fear but a deep sense of loathing that made Kate want to stand clear. "I don't see as we have anything much to say to each other."

"Oh, I do, my dear." He leaned in, bracing his arms up on the bar.

"Say it then and be done with it."

"I know what you're trying to do and it won't work. You think that spending a little money on the school will ingratiate you to the town? Well, I have a whole lot more money than you, a bankful at my disposal and I can see that no one steps one foot into this bar again."

Kate stood her ground, undaunted by his threats.

"You didn't scare my mama and you don't scare me."

"I don't?" He grinned as though she was an innocent, small child. "I should. I could run you out of town or…I could offer you something better."

Kate wouldn't ask. She didn't like the way the banker leered at her.

"Your mama wasn't smart enough to take me up on my offer, but you, Kate, you're a whole lot smarter than she was. And even a mite prettier."

She leaned in close, setting her fists firmly on the bar. "Don't talk about my mother." She surprised herself at the threat she put in her tone.

"Fine, then let's talk about you." He grabbed hold of her wrist. "I can run you out of town, dear, or we can…come to an agreement."

Kate struggled to release her arm from his grasp. Wesley kept his grip firm.

"My daughter has her sights set on Cole Bradshaw. The sheriff seems to be a bit…confused right now."

"That has nothing to do with me," she said, yanking hard to finally pull away from his grasp.

He only smiled at her small win. "Oh, I think it does. I'm a man, my dear. I know what he sees in you. I see it too. Now, the sheriff doesn't really want you, but I do. I'll buy you out of the saloon and get you a pretty little house far outside of town. All I ask is that you greet me cordially when I make my nightly visits."

Kate gasped and hauled her hand back, landing a full smack on Wesley's round cheek.

Fury flashed in the banker's eyes. He rubbed his jaw. "Your mama refused me and look what happened to her."

Kate knew anger just as powerful as his and she fairly trembled with it. "Are you saying you burned us down?"

"No, I didn't burn you down. I'm a businessman, Miss Malone. I wait for opportunities. And when your mama needed a loan, she didn't get it, now did she?"

"You snake! You tried to blackmail her."

"She should have taken me up on my offer."

Kate understood fully what her mama had never shared with her before. She now knew that Wesley was behind Louisa's financial troubles. She felt great pride knowing Louisa had held her integrity intact. As much as her mother loved the Silver Saddle, she wouldn't compromise her ideals. And neither would Kate. Ever.

"Get out!"

"You'll change your mind. You'll see. This town will never accept you or your saloon." The iron door slammed closed when Wesley walked out and Kate slumped over, needing the solid wood bar to hold her up.

Cole leaned up against the wall of the general store, calling himself a damn fool, but that didn't stop him from watching Edward Wesley enter the Silver Saddle after the town council meeting and it didn't stop him from waiting until the man left with fury written all over his face, minutes later.

Cole pushed away from the wall and headed for the saloon. Without a breath of hesitation, he pushed open the door to meet with a misty-eyed Kate.

"I should learn to keep that door locked until opening time." Kate frowned and turned away from him.

"That's a fine greeting, Kate."

She didn't respond. He didn't like the look he'd seen in her eyes just then or the way her shoulders slumped with seeming defeat. It wasn't like Kate. Something or *someone* had upset her.

"Kate?"

Cole studied her from the back and noted her trembling. He glanced at the door and wondered if Wesley had much to do with her mood. She walked over to the bar and put her head down. "I wish you'd just go, Cole."

Cole sidled up next to her. "I will, soon as you tell me what's wrong."

She shook her head. "Nothing's wrong, nothing at all."

Cole blew out a breath. His head told him to leave it be and do as Kate had asked. But Cole never much listened with his head when it came to Kate. He turned around and braced his elbows against the bar then shot her a sideways glance. "Remember when mean old Ruby Larue chased you off her property 'cause you were the saloon's gal's daughter? She said she didn't want your kind touching foot on her land.''

Downcast, Kate nodded. "I remember. I only wanted to pick a peach from her tree."

"You wouldn't tell me then either that you were troubled. You kept on saying, 'Nothing's wrong, Cole.' But I didn't believe you, on account of your body trembled and your face took on this sad, angry, hurt look. That's about the same look you've got on your face now."

Kate didn't say a word.

"I finally got the truth out of you."

"I didn't want to say…it was so humiliating."

"I fixed her good though, didn't I?"

A smile began to surface on Kate's face. "You snuck onto her property one night and picked all of her peaches. She went to her grave believing it was me who stole all of her fruit."

"Jeb and I got sick eating all them peaches. Had to get rid of the evidence." Cole grinned at the recollection.

"And you left a bushel on my doorstep. We ate peach pie for weeks after that."

They stood in silence for a moment, each deep into the memory. When Kate didn't offer an explanation, Cole pushed further. "I saw Edward Wesley leave here in a huff."

Kate's body stiffened. "He's an unbearable man."

"I know you don't like him, Kate. What'd he do?"

Kate snapped her head up and met his eyes with determination. "Cole, let it alone."

Cole was now certain Wesley had something to do with hurting Kate. He rubbed tension from the back of his neck. "Did he threaten you in any way?"

Kate shook her head. "Not really."

"Then it's something else?"

"I'm not going to say, Cole. Please, forget it."

"There was a time when we shared everything, Kate."

Kate moved to the door and opened it. "Those times are over, Cole. We're different now." It was his invitation to leave and he took it, realizing that he and Kate had lost something rare and precious somewhere along the road to adulthood. She didn't need him looking after her anymore. She was a fine, capable woman who could deal on her own with whatever life put in her path.

Cole strode to the door and looked her deep in the eyes. "If you need me I'm right here, Kate."

Kate nodded and closed the door behind him. She couldn't confide in him. She had too much pride to tell Cole about the indecent proposal Wesley had offered her. He'd humiliated her, just as Ruby Larue had, but that hadn't been the worst of it. Kate's hatred ran deep for a man who'd blackmail a woman then run her out of town unfairly because she'd rejected him. Yet Louisa Malone had stood up to the man, just as Kate had.

She shuddered, unable to imagine having that

man's hands on her. Even the Silver Saddle wasn't worth that degradation. Kate muted her cries for her mother's unjust treatment. And she bit back her fury at a man who wielded his power over women simply because he had the opportunity.

Kate sat down again, running a hand through her hair and thinking back on Cole's parting words. *If you need me I'm right here, Kate.*

She needed him, but not to fight her battles. She needed his respect, his acceptance, his love. All of the things he couldn't give her.

Chapter Eighteen

~~~~~~~~

Kate ushered Nora inside her house and offered her a seat in the parlor, pleased to have her good friend's company today. "I'm so glad you decided to pay me a visit, Nora."

Nora's sweet smile was a balm to Kate's stormy and unsettled feelings lately. "It's good to see you, too."

"Would you like a glass of tea or coffee? I just pulled a fresh batch of biscuits out of the oven."

Nora clutched her stomach. "Oh, not right now, Kate, but thank you. Abe and Jethro are stuffing me full of food from the moment I rise in the morning until nearly bedtime. One would think I'm growing a baby heifer in my belly, instead of a tiny little child."

"I can sympathize with the men, Nora. Every time I see you, I want to make sure you'll not go hungry."

"Well, with those two hovering constantly, trust that I'm never hungry. They see to it."

"I'll try to remember that."

Nora tugged something out of her handbag. "Kate, I'm actually here on a bit of business, representing the Cable Brothers Livery. Abe thought I'd enjoy speaking with you on this matter."

Puzzled, Kate tilted her head. "What business is that, Nora?"

"Well, we've all heard about your generous contribution to the school the other day. Kate, how kind of you," Nora said sincerely, "helping out when you've barely made any money at all. My goodness, the entire town's clamoring about what you've done."

"I didn't do all that much, Nora. The school needs a great deal. I hoped that with my help, at least, the children would get the readers they need."

"And they shall. You see, we want to join in, too. The livery is doing good business and Abe and Jethro felt it's time to give something back to the town. No better way than to donate to the school. After all," she offered with a pat to her stomach, "our little baby will attend that school one day." Nora handed Kate an envelope.

Kate peered inside. "There's quite a bit of money in here."

"It's the amount Abe came up with. Abe said it's a portion of the month's profits. He hopes to match that amount each month."

"But, with the baby coming and all, won't you need this?"

Nora smiled. "I have everything I could possibly

want in life, Kate. Take the money and use it to do more good. And I have other news that will please you. Mrs. Whittaker from the millinery will also be contributing. You know, she had thoughts of selling her shop, though I think the woman wouldn't know what to do with herself if she did sell. She does love those hats. She told me she'd be honored to donate some of her profits for the good of the town. I don't think I've ever seen her this excited about anything in a long time. It's giving her a reason to keep her shop open. I wouldn't be surprised if more people came forth."

Kate sat thunderstruck, awed by the generous gesture. "This is…" Tears stung her eyes. Kate hadn't expected her small gesture to develop into anything so wonderful.

"Unexpected?"

"Well, that too," Kate said with a smile. "But I never thought that my simple act would escalate into this. There are others we can help with this money, too. Mr. Dresden broke his leg and can't farm his land. He's already in debt to the bank. And the widow Gainsley has six children to feed."

Nora grinned. "Kate, see what you've started? Only good can come from this."

Later that week, Kate had two more visitors and was pleasantly surprised when they offered a small amount from their profits, as well. Not only would the saloon, livery and millinery be contributing, but the blacksmith and the barber, too. The school would have all the repairs it needed now and many families who struggled, due to called-in loans from the bank, would have a second chance to survive.

Friday evening Kate left for the Silver Saddle with high spirits. Her feet barely touching the ground, Kate seemed to float on air as she made her way to her saloon. She felt light and happy, filled with a deep sense of accomplishment. For the first time since coming back to Crystal Creek, true and genuine hope filled her heart.

Earlier in the day, Kate had paid a visit to the Dresden family and offered them financial aid to tide them over until Mr. Dresden recovered from his injury. Pride kept him from accepting initially, but with a little coaxing on Kate's part, he'd finally agreed. Both Kate and Mrs. Dresden pointed out that, once he got on his feet again, he could pay some monies back in the form of donations to others in need. Kate didn't want repayment, but she did understand a man's pride.

When Kate reached the Silver Saddle, a surprise awaited her. The saloon was filled with cowboys as usual, and a handful of drifters who'd move on either today or tomorrow to where they were headed, but what struck a chord deep in her heart was that the locals, businessmen and shop owners had come in, too.

Kate strolled over to the bar and lifted a brow to Josh.

"Could've knocked me over with a bluebird

feather," he said with a shrug. "One by one, they came in, asking for a drink, claiming they're helping a neighbor."

"Helping a neighbor?" Baffled, Kate pierced him with a look.

"'Have a drink, help a neighbor,' one of 'em said by way of explanation."

Kate furrowed her brows, then finally, after some thought, she caught on. "Oh my! I see now. How wonderful!" Delighted, Kate glanced across the saloon to smile and nod to her new patrons, many of whom had once protested the saloon's reconstruction.

"Kate, it's a real good thing you're doing, helping folks out."

"It's not just me. Many others have joined in. I had the idea when I saw the school in such sorry condition, but I couldn't have done so much alone."

"Still, you've started up something and looks to me that the town's all but forgiven you for daring to rebuild the Silver Saddle." Josh winked, the gesture so rare on the brawny man, it endeared him to her even more.

Kate sighed and thought that forgiveness was a good thing, but a dose of faith and determination was decidedly even better.

Meggie stood atop her mattress and lifted her arms up as Cole lowered her nightclothes down, readying her for bed. "There you go, Megpie. All set now. Jump on down and get under the covers."

Meggie bounced a few times on her bed, giggling gaily then plopped down as she was told and snuggled under her blanket. Cole leaned over, tucking her up to her chin. "Daddy, are we gonna have pie and cookies and play all sorts a games at the cel-bration?"

"Sure thing, sweetheart. And Daddy's gonna lift you up high in the sky so you can see above everybody's heads at the horse races."

"You're gonna win, right, Daddy?"

"Nah, I don't wanna ride in the horse race. I'm gonna win the shooting match. Your daddy's pretty doggone fast on the draw."

Meggie grinned. "Is Miss Kate gonna be there?"

Cole hid his frown. It was a question he'd been wondering himself. Kate was hardly speaking to him lately, so he didn't really know what her plans were. Most all the townsfolk usually showed up for the festivities. Shops closed and business pretty much came to a dead halt on Founder's Day. "I suppose she'll be there, Megpie."

"Goodie!"

Cole cast his daughter a thoughtful look. "You like Miss Kate, don't you?"

Meggie nodded eagerly. "Uh-huh. She has fun games and we make cake. And she teached me things."

"Yeah, she has fun games." Cole never minded spending time with her in his youth. Kate always entertained. She was one to make a day interesting just by being Kate.

"Do you like her, Daddy?"

"Miss Kate?"

Meggie bobbed her head.

"I like her." Cole's feelings for Kate were muddled, confused and more than a little perplexing, but one thing he knew for sure, he definitely liked her. Far too much. She was the only woman he thought about, the only one who claimed his mind both night and day. "Now, it's time for sleep." Cole lowered the lantern light and bent to kiss her good-night.

Meggie wrapped both arms about his neck and hugged tight. "Night, Daddy."

"Night, Megpie." Cole stood, overwhelming love filling his heart as he gazed down at his child. But the peace didn't last long. It never did. A nagging thought haunted him more and more lately. Meggie needed a mother. He'd promised Jeb. Hell, he hadn't found the last of the marauders who had taken both parents from his child, but the very least he could do was see to the child's upbringing. Mrs. Gregory wasn't going to be around too much longer.

Just then, as though she'd read his thoughts, Mrs. Gregory appeared in the doorway. She whispered, "The little darling asleep?"

Cole nodded and walked out the door, a sense of melancholy sweeping though him. "She is."

"Shall I be going then?"

Emptiness engulfed him and a wild forbidden loneliness that Cole usually fought down surfaced. He needed a drink. Truth be told, he needed to see Kate.

It had been days since he had set eyes on her. Something within him compelled, pulling at him with ferocity. He couldn't much explain it, but he *had* to see her. "Uh, would you mind staying half an hour more? I have...some business to tend to. I won't be long."

Mrs. Gregory smiled a knowing smile. "Wouldn't have anything to do with that lovely girl down at the saloon now, would it, Sheriff?"

Cole relented, grinning. She might be old, but Mrs. Gregory had a keen, insightful mind. "Might be."

She shuffled him quickly toward the door. "Go on. Take your time. I don't have a man to go home to. I can stay for as long as you need."

Grateful, Cole planted a chaste kiss on her plump, rosy cheek. "Thanks, Mrs. Gregory."

"Ah, go on now," she said, shooing him out the door. "I'll be right here when you get back."

Cole chuckled and headed straight for the saloon.

Kate sat down by Shady on a high-back chair on the small stage, her mood bright. She peered out to the crowd of patrons, many of whom she recognized as regular customers now, and smiled. The Silver Saddle prospered despite the odds she'd been up against; the unjust town ordinance, a powerful vindictive banker and many naysayers who had doomed her saloon from the very start. Still and all, her business flourished. Her mama would be proud. And Kate had good feelings about using a portion of her profits to help people in need.

Only yesterday, she'd met with Crystal Creek's most recent widow, Mrs. Gainsley. The woman had cried great tears of relief and gratitude when Kate handed her enough money to see her family through another season. But Kate couldn't take all the credit. She had others to thank for pitching in and helping. She noted many of them sitting in her saloon right now.

Kate began to sing as a quiet hush fell over the room. Men carefully turned their chairs toward the stage, others at the bar stopped talking to swivel their heads her way.

Lyrics poured out of her with great ease, the song a happy ballad about a wandering cowboy finding his true love. Through a haze of smoke and muted sounds Kate noticed the iron door opening. Cole walked in, his attention focused solely on her. Big Josh poured him a whiskey and he sat down at a back table.

Kate continued to sing, her heart thumping erratically at the sight of him. At times, Cole simply startled her with the intensity of his liquid-blue eyes and sure demeanor. He held her captivated, their eyes meeting, touching as though she was singing to him. Only to him.

Kate's breath caught and she missed a verse, but nobody seemed to notice, so she continued on with the song. She tore her gaze away from Cole to scan across the room, to break the hold he had on her, to gather her courage. But each time she darted a glance his way, his gaze beckoned, caressing her softly and making her tingle in private areas of her body.

Cole wielded his power in a most subtle way, with a mere movement of his hands, a mere shift of his body. He had her heart, she'd given him her innocence, but that hadn't been enough. She should conjure up well-deserved anger toward him, but tonight, with the way he looked at her, the way his body called out for her, all Kate could do was melt into his gaze and allow the feelings to flow naturally.

Applause broke out when Kate finished the song. The crowd demanded another. Cole sat quietly, watching her intently. Kate felt him close, though five tables and two dozen men separated them. She began singing another tune, one similar with a soft, low melody that spoke of hope for a wayward drifter.

Three more songs followed, and by the time Kate finished singing, she was a mass of wanton desire. Cole hadn't taken his eyes off her and she...she couldn't rightly think straight from the sheer and potent passion his deliberate scrutiny evoked.

He stood then, gazed into her eyes once more then tipped his hat. Kate watched him turn and, with smooth, efficient steps, he exited the saloon, leaving Kate feeling so very alone in a crowd full of men. The only man she wanted was gone from sight and emptiness created a hollow ache in the pit of her stomach.

"Cole," she breathed quietly.

But he was gone and he wasn't coming back.

* * *

Kate sat in church on Sunday morning with Nora by her side. Her insides quivered with a queasy feeling. She shouldn't be this nervous, yet her heart pumped over itself, pounding up near her ears.

She'd asked Reverend Pritchard for a special favor and nervously awaited his sermon to be over. With a turn of her head, Kate noted Cole and Meggie sitting on the other side of the aisle. Interestingly, Cole hadn't walked in with the Wesleys. They sat up in front by themselves today.

Meggie caught her attention, rushed to the end of the pew and waved. The child's cherub face broke into the sweetest of smiles. Kate lifted her hand and waved back. Meggie lingered a bit, then walked back to her father and crawled up onto his lap.

Kate didn't make eye contact with Cole. She didn't need him adding to her queasy stomach. She had enough to deal with right now.

"And now, ladies and gentlemen of the congregation, I've had an unusual request by one of our members." The reverend smiled and looked her way. "Miss Malone would like to address you one and all. Come up here, please. You have everyone's attention."

Kate noted that she did. All heads had turned to gape at her with curious stares. Nora whispered, "Go on, Kate. You're doing a good thing. You just go on up there and make your announcement."

Kate stood and straightened out her cream gown laced with tiny seed pearls along the collar and sleeves. It was one of the finest she owned. Today, especially, she wanted to look her best. She made her way along the pew, and once she'd reached the end of the aisle, without conscious thought, she looked straight into Cole's questioning eyes. She took a breath then, watching his eyes soften on her, giving her strength, bolstering her resolve. Cole, her friend, seemed to know she needed him. He gave her the slightest nod and even though he didn't know what she was about, his encouragement had her heading up to the pulpit.

Reverend Pritchard took her hand and guided her to the front. She faced the congregation and found many friendly faces. "I wanted to thank Reverend Pritchard for allowing me this time to speak. There are a few things I'd like to say. As you might have heard, several of our citizens of Crystal Creek have contributed a portion of their business profits in order to help others in need. The school, for one, will be first on the list to have repairs done, and Miss Ashmore has informed me that all supplies needed for this school session will be provided. I'm pleased to say that the children will have the readers and workbooks they need and will have decent seating and tables to work on.

"Since many of you have come forth to join in with your generous contributions, I believe that we should start up the Crystal Creek Community Fund. Mrs. Whittaker has graciously agreed to hold the monies in her safe, to be distributed as needed to the citizens of this town. The Community Fund is meant to temporarily help folks or institutions that are struggling, and the contributing members will make decisions regarding how the money shall be dispersed. We should probably take it to a vote to place someone in charge. We could do that later on—"

"I vote for you, Miss Kate. It was your idea. You were the first to come forth for the school. You should be in charge," Mr. Teasdale interrupted.

"I second that," another man said.

Hands went up then, and it appeared that the vote had been cast. Overwhelmed, Kate accepted. "Well, I suppose, if you all think I can do an adequate job, it would be an honor to head up the Fund. I have ample room at the saloon for the meetings."

After a momentary pause to gather her thoughts, Kate continued. "Also, from now on, the Silver Saddle will close on Sundays. It's a day for worship, a day meant for family and friends." Kate smiled, looking out at the women nodding their heads. The men, though, revealed no such sentiment. "I want to thank all of you again for taking hold of my idea. It's something I hadn't planned but I'm grateful for. I do believe the Community Fund will do a world of good."

Afterward Kate stood just beyond the church steps with Nora and the Cable brothers. She'd had several families come up to thank her and commend her idea of the Community Fund. The Wesleys hadn't, of course. Mr. Wesley had taken his daughter's arm when it appeared she'd like to come over to say something and they'd pressed forward into the crowd. It turned Kate's stomach just seeing the man. She felt immediate remorse for Patricia. The young woman probably didn't have a notion as to her father's true nature.

"You look disappointed that Patricia didn't come over to speak with us," Nora said to Jethro.

Jethro found Patricia easily in the crowd, his eyes seeming to focus on the sway of her backside. "I just wanted to knock some sense into her head. Fool woman thinks she's ready to race her horse. Actually wants to enter into the horse races tomorrow at the celebration."

"So your lessons aren't helping?" Abe prodded with a sly grin.

"She's a stubborn one. It's hard to teach her anything. She thinks she knows it all," Jethro replied.

"You're not going to let her enter, are you, Jethro?" Nora seemed genuinely concerned.

"It's not up to him, sweetheart," Abe reminded.

Jethro shook his head. "She's not ready to race a horse, that's for sure. She can barely mount her mare. I have to stand there and make sure she doesn't fall off. Half the time, she does."

"And you catch her?" Abe asked with a lifted brow.

"Of course. Can't let the woman fall." Jethro seemed truly perplexed. "She's not a fast learner."

Nora smiled, looking toward Kate. "I wouldn't think Patricia is all that clumsy and I do believe she's quite bright."

Kate chuckled. "Yep. I'd say Patricia Wesley pretty much knows what she's doing."

Jethro frowned. "What?"

Kate took hold of Jethro's arm. "Nothing, Jethro." Kate supposed he'd find out soon enough. Men sometimes weren't all that intelligent when it came to figuring out about women. "Let's have supper. You're all invited over to my house. It's my turn to cook."

Kate sat in the quiet of her parlor, working on a quilt for Nora's baby. She rarely found the time needed for such things, but she wanted terribly to surprise Nora with the gift before the baby arrived. The Cables had left an hour ago after sharing the Sunday meal and Kate felt energetic enough to work clear into the night if need be. She didn't have to rise early in the morning. Tomorrow, the saloon would be closed in honor of Founder's Day and those festivities didn't start until noon.

A soft knocking at her door didn't surprise her. Jethro had left his hat here after supper and she assumed he'd come to claim it. Kate had to admit, as she lifted the tan suede hat from a peg by the door that it looked kind of nice having a man's belongings around. It sort of made Kate feel as though *she* belonged. Silly thoughts, she mused, and opened the door wide. "I bet you came for this, Jethro," she said happily.

Cole stood frozen on the porch, his gaze fastened to the Stetson she held.

Shocked, Kate's heart raced. "Oh, Cole. I wasn't expecting you."

He held his own hat in his hands. Fingering the brim, he said, "That's obvious, Kate."

"What are you doing here?" she asked, then a thought struck. "Is Meggie sick again?"

Cole shook his head. "Nope. Meggie's just fine. I came to ask you something. May I come in?"

Kate stepped away from the door and allowed him entrance. He took a few steps into the parlor. Kate noticed him staring at the sofa. No, not the sofa, she decided. Cole was gaping at the baby's quilt she'd left on the sofa. "Cole?"

His head snapped up. With intense perusal, he searched her eyes then his gaze drifted lower to her abdomen. Kate had never seen that stark expression on his face. Suddenly it dawned on her what he might be thinking and she blushed clear down to her toes. "It's a gift for Nora's baby."

Cole nodded and turned away, but not before Kate observed his expression change. She'd expected relief, but didn't believe that's what she'd witnessed at all. Had she imagined disappointment in those clear blue eyes?

Cole cleared his throat. "It's a fine thing you're doing, Kate. The Community Fund is a good idea."

"Well, there are many to thank for that. I only tried helping Miss Ashmore and the school, then more and more people offered to make donations."

"I heard Mrs. Gainsley was ready to move off her land before you gave her some hope."

"Oh, Cole, she has six children. They are the sweetest things. Her boy Troy is the oldest at eleven.

And you should see him around the house. He tries to make up for everything and be so grown-up. Mr. Becker says he might be able hire him part time when the store is busy.''

"That's real good, Kate.''

Cole's smile affected her insides. He looked so handsome today, still in his Sunday clothes—a clean white shirt under a stitched leather vest and tan trousers. She liked that he always wore his gun and his badge. He was Cole Bradshaw, Sheriff of Crystal Creek, without a doubt. He'd attained his dream. And now, so had Kate. Yet, neither one was truly happy, she surmised. "Is that what you wanted to talk to me about?''

"Uh, no. Not that exactly.''

Kate waited.

Cole cleared his throat again. "I, uh, came to ask you to the Founder's Day celebration. I'd like you to join me and Meggie tomorrow.''

A dozen emotions rushed forth and she nearly gasped aloud. Kate recalled the one Founder's Day she'd prayed for Cole's invitation, only to be disappointed upon learning he'd asked Patricia Wesley. But tonight, here he stood with hat in hand, asking her all proper-like to go. She'd like nothing more. She wanted to spend her days with him…and her nights. "I've already accepted an invitation to go with the Cables.''

Cole flinched as though he'd been struck. He stared down at the hat she still held in her hand. "You're going with Jethro, then?''

There was accusation in his tone, though Kate thought he struggled not to let it show. How could he ask that, Kate wondered. Didn't he know that what she'd given to him, she'd not ever give to another man? "I'm going with *all* the Cables. They've become like family to me, Jethro included."

Cole nodded and took a deep breath. "Fine. Well, I hope you have a good time tomorrow."

"There's no reason we can't...uh, well, I'd like to spend some time with Meggie."

Cole grinned, a charming lift of his mouth that brightened his entire face. "She'd like that too."

"Wonderful. Then I suppose I'll see you both tomorrow."

Kate walked to the door and opened it. "Good night, Cole."

Cole hesitated a moment, his gaze lingering on her. Kate felt an immediate rush of heat under his perusal. He nodded then strode to the door. "Night, Kate. See you tomorrow."

Kate closed the door after him and smiled so hard she was certain she beamed. It had been a long time coming, perhaps years too late, but Kate's heart still warmed to the notion.

Cole Bradshaw had finally invited her to the Founder's Day celebration.

Chapter Nineteen

As always, the Founder's Day celebration was held in a large clearing just outside of town where green grass was in abundance and tall sugar pines provided shade from the day's sun. Kate and Nora set a patchwork quilt that Kate had brought from home under one of those pines and lowered themselves down to watch the festivities.

Abe and Jethro were right behind them, carrying baskets of food and a pitcher of lemonade. "Here you go, ladies," Abe said, handing Nora a basket. Jethro, in turn, delivered a basket to Kate along with the lemonade. "If you two will excuse us, Jethro and I have a log-splitting contest to win." Abe kissed Nora's cheek with affection and the two men took off.

"C'mon, Nora, we have to see this." Kate bounded up from their spot and bent to lend Nora a hand. Her growing stomach was the size of a small ripe melon now and, though she still moved gracefully, Kate knew it took some effort. Nora graciously accepted her hand and together they headed to the other end of the clearing where the contest was ready to begin.

The two-man teams were settled by a cropping of trees and whoever chopped their massive log up first would be declared the winner. While the entrants were being organized and handed their axes, Kate scanned the grounds for Cole and Meggie. Although she didn't locate them, she did manage to ensnare the attention of Patricia Wesley. She stood with a group of young ladies, many of whom turned to wave at Kate. Patricia didn't wave; instead, she lifted her skirts and headed her way.

Kate braced herself for the encounter. None of her conversations with Patricia were ever pleasant. "Here comes Patricia," Kate said softly, but Mrs. Whittaker, who stood nearby and was explaining her latest bonnet creation had taken Nora's attention.

Patricia approached with a smile. "Hello, Mary Kat—" she began, then started again. "Hello, Kate."

Kate raised a brow. "Good afternoon, Patricia."

"It's a pleasant day for such an outing, wouldn't you agree?" Patricia was in an especially gay mood. She'd never been this cordial before.

"Yes, the weather is cooperating."

"I wanted to come over after church yesterday to commend you, but Father whisked me away quite swiftly, I'm afraid. I'd wanted to say that it took a great deal of courage to stand up in front of all those people and make your announcement. I, for one, thought that you handled yourself quite well. You can count on my support with the Community Fund. Jethro tells me that you were the first to help out with the school. Something should have been done months ago. If I had known the state of disrepair in our school, but well, you took action and that's quite impressive.''

Dumbfounded at Patricia's sincere tone, Kate smiled. "Thank you. I did what needed to be done."

"Yes, well...some of us women should take heed."

"Whatever do you mean?"

Patricia smiled ruefully. "The entire town was against you, Kate, but you didn't let that stop you from doing what was in your heart."

"I'm stubborn," Kate said with self-mockery.

"You're determined. There is a difference. And smart enough to be successful. I have a dream of my own...to open a shop, a specialty store just to suit women's needs, with the latest fashions from Europe and the East, but Father..."

Kate frowned at the mention of Edward Wesley. "He's opposed."

"In the worst way. He wants to see me married. Says it's a woman's only place. I don't see that it's all that wrong for a woman to want to achieve something in life, too. Jethro doesn't think..."

"What doesn't he think, Patricia?"

"Well, he doesn't think it's wrong. He believes that women have rights."

Kate understood all too well Patricia's dilemma.

Kate had grown up fighting that very same battle. "You should do it, Patricia. If that's what you want, it's—"

Kate was interrupted by the announcement that the contest was ready to begin. All conversation came to a halt and heads turned toward the five teams ready with axes in hand.

Abe shed his shirt, but it wasn't until Jethro did the same, tossing it aside, that Patricia gasped. "Oh," she said on a breath, trying hard to conceal a gaze fixed solely on Jethro's bare chest.

"It's a warm day," Kate offered, noting that Jethro Cable was a fine male specimen. It was clearly evident Patricia agreed.

With her gaze still fastened on Jethro, Patricia fanned herself. "And getting warmer all the time."

Kate chuckled as the men began chopping timber.

An hour later, after having lunch with the Cables, Kate found herself on the start line sharing a stiff burlap sack with one of the school children, a little girl named Henrietta. Other adults were paired with children and, as Kate looked down the line, she saw Cole in the same situation with a small boy just ten feet away. Thin rope wrapped the burlap around their adjacent legs, leaving the outer leg free. The "three-legged" race would determine the fastest, with the winner breaking the ribbon across the finish line about fifty yards away.

"Are you fast, Henrietta?"

"Yes, ma'am."

"I thought so," Kate said truthfully. She saw the same spark of grit and resolve in this child's eyes that Kate had had while growing up.

"I like to win, Miss Malone."

Kate grinned. "No more than I do," she said.

"C'mon, Kate!" Abe and Jethro shouted at various times from the sidelines. Sure, the men had their first-place award for winning the tree-splitting contest and now they expected nothing less from her.

Mr. Becker headed this event. He took his position at the finish line and all eyes were on him.

"Henrietta, just do your best. Win or lose, as long as you always do your best, you can hold your head up," Kate reassured.

"Yes, ma'am."

Then with a playful wink, Kate added, "But unless you're hurt, don't stop for anything, okay?"

The ten-year-old smiled wide. "Okay."

Kate gave her a reassuring hug. "Looks like it's time."

Mr. Becker waved his arms up and shouted, "Get ready, get set. Go!"

Kate took off, lifting the child with her. Henrietta didn't flinch, keeping up without fail.

Kate looked over and found that two contestants had already dropped out, tripping over themselves and landing in a heap. She heard their laughter from behind and pushed ahead.

"Hang on, Henrietta. We're in first!" Kate forged

forward, but from the corner of her eye she noted another pair coming up from behind. Cole and his teammate!

Kate kept her composure and her balance. That was essential and she strode with big steps, tugging Henrietta along with her strides. Laughter and shouts of encouragement filled the air. Others fell, but Cole kept coming. They were side-by-side, neck and neck with her.

"Come on, Henrietta," Kate said, moving along at an incredibly fast pace. Good thing Henrietta was made of solid tenacity because another child would have fallen by now. Bless her soul, Henrietta was just as determined to win as Kate.

Cole shouted, "We've got you, Kate."

"No, you haven't!"

Familiar competitiveness returned as though it had never left them. Kate didn't want Cole to win. Cole had to show Kate up. That was the way with them— two souls butting heads, comparing skills, always trying to best the other.

Kate noted the fierce resolve on Cole's face, the sheer strength of him moving just as fast she was. He'd beat her for sure, if not for his young partner. Cole was attuned to his capabilities and wouldn't push him further than he knew the boy could go.

They hit the ribbon at exactly the same moment, Mr. Becker declaring both teams in a tie.

"We did it, Henrietta! We won!"

The girl giggled and grinned and Kate's heart filled with joy.

"Congratulations, Kate," Cole said, coming over to them with the boy.

"You too, Cole. We both won this time. Couldn't have done it without Henrietta." She turned to the girl. "Have you met the sheriff yet?"

"No, ma'am."

Kate braced her arm on the girl's shoulder. "Sheriff Bradshaw, this is Henrietta Wilkins."

"Pleased to meet you. And this is Keith, Mrs. Gregory's grandson. He sure kept up with me. I've got to give him credit."

Kate looked down at the blond boy. "Hello, Keith. I know your grandmother. She must be proud of you."

"Yes, ma'am. Grandma says she's always proud of me."

"I bet she is." Kate smiled and began untying their legs, but her skirts got in the way. "Oh, pooh!"

"Here, let me." Cole bent down, pushing her skirt aside, and untied the rope that held the burlap sack. The soft brush of his hand on her bare leg created a pleasant tingling, but with the task done, Cole removed his hand all too quickly. "There you go."

He untied his own sack and they sent Keith and Henrietta to pick up their first-place ribbons.

"Where's Meggie?" Kate asked, scanning the grounds.

"I'm right here," Meggie said, coming up from

behind Kate with a giggle. Mrs. Gregory was only steps behind. "I sawed you win, Daddy. You and Miss Kate!"

"That's right, Megpie. We tied. That means we finished at the very same time." Cole lifted Meggie up and planted a big kiss on her chubby cheek.

"Keith is thrilled. It's his first ribbon ever," Mrs. Gregory said, smiling her greeting to Kate.

When Cole put Meggie down, she took Kate's hand. "I wanna play with Miss Kate now."

"Maybe she can take you over to the shooting match, darlin'. That's about to start," Cole said, glancing at Kate.

"I'd love to," Kate said immediately.

Meggie bobbed her head up and down. "My daddy's gonna win."

Kate smiled. "I'm sure he will. Your daddy used to practice and practice when he wasn't much bigger than you, Meggie. And now, well, nobody can beat him."

"Well, I don't know about that, Kate," Cole said modestly.

"Well, let's all head over there," Mrs. Gregory interjected. "Keith and the others can't wait for the contest to start."

They all began walking over to the area designated for the shooting match. Cole put Meggie atop his shoulders and Kate was right beside him. "You're gonna win, Cole. No doubt about it," she declared quietly, so only he could hear.

Cole's face broke out into a big, wide grin. "If you say so, woman. Wouldn't want to disagree with you about a thing today."

The sun dipped in the late afternoon and shadows danced across the clearing. The air was cooler now and the festivities continued as the fiddler's vivacious tunes had the crowd bringing their hands together in time to the music. Kate stood with Nora, clapping, watching Jethro and Patricia on the dance area...arguing.

"That's not the proper way to hold a lady," Patricia instructed.

"It's the way I do."

"Well, you might, and I do mean *might* know a thing or two about horses, but you certainly don't know how to hold a woman during a dance."

"I haven't had any other complaints," Jethro countered.

"You've only danced with Mrs. Whittaker and your sister-in-law, Nora. I doubt either one would want to correct you."

Jethro's face lit with amusement. "You noticed who I danced with?"

Patricia's face flushed rosy red. "And I suppose you didn't note with whom I've danced?"

"No, no I didn't." He scratched his head. "Who did you dance with?"

"Nester Gunderson and Casey Kelper." She folded

her arms around her middle and didn't attempt to take another step.

"That wasn't Casey, it was his brother, Justin," Jethro argued.

"Oh? And you say you didn't notice," Patricia said boldly. It appeared she had the upper hand now. Jethro stumbled with an excuse, but finally took Patricia in his arms and swung her around the dance area.

Nora and Kate chuckled. "And I thought you and Cole were stubborn," Nora declared, shaking her head.

"Those two can surely put anyone to shame."

When the music stopped, Jethro led Patricia back to her father and then headed their way, his face a mass of frustration.

"How was your dance with Patricia?" Nora asked.

Jethro grimaced, a distinct downturn of his full lips. He rubbed the back of his neck. "That woman…I'm either gonna strangle her…or marry her. Haven't decided which."

"Jethro!" Nora exclaimed. "Did you hear what you just said?"

"What?" He appeared truly startled.

"You want to marry Patricia," she stated.

"Well, I, uh…" Once he realized what he had admitted, a giant-size grin broke onto his face. "Damn, did I say that?"

"You did," Kate and Nora both replied.

"And it looks like that Gunderson fella is about

ready to ask Patricia for another dance," Kate added. "Are you going to let that happen?"

Jethro took a deep breath. "Ah, she'll only try correcting me again if I go over there."

Nora took his arm and gave him sage advice. "Don't go then, Jethro. You don't need a smart, pretty woman giving you all that attention."

"No, I wouldn't think you would," Kate stated. "Let some other man listen to her."

Jethro pursed his lips and narrowed his eyes, darting a glance first at Nora then at Kate. "I think I'm being shanghaied here."

The women eyed each other and grinned.

"All right, I'm going. But I might just come back with a noose around my neck for murder, or, or—"

"A ring on your finger?" Nora asked.

Jethro strode toward where Patricia stood, shaking his head all the way.

Later, Cole held Kate in his arms as the fiddler played a lazy, tranquil tune that required the barest of foot movements.

"I told you, you'd win," Kate said, gazing up into his blue eyes. When she looked at him like that, as though he could conquer the world, Cole's gut reaction was to never let her go. She'd stolen his heart somewhere between being best of friends and on opposite sides of the law. Jumbled feelings swirled around inside his head, leaving him confused mentally, but the rest of him sure knew what it wanted.

"Didn't want to make you out a liar, Kate." Cole applied slight pressure on her waist, bringing her closer. He breathed into her hair, so soft and curly, all those coppery waves floating down her shoulders.

"Mmm," Kate mumbled as she flowed with him. "You're a good man, Cole Bradshaw, even if you are mule-headed."

"Me? Mule-headed? I'm not the one who insists on…" Cole stopped himself. He had Kate right where he wanted her, where he *needed* her—in his arms. He wasn't about to engage in battle now. Not this time. It had been too long since he'd held her.

"What do I insist on?"

"Nothing, Kate," he said, swinging her around in a full circle. "It's not an argument I can win."

Kate laughed, the sound so sweet, so melodious to his ears, Cole found he wanted to keep Kate laughing and happy for the rest of their lives.

"You're also a smart man."

Cole grinned and tugged her up against him. They brushed against each other, burning up with desire. When the music stopped they stood together, staring into each other's eyes, smiling.

Nora came up with Abe, breaking the special moment. "Jethro wants to escort Patricia home," Nora said with glee, "and this time, he didn't have murder in his eyes."

"I bet not," Kate said, blinking, seeming to come back from wherever her mind had been. Hopefully, it had been on him.

"Abe and I will take you home, whenever you're ready, Kate."

Cole took Kate's hand. How easily it slipped into his, the fit perfect. "I'll take her home," he announced, staking his claim. He didn't want his evening with Kate to end.

Kate nodded as her gaze searched through the crowd. "I'd like that, but where's Meggie?"

"Little darlin' fell asleep a while back. Mrs. Gregory was just as tuckered out. They went on home," Cole answered.

Both Nora and Abe gave Kate a hug. Abe shook Cole's hand.

"Well, then, good night to you both. It was a fun day, wasn't it?" Nora asked, handing Kate back the quilt she'd brought for today.

They both agreed and watched as Abe and Nora left the festivities. Cole turned to Kate. "Are you ready to go?"

"Yes, it's late. I should probably get home, too."

"Mind if we walk back along the creek?"

"I'd love to. It'll be peaceful and quiet there after all this activity."

"Lots of stars out tonight." He took the quilt from her, throwing it over his shoulder, grasped her hand again and together they left the clearing.

Kate enjoyed her quiet time with Cole. They were comfortable enough with each other not to need conversation to fill the silent moments. He held her hand as they walked along the banks of Crystal Creek. The night air was crisp now, and the sound of rushing water lapping over rocks and fallen timber brought back so many childhood memories. Kate turned her attention to Cole, his profile, the strong jaw, dark eyes and the stubble of a beard appearing now, making him look more like a dangerous outlaw than a lawman.

She found it hard to concentrate when he was so close. "I love it here," she said finally.

"So do I."

"We've shared so many great memories right here."

Cole flashed her a devilish smile. "You mean our races when I'd beat you all the time?"

Kate's chuckle resounded against the surrounding trees. She wasn't in the mood to disagree. Serenity washed over her—she felt at peace with Cole by her side. "Yeah, you used to beat me. But not always."

"Mostly," he teased.

Kate smiled. "Look, there's our rock," she blurted out when she spotted it. The ancient great chunk of granite hadn't changed through the years. It was the one constant in a world full of recent change.

"Wanna sit for a while?"

Kate nodded. "Sure." She found a flat spot and planted herself down. Cole sat beside her, but his attention was drawn to the creek waters. He stared out, deep in thought, his arms braced along his thighs as he leaned forward.

"I meant what I said the other night, Kate."

Kate lifted her brows. "You said a whole lot the other night, Cole."

Cole turned to her then, his eyes dark with passion. "You're my woman, Kate."

Kate's heart hammered. Each time he said that, she wished there was a new road for them to take—a way for them to reach each other. She knew his words as truth. She *was* his woman. And there was no other man for her but Cole. Yet, they were separated by something powerful, something hard to overcome and something perhaps stronger than both of them combined—their beliefs.

"I know," Kate acknowledged softly.

Cole blew out a breath. "Glad you're not disagreeing about that, or I might have to show you again."

Kate recalled the last time Cole had proved his point, the night he'd nearly buckled her knees with his kisses. "Show me what again?" she asked all too coyly.

Cole's grin was pure sin. He threw down her quilt, slid her onto it then pressed his body next to hers. "This," he said, taking her in a sweeping, long, passionate kiss.

Kate was consumed with desire, a fire burning low and deep, her body filled with familiar yearnings for Cole and what it had been like to have him deep within her.

Cole worked magic on her, kissing here, caressing there, hiking up her skirts to touch her everywhere.

Kate whimpered and Cole groaned and soon there was a wild frenzy of motion. Thrills of pleasure lent way to clothes being pushed down, to Cole taking a place above her, to him finding her core and with one deep thrust, joining them instantly. The ache of their long separation was gone. They were together in heat and passion.

Cole put his mouth over hers, kissing her sweetly. "I love you, Kate." He thrust again, lifting her with him, and kissed her. "I love you so much I can hardly bear it."

Kate closed her eyes and relished the words she'd craved for so many years. Cole loved her. "I love you too, Cole. I always have."

There, she'd finally admitted it. To herself and to him, but rational thoughts gave way to more potent sensations as Cole made exquisite, earth-shattering love to her. Right there, beside smooth-running creek waters, under the most beautiful twinkling stars.

Afterward Cole bundled her up in the quilt and walked her home, stopping every so often to speak of his love, to kiss her again. Kate wanted the night to never end. She was ensconced in a blissful state that she knew would shatter all too soon, because Cole loved her but he still didn't want her. He still hadn't accepted the woman she'd become.

No proposals came this night. No declarations of a future together. Cole's face was a mass of confusion when he'd said his final goodbye at her door. So much so that Kate ached for him as much as for herself.

She loved him more than ever now, but it was futile, almost pointless to try to find a single ray of hope. Cole's convictions outweighed his love for her. She witnessed his struggle and knew he'd been defeated by his own self-induced code of honor.

There would be no happily-ever-afters for Kate Malone. The sooner she faced that sorrowful fact, the better she'd be for it.

Chapter Twenty

Cole spent a sleepless night. He awoke bone weary, but he'd come to a final decision about Kate. They couldn't go on having stolen moments like last night. Wonderful as it had been, it wasn't fair to her. It wasn't fair to either of them. Yet, neither one could deny the passion that existed between them. He knew once he'd arrived home last night, he'd have to make a decision that would alter the course of both their lives. He had Meggie to think about. And his promise to Jeb.

Cole knew what he had to do.

He washed up and donned his clothes, took time to have breakfast with Meggie then kissed her goodbye and headed off to the jail. Later, once the saloon opened, he'd speak with Kate. He couldn't fathom going to her house this morning, seeing her all dewy-eyed and sleep tousled. The temptation would be too great and he was certain they'd end up making love again. That would settle nothing, other than to ease the ache that seemed to be a constant with him lately. No, Cole had to meet Kate head-on, where there'd be no further temptation. He'd bide his time and see her later, at the saloon.

The Silver Saddle was more crowded than ever before. Business boomed and Kate attributed that fact to having been closed yesterday for Founder's Day and having more than a few ranchers and cowboys stay overnight in town after the festivities.

They'd come in claiming their throats were parched from drinking nothing but lemonade and iced tea the day before. That was all right by Kate. The more money the saloon made, the more profits they earned, which meant extra cash to donate to the Community Fund. She liked knowing her profits were doing the town some good and was proud of the slogan, Have A Drink, Help A Neighbor.

She'd been serving up drinks all day long, which helped keep her mind off Cole. Lord above, she did need to keep from thinking about him. He consumed her thoughts lately and even after last night, nothing had been settled between them still. Her heart seemed to truly ache. No, it was better not to think about Cole tonight. With that in mind, Kate strode up to the bar and placed an order with Josh.

"I don't like the look of those strangers over there. Want me to serve up their drinks?" Josh asked.

Kate knew whom he was speaking about. Three men that she'd never seen before in Crystal Creek sat at the far table. One man, who had a scar the size of her pistol running down his cheek, made her shiver. She didn't understand it much because she wasn't one to judge someone solely by appearance, but he had a cruel, embittered face. Still, they were her customers. "Probably just drifters, Josh. I'll handle it."

Kate took up the drinks and carefully laid them down on their table, just as the mean-faced man's arm came out, knocking them to the ground. Glass splintered onto the floor and whiskey streamed out like a running river. The man grabbed her arm and yanked. "Damn clumsy, woman," he said, growling into her face.

Kate tried yanking her arm free, but he held firm. "Let go of me!" She glanced at the bar, but Big Josh's back was turned away, and apparently he hadn't heard her over the noise of the crowd.

The man stood and slapped her face. "Shut up!"

Stunned, Kate's face burned with pain. She cried out. Cole pushed his way through the crowded room with his hand on his gun. "Let her go!" There was murder in his eyes.

A smug expression stole over the man's face. He grabbed Kate even harder and brought her up against him. Her attempts to fend him off were useless. The man held her with an iron-tight grip. "I say she stays with me, *Sheriff Bradshaw.*"

The saloon customers removed themselves from the situation as best they could. Some ducked under tables, others headed out the door. Many stood stone still as the room became eerily silent. Cole spoke quietly, with deadly calm. "Then I'm gonna have to put a bullet between your eyes."

Kate gasped. "No, Cole!"

"Seems your woman doesn't want you to die," the man said almost gleefully, nudging Cole on.

Cole's face had a resigned look about it, as though he knew this day had to finally come, as though he expected to be in this situation. But there was also pure determination in Cole's glare. He wouldn't back down.

Kate's insides churned with dread, realizing she'd caused this trouble. Cole had warned her countless times that she had no business reopening the Silver Saddle. He'd warned her that rowdies would cause turmoil in this town. And now, Kate bore witness to Cole coming head-to-head with a dangerous man.

"I'm not going to die. You are. Let her go."

"I think I sorta like her. The boys here tell me she's your woman." His grip tightened with one hand, while the other ran through her hair. "All this soft red hair. I bet it feels real good flowing over a man's body."

A tic worked in Cole's cheek. He stood rigid and Kate could see his restraint, his anger being contained, just barely. "You like hiding behind a female?"

Kate felt the man's body stiffen. Cole knew how to prod him. She prayed for his safety, being more fearful for him than for herself.

"You calling me a coward?"

"I am. Let her go and we'll see what kind of man you are."

Swiftly the man shoved Kate away and went for his gun. Kate stumbled to the ground. Shots rang out. Panic seized her, clutching at her heart when she realized what it meant that there had been more than one shot.

She bounded up. "Cole!" She found him lying on the floor and rushed to his side. A bullet had pierced his chest and blood oozed out, mingling with the whiskey on the ground.

He lifted his head up slightly. "Kate," he said softly, before passing out.

Kate paced the doctor's office, tears stinging her cheeks from all the crying she'd done. Big Josh was there, trying to give her comfort, but nothing could put her at ease until she knew whether or not Cole would survive.

He'd shot the man dead, though not before taking a bullet in the chest. Cole was a fast shot, but it had been her fault that he was lying in there, fighting for his life. She'd seen his hesitation, a split second of indecision, making sure Kate was truly out of his line of fire before taking his shot. Otherwise, the man wouldn't have had the chance to make a clean shot.

Everything was her fault.

Kate couldn't deny it. Cole had warned her about the saloon. He'd cautioned her time and again about the drifters and drunks who would bring nothing but trouble to Crystal Creek. Kate hadn't heeded anyone's advice. She'd been too determined and too bullheaded to listen to reason. She had gone up against the entire town and now the man she loved above all else might not live.

She'd lose him forever.

And Meggie. Oh poor little Meggie. Hadn't she had enough loss in her young life? Kate was responsible for it all. What would happen to that sweet child if Cole should die?

The very thought of it was unbearable.

Kate prayed to the Lord to spare Cole's life. She prayed and prayed to the Almighty. "He's a good man. Don't take him yet," she chanted over and over.

Big Josh shook his head. "It ain't your fault, Miss Kate. The sheriff wasn't about to let that man hurt you."

Kate cried harder. "He's forever protecting me."

"That's what a man does when he cares about a woman."

"I gave him no reason to care, Josh. I've caused him nothing but trouble."

"He was doing his job. As sheriff of this town, he had to see to keeping the peace." Josh shook his head again, repeating, "It ain't your fault."

But deep down straight into her soul, Kate knew she was to blame. And she vowed to never forgive herself if Cole died.

The doctor came out, wiping his hands dry on a

cloth. Kate winced, seeing Doc Royer's shirt colored with Cole's blood. "I got the bullet out, but the sheriff's still unconscious. I can't say for sure he'll make it. Depends on how he does during the night."

"Can I see him?" Kate asked, straightening and wiping away her tears.

"You can, but don't be alarmed. He's pale. He's lost a good deal of blood."

"Okay," she said quickly. She'd agree to anything to see Cole, but she did brace herself for the worst. Kate followed the doctor into the room where Cole had been operated on. The narrow examining table barely contained Cole's frame. "If he makes it through the night, we'll move him to a more comfortable bed."

Kate bit back her horror, seeing that Cole, usually so vital and alive, looked pallid and weak. "Cole," she said on a breath, "I'm here." She took his hand, noting how limp it felt in hers.

"I'll be staying here overnight. I won't leave the sheriff in this state," Dr. Royer said.

"I'm staying too. I won't leave his side. Just tell me what I need to do."

"Fine. I'll show you what to do if he spikes a fever."

After several minutes, Kate left the room to speak with Big Josh. "I'm okay, Josh. You don't have to stay. I'm spending the night here. But I need a favor. Will you check with Mrs. Gregory at the sheriff's house and make sure she and Meggie are okay? I'm sure someone's notified them. I hope the child was asleep and didn't hear the worst of it."

"I'll head there right now and come back shortly to let you know how they're faring."

Kate wrapped her arms around Big Josh's middle, as much as she could, which seemed only halfway. "I can't thank you enough. You've put up with my ranting and crying. You've always been by my side. I consider you a dear friend."

He hugged her tenderly and patted her shoulders. "Don't you worry none, Miss Kate. The sheriff is tough. He'll make it."

"I'm praying, Josh. I'm praying hard. I only hope the Lord hears me."

"That's what He does best. He hears us."

Kate nodded. "I know." She broke off their embrace and looked up at him. "I'll be waiting to hear about Meggie."

With that, Josh took his leave and Kate went back to Cole's room, pulling up a chair. Before taking a seat, she bent to kiss his cheek and stroke his hand. "Don't you d-dare d-die, Cole Bradshaw," she said with a wobbly voice. "Don't you dare l-leave this w-world without me."

An hour later, a soft knock at the door startled Kate. "Come in," she said quietly, going to the door.

"How is he?" Big Josh asked.

"The same. He hasn't come to yet. Doc Royer gave him some laudanum for the pain in his chest a while back. But he hasn't so much as twitched. He's breathing shallowly.''

"His body is getting the rest it needs," Josh offered.

Kate glanced at Cole again. She couldn't bear to take her eyes off him for fear that his shallow breathing would stop altogether. "How's Meggie?"

"I spoke with Mrs. Gregory. It's a lucky thing that Meggie went to bed early tonight. Mrs. Gregory got the news about the sheriff, but little Meggie doesn't know anything yet. I have to say, that woman is beside herself with worry."

Kate understood Mrs. Gregory's concern. The three of them had been like a family. "She's quite fond of Cole and his daughter."

Kate stared at Cole's motionless body. Good Lord, he deserved a real family. It was what he'd always wanted. He deserved a proper wife—a woman who'd be there from morning until night for him. He deserved a woman who didn't have grand plans in her head other than keeping him happy and giving him children. Kate had been all wrong for him. He'd been right not to accept her. What his shooting had finally knocked into Kate's mule head, he'd known all along.

She wasn't the right kind of woman for him.

And now, because of her, he might be taking his last breaths on this earth.

"Miss Kate?"

Kate came out of her musings and lifted her eyes

to her friend. "Oh, Josh. I'm sorry. Did you say something?

"I was saying that Mrs. Gregory is gonna come see him tomorrow."

"That's good. As long as she doesn't bring Meggie. She shouldn't see her father..." Kate stopped and inhaled deeply, unable to go on without shedding more tears. She blinked them back. "She shouldn't see her father like this."

Morning dawned, a tiny ray of sunlight streaming into Cole's room from a hole in the window shade. Kate shifted uncomfortably in her chair. She hadn't slept much, if at all. On and off all night, she and Doc Royer had administered to Cole. Kate kept checking his breathing while the doctor monitored his pulse for a steady heartbeat and peered into his eyes. Thankfully Cole had survived the night, but Kate had listened intently and he hadn't moved or made a sound during the long torturous hours since he'd been shot.

"Kate, are you in there?" Nora's voice soothed her nerves and Kate rose to open the door.

"Oh, Nora." Kate fell into her arms and hugged her friend tightly. "Thanks for coming."

The two embraced for a long, drawn-out moment. Kate had never been so happy to see anybody in her life. She needed Nora's sweet comfort and encouragement right now. Kate was so weary and Nora always knew how to make her feel better. "I'm so very sorry to hear about Cole. How is he?"

Kate spoke softly, telling Nora the details of the shooting and of the night she'd just spent watching over him. "He's so still, Nora. He's barely breathing."

Nora took Kate's hand and walked over to see Cole. "Oh dear, he is still, but Kate, he looks to be recovering. There's some color in his face."

It was the first sign of hope she'd had. Kate stared at Cole and, sure enough, he appeared to have gained a bit of color overnight. "I think you're right, Nora. He looks better. Oh, I've been praying for that. For anything."

"He's going to recover, Kate. Cole's a strong man and he's got a lot to live for." Nora cast her a knowing smile.

Kate shuddered and shook her head. "He's got Meggie. He's got the job he loves. But that's all, Nora. It's over for him and me. I'm not going to pretend this wasn't my fault. I'm to blame for his getting shot. If Cole survives and I pray he does, he won't have to worry about me ever again."

Deep lines wrinkled Nora's forehead. "Kate, I've never heard you speak like that before. Of course Cole will worry about you. He cares for you. After I saw the two of you together during Founder's Day, I'm sure that he loves you. And you love him fiercely. I know that. Nothing was your fault, Kate. Especially not the shooting. You didn't know that would happen so don't talk crazy.''

Kate let the subject drop. Nora would be loyal to the end, but Kate wouldn't let anyone convince her otherwise. She'd caused Cole's injury almost as if she'd raised that gun and pulled the trigger herself.

''Nora, you're a good friend,'' was Kate's only reply.

Nora frowned. ''Kate, I don't like that look in your eye.''

''I'm worried, is all,'' Kate said, then changed the subject. ''I do need a favor. Do you think you might watch Meggie for Mrs. Gregory? Big Josh said she wants to come see Cole this morning. It wouldn't be for very long.''

''Of course, Kate. Anything I can do to help out.''

''I don't think Meggie knows yet. It's best not to tell her until Cole comes to.''

''That's probably a good idea. I won't let on. It'll be hard, but I'll think of something.''

''She'd like to talk about the baby. She wants a real family just as much as Cole does.'' Kate bit her lip and blinked back yet another round of tears. ''She's, uh, she's hoping to have a brother or sister one day. I know she'll have lots of questions for you.''

Nora chuckled softly. ''And just how will I answer *those* kinds of questions?''

Kate patted her hand. ''Like you said, you'll think of something.''

* * *

It was three o'clock in the afternoon when Cole finally stirred. Big Josh and Dr. Royer had moved him earlier in the day from the narrow table to a bed in another room in the doctor's office. Kate had dozed a bit but always with an ear close to listen for Cole's breathing.

She witnessed him shift a bit and his eyes fluttered, as though he was trying to open them. Then he spoke. It was a low, nearly inaudible sound, more like a mumble. "Kate."

Kate rushed to his side, kneeling by his bedside. "I'm here, Cole." She took hold of his hand and squeezed gently. "I'm here," she said again, this time elated that he was coming out of his unconscious state. "I'll go get Doc Royer."

"No," he said, and she thought she felt the slightest pressure on her hand. "Don't go," he said on a breath.

Tears flowed freely now, but they were tears of joy and relief. Kate held his hand and wiped down his brow. He still felt cool to the touch, with no sign of high fever, which according to Dr. Royer was a good thing. He'd hoped that Cole's young body would fight for survival and it had.

"Thank the Lord, Cole. Thank the Lord you're coming to," Kate whispered. She sat with him the rest of the day. He spoke only once more, but color had come back to his face. He'd moved around a bit, searching for comfort, and dozed on and off during the evening hours.

Nora had stopped by as the sun had begun to set, thoughtfully bringing Kate food, a platter of bread and cheese along with beef stew from dinner. Kate had little appetite, but Nora had stood by and made sure Kate put something substantial in her stomach.

Dr. Royer admonished her for not going home to get some sleep, claiming he didn't want another patient to tend to, but Kate couldn't leave Cole, not until she was sure he would make a full recovery. She stayed the night again, much to the doctor's dismay, and in the morning Kate received the news she'd been hoping for. After a long examination, the doctor told Kate that Cole was out of immediate danger. With proper rest and care, he'd be up and around in a week's time.

Kate sat by his bedside, watching him sleep for a long time, willing herself to rise from the bed and do what she knew in her heart she had to do. Guilt ate at her unbearably. Kate was out of options. She couldn't live here, knowing she'd placed Cole in such danger. She couldn't forgive herself. With a gentle brush of her lips, she kissed him tenderly and heard him mumble something sweet. The sound tore at her heart. ''Goodbye, Cole,'' she whispered, almost silently.

She knew this would be the last time she'd see the man she loved.

Chapter Twenty-One

Kate sat in Cole's parlor and spoke quietly with Mrs. Gregory. "I need to know that Meggie will be taken care of while Cole's recuperating."

Mrs. Gregory served her a cup of tea and didn't flinch at the bold question. Kate had no time to be subtle, she had to know about Meggie's well-being first. "She will. I've had many offers of help, but between Caroline and myself, the child will be well taken care of."

Kate blew out a breath in relief. "I understand this is a hardship for you, Mrs. Gregory. You had plans of moving into your daughter's home soon. I want to thank you for your loyalty to Cole."

With a wave of her arm, she offered, "No thanks necessary. I'm fond of them both and prayed for the sheriff's recovery. Moving in with my daughter can wait for a time. I wouldn't leave Meggie now. She needs me and so will the sheriff once he comes home."

"Nora said she'd be happy to spell you from time to time. She's good with children and she truly cares for Meggie."

Mrs. Gregory sipped her tea. "And what of you, my dear? I get the feeling the sheriff would like having your company. I know Meggie would enjoy having you here. Will you be stopping by from time to time?"

An ache developed in her stomach. She managed to keep tears from filling her eyes, but she knew Mrs. Gregory noticed her distress. She shook her head. "No. I won't be coming by, I'm afraid."

"Oh, I'm sure the sheriff will be disappointed," Mrs. Gregory said, clearly perplexed. Kate knew she'd confused the woman. But Kate couldn't divulge her plan to anyone yet. Soon everyone would understand.

"I'd like to see Meggie now, if you don't mind. Is she awake yet?"

"Well, she should be by now. The little one likes to sleep late. Let me check on her."

After several minutes, Meggie came out of her room, rubbing her eyes. "Here she is. Say hello to Miss Kate." Mrs. Gregory exited the room then, giving them a bit of privacy.

Little Megpie, dressed in a wrinkled nightgown with her blond hair sticking up in several places had the sweetest expression on her face. Kate had never seen a more adorable picture. As soon as Meggie noticed her, she came over and crawled right onto her lap.

Kate stroked her hair. "Good morning, Meggie."

"Morning." She snuggled closer in and Kate wrapped her arms around her.

"I came to see how our little girl is today."

"Fine. Daddy's at the doctor's."

"I know. He was hurt, but he'll be home soon. And I bet you're going to take really good care of him, too."

Meggie nodded. "I want to make Daddy a cake."

"Oh," Kate said, recalling the last time they had baked together, "he'd like that."

"Will you help?"

Kate hesitated. She knew this would be hard. "Mrs. Gregory can help you. I'm sure she'd love to. She's a wonderful cook."

Meggie whined, a rise of her small, soft voice that indicated her displeasure. "I want you to help me."

Kate's heart ached. She knew she couldn't bear to leave the child disappointed. "Meggie, listen, just in case you don't see me doesn't mean I'm not thinking about you. I'll be thinking about you all the time. But to remind you, I brought you a little present." Kate dug into her reticule and brought out a gold locket and chain. "This was my mother's, Meggie. I want you to have it now. It's very special to me. And so are you."

Meggie's face beamed with joy when Kate handed

her the locket. The child held it carefully, inspecting it from all angles. "It's pretty."

"It's yours now. Would you like me to put it on you?"

Meggie nodded eagerly.

"Okay, there," Kate said, once she fastened the locket around Meggie's neck. "I hope you'll always think of me when you wear it." She hugged Meggie tightly and stood abruptly. She didn't want the child to see her dismay. "I love you, Megpie."

"Love you, too," she said, too interested in fingering the locket to notice Kate's sad smile.

"Well, I'd better get going. Remember, you take care of your daddy and love him up real good. He's the best daddy in the world."

"'Kay. Thank you for the present, Miss Kate."

Kate left Cole's house quickly after kissing Meggie goodbye and headed straight for Nora's. It would be her last stop before leaving Crystal Creek.

Cole pressed his eyes open, fighting off the haze of cloudiness that had engulfed him. His chest burned, the ache bringing back recollections, fuzzy as they were, of trouble at the saloon. He pushed himself up on the bed, ignoring the knifing pain to his upper body, and noted that he wasn't home. He'd been in and out of consciousness for days, but today he recognized Doc Royer's office. How long had he been here?

A vague and fleeting memory of Kate—her scent,

her touch, her soft voice soothing him—floated into his mind like an enchanting dream. She'd been with him throughout most of the time, he was certain. But as he glanced around the room, moving his head only slightly to ward off any dizziness, he found that he was alone.

He closed his eyes and vivid recollections of the shooting surged forth. A man with a scarred face held Kate, hurting her, and Cole had shot him. Cole's eyes opened wide then, remembering. He knew that man.

Dwight Sloan.

Cole had known who he was when he saw him at the saloon, straight away. Seeing him put his hands on Kate, knowing what he was capable of, how he'd been party to Jeb and Lydia's murders had Cole itching to pull the trigger. First and foremost, he'd made sure that Kate was safely out of the way before taking the shot.

He recalled downing the man. Cole hadn't missed, his bullet had entered right in the chest, into his heart. Cole felt no remorse, only relief that Kate was safe now and that finally he'd avenged Jeb's death.

Had the man come back out of revenge? That had to be the reason. Cole had been key in catching and jailing Sloan's brother, who'd been found guilty and hanged. But Cole felt he'd been manipulated from the start. The calculating man knew who Cole was. He'd probably waited for the exact right moment when Cole showed up at the saloon. He must have known about Kate, too.

Either way, the man would have found a way to draw Cole out, sometime, somewhere.

Cole closed his eyes and wondered where Kate was, and he thought of Meggie. He prayed his young daughter wouldn't take his injuries to heart. Meggie, sweet Meggie, wouldn't like seeing him all bandaged up. He hadn't recalled her coming here, although his memory of this time was vague. But one thing he was sure about was that once he got out of this bed, he'd be heading straight home, to Meggie and to Kate.

Cole dozed off then, waiting and wanting Kate by his side.

Not more than an hour later, Cole got his wish. He heard the door opening and the swish of skirts. His heart rate escalated. He needed to see her in a bad way. "Kate?"

He sat up in the bed, but it was Nora Cable by his side and she had tears in her eyes.

"Nora? What's wrong? Is it Meggie, Kate?" Desperation settled in his gut, seeing Nora so distraught. Something had happened to someone he loved.

"No, it's not Meggie. She's just fine, Cole. Mrs. Gregory is taking good care of her, as usual."

"That's good." Cole relaxed a little. "Where's Kate?"

Nora swallowed hard. She shook her head. "I tried to stop her, Cole. Honest. But she's gone." Nora shed big tears now. They ran down her face in streams.

Overwhelming dread seized him. "Where'd she go?"

"She left on the train not ten minutes ago. She closed up the saloon...and left town."

Cole didn't excuse his foul language. He cursed up a storm. "Why the hell did she go, Nora?"

"Oh, Cole, she blames herself for you getting shot. I couldn't convince her otherwise. She left you a note." Nora reached into her pocket and took out a piece of parchment.

Cole scanned the note quickly then balled it up in his fist. He'd gotten the gist of what was in her fool head. "Where? Tell me where she went."

Cole sat up, swinging his legs off the bed and onto the floor. He winced in pain but kept moving. He hoisted himself up and, although his legs felt wiry, he stood tall.

Nora let out a loud gasp. "Cole, what are you doing?"

"Get me a shirt, Nora. I'm going after her, soon as you tell me where. Did she go back to Los Angeles?"

"No, I don't think so." Nora stopped talking to shake her head at him. "You can't ride in your condition, Cole."

"What I can't do is let Kate get away. Now, are you gonna help? I need a shirt."

Nora opened up drawers and finally found a man's shirt. She handed it to him and helped him on with it. With nimble fingers, she buttoned it up carefully over his bandages. "I think the train was headed north a ways. It was the first one out this afternoon."

"Aw, hell. Nora, do me a favor. Have Jethro saddle up my horse for me and bring it here."

Nora stared at him a moment. "I want her back, too, Cole, but you're in bad shape."

"I'll be in worse shape if I don't find her, Nora."

Thankfully Nora seemed to understand his desperation. He read it in her eyes, in her worried expression. Cole knew he'd be no good for anything without Kate by his side.

"I'll hurry," Nora said, and left the room quickly.

Kate had boarded the train that departed Crystal Creek half an hour ago and hadn't looked back. She couldn't bear to, for if she had, she would have been tempted to return to everyone she cared about. She'd found love in Crystal Creek with Cole and Meggie. She'd also made the most wonderful friends in the Cables. Leaving Nora and knowing she'd not ever see her new little babe hadn't been easy. Nora had pleaded, but Kate knew what was best. She couldn't have Cole, and she couldn't very well stand by and watch the man she loved marry another. Eventually, Cole would, for Meggie's sake if not his own.

Kate hugged her valise to her chest and stared out the window wondering what San Francisco would be like. She supposed she could always get a job of some sort in a hotel. She'd had many years of experience while working with her mama in Los Angeles.

Kate would have to make a new start and try to find a shred of peace in a place where she knew absolutely no one. She was alone now, completely. Mama had always said, "Don't dwell." But Kate knew she'd not see a truly joyous day again without the ones she loved by her side.

The Southern Pacific pulled up to its next stop, Grass Valley. Kate stared out the window, viewing the town, and noted several travelers making their way from the depot. There she spotted a man on horseback nearly slumped over. Initially she believed she was seeing things, her mind dulled from sadness and heartache. It couldn't possibly be. But once she recognized the man, who seemed to be searching the windows of the train with dogged persistence, her breath caught. "Cole."

He nearly fell from his horse then, his face pale, his body weakened. Kate picked up her valise and dashed outside. She reached him just before he plunged off his horse. She took the brunt of his weight and helped him down. Without a word, with fear in her heart that he'd done himself even more injury, she guided him along then propped him up against the wall of the depot, where he let his weakened legs buckle as he sank down onto the dirt.

Kate blinked her astonishment back and bent to him. "Cole," she breathed out, wiping away sweat from his brow. "Why did you come after me? I've been nothing but trouble for you."

"Hell," he said softly, after taking a deep steadying breath, "I ought to arrest you again. Must be a law about leaving a man twice in his lifetime."

"I almost got you killed," she admitted regretfully.

"No." The slow shake of his head took great effort. "It wasn't your doing. That man wanted me dead. Didn't matter where or when."

"I don't understand."

"That was Dwight Sloan. I jailed his brother, who had been tried, convicted and sentenced to death. Sloan wanted me dead, to avenge his brother's death, just as I wanted him dead to avenge mine. I recognized him the moment I saw him with you. I knew I'd finally have my revenge, but what I hadn't planned on was having you in danger."

"You didn't shoot him right away. You hesitated."

"I couldn't chance it. I had to make sure you were clear of him," he said earnestly.

"But don't you see, you put your life in danger for me."

"I'd do it again, Kate. You have to know that. And Sloan would have found me, sooner or later. I'm sure of it. None of this was your doing."

Kate shook her head fiercely. "I didn't listen to your warnings. If I hadn't been so stubborn I would have seen the dangers. Nobody wanted the saloon to reopen."

"Kate, you've done more good with that saloon than anybody in the entire town. You've taught them all a lesson in compassion…a lesson long overdue. You have such a giving heart. I love you for it. Hell, I just plain love you." He reached up with a hand to graze her cheek.

Kate gasped when she saw blood soaking his shirt. "Cole, you're bleeding again," she cried.

"Reach into my pocket, honey."

With a questioning look, Kate felt inside his pocket. Tears stung her eyes when she lifted out the thin strip of once-white petticoat, stained with his blood. It was the cloth she'd used to wrap his hand after he'd deliberately slashed it that day by the creek, the day they'd claimed friendship forever, the day she'd fallen in love with him. "You kept it all this time," she said, taken aback. Tears streamed down her cheeks now.

"It's always with me," he muttered, taking her hand and bringing it to his mouth. He pressed a kiss on her palm then wiped away her tears with the pad of his thumb.

"I love you, Cole." She stared deeply into his eyes.

"Glad to hear it, sweetheart."

Kate took the piece of material and anchored it to his wound, wrapping it tightly. Then she reached into her bag and produced the other half of the bandage she would use on him, the plaid piece of material he'd used to wrap up her hand, that same day, years ago. She lifted it to his wound to help stop the bleeding. "It's always with me," she said softly, repeating his words.

His smile melted her heart. And when he kissed her soundly on the lips, she couldn't control her giddy trembling.

"I was wrong, Kate, about the saloon," he began with a somber tone. "I fell in love with that devilish imp of a girl who wanted to beat me at everything, all the time. You're strong and capable, Kate. I don't want you to change a thing. I need you for my wife and I love you the way you are. You can own ten saloons for all I care. That's what I'd planned to tell you the night of the shooting. I wanted to ask you to marry me."

"Oh, Cole," Kate said, elation stealing into her heart.

"So, will you, Kate? Will you marry me?"

"Yes, yes." Kate eagerly accepted his proposal. "I'll be your wife. And we'll see about the saloon, Cole. I have some ideas on the matter. Perhaps taking on a partner, someone who'd run the place for me would work. Big Josh has expressed an interest. Besides, even one saloon might prove to be too much when we..."

"Have babies?" he asked, a hopeful look in his expression.

Kate nodded, unable to speak. She didn't know for sure, but wondered if she might already be with child. Sweet warmth coursed through her body at the thought of carrying Cole's child.

"I want babies with you," he admitted softly.

"Heaps of them?" A smile emerged as Kate remembered Cole's wish from years earlier.

Cole nodded. "Heaps, but for now, you, me and Meggie...we'll be a real family."

He took her hand, entwining it with his. The thin, faded line of the mutual wounds on their palms beating together to the tender pulse of love. "Friends forever," he said, gazing softly into her eyes. "And love," he added.

"And love," she said on a blissful sigh. The sheriff and Kate were finally where they belonged.

Together.

* * * * *

COMING NEXT MONTH FROM

HARLEQUIN HISTORICALS®

- **TEMPTING A TEXAN**
by **Carolyn Davidson,** author of THE TEXAN
When beautiful nanny Carlinda Donnelly suddenly shows up and tells the ambitious and wealthy Nicholas Garvey that he has custody of his five-year-old niece, he couldn't be more shocked. But before it's too late, will Nicholas realize that love and family are more important than financial success?

    HH #647 ISBN# 29247-3 $5.25 U.S./$6.25 CAN.

- **THE SILVER LORD**
by **Miranda Jarrett,** book one in *The Lordly Claremonts* trilogy
Behind a facade of propriety as a housekeeper, Fan Winslow leads an outlaw life as the leader of a notorious smuggling gang. Captain Lord George Claremont is an aristocratic navy hero who lives by his honor and loyalty to the king. Can love and passion join such disparate lovers?

    HH #648 ISBN# 29248-1 $5.25 U.S./$6.25 CAN.

- **THE ANGEL OF DEVIL'S CAMP**
by **Lynna Banning,** author of THE COURTSHIP
Southern belle Meggy Hampton goes to an Oregon logging camp to marry a man she has never met, but her future is turned upside down when her fiancé dies in an accident. Without enough money to travel home, Meggy has no choice but to stay in Devil's Camp, even if it means contending with Tom Randall—the stubborn and unwelcoming log camp boss who's too handsome for his own good!

    HH #649 ISBN# 29249-X $5.25 U.S./$6.25 CAN.

- **BRIDE OF THE TOWER**
by **Sharon Schulze,** the latest in the *l'Eau Clair* series
On his way to deliver a missive, Sir William Bowman is attacked by brigands. More warrior than woman, Lady Julianna d'Arcy rescues him and nurses him back to health. Julianna suspects the handsome knight may be allied with her enemy, but she can't deny the attraction between them....

    HH #650 ISBN# 29250-3 $5.25 U.S./$6.25 CAN.

KEEP AN EYE OUT FOR ALL FOUR OF THESE TERRIFIC NEW TITLES

HHCNM0203

CHARLENE SANDS

resides in Southern California with her husband, Don,
and two children, Jason and Nikki. Her love of the
American West stems from early childhood memories
of story time with her imaginative father. Tall tales of
dashing pirates and dutiful sheriffs brought to life with
words and images sparked her passion for writing.
When not writing, she enjoys sunny California days,
Pacific beaches and sitting down with a good book.
She loves to hear from her readers. Contact her at
charlenesands@hotmail.com, or visit her Web site at
www.charlenesands.com.